Sleet Kitten

By S.J. Tilly

Sleet Kitten

Sleet Series Book One

Copyright © S.J. Tilly 2021
All rights reserved.
First published in 2021

No part of this book may be reproduced, stored in a retrieval system or transmitted in any form or by any means, without the prior permission in writing of the publisher, nor be otherwise circulated in any form of binding or cover other than that in which it is published and without a similar condition, including this condition, being imposed on the subsequent purchaser. All characters in this publication other than those clearly in the public domain are fictitious, and any resemblance to real persons, living or dead, is purely coincidental.

Cover: James Adkinson
Editor: M. Penna
Copyeditor: Scott Pearson

This book is dedicated to everyone who's ever embarrassed themselves in front of a crush. We can't change the past. But we can laugh at it.

CHAPTER ONE

KATELYN

"Well, fuckity shits on a stick. Isn't that just great?" I grumble, thinking how tonight just went from dull, to bad, to worse.

"What did you say?"

I glance over to see an older gentleman standing beside me, critically eyeing the chicken skewer in his hand.

"Oh, um..." I quickly scoop up the heel that just broke off my favorite pair of shoes and hold it up between us. "Just cursing out my footwear."

The man narrows his eyes before giving me a nod. "Ah, well, nothin' a bit of crazy glue and a well-placed nail can't fix."

I resist a shudder at the idea of putting my foot anywhere near a shoe held together with a *nail*.

"I'll keep that in mind." I give the man a small smile and hobble past him before I can get sucked into yet another long-winded conversation I couldn't be less interested in.

I promised my mom I'd come here tonight, and I've fulfilled that promise. But I am officially over this party. And honestly, to call this a *party* is an insult to all fun parties everywhere. This is more of a rubbing elbows, gaining voters, and pocketing fundraiser checks event. *Not* a party.

Sure, I'm proud of my cousin Daniel for announcing his run for Minneapolis City Council. And if I lived within the city limits, I'd gladly vote for him. But I don't. And I'm not loaded enough to be a donor. I'm strictly here for support as the sole family representative. Alex, my brother, is an asshat... so I'm not surprised he bailed. Everyone else is either out of town, lives out of town, or knew about this with enough of a heads-up that they were able to make up excuses to get out of attending. Me? I didn't know about any of this until yesterday afternoon. My aunt called asking me to *please attend* since, like the cold-weather-pansy that she is, she's already down in Florida for the winter. So, long story short, she guilted me into making an appearance.

    I doubt Daniel would've even noticed if I didn't show up. This condo we're in has got to be around 5,000 square feet, and it's nearing standing-room-only. I don't know where my cousin got the guest list. These are not his typical beer-swilling friends I've met before. I think I heard something about this place belonging to a professional athlete. My guess is that *Mr. Athlete* played a role with the invitations, because the crowd is definitely highbrow. Much like the penthouse itself.

    I'd showed up late enough that the socializing was in full swing when I walked through the front door, and instantly felt like I'd stepped into a photo shoot half made up of gorgeous twenty-and-thirty-somethings, polished and plucked within an inch of their lives. I bet any one of them could enter a crime scene and not leave a piece of hair, DNA, or lint behind. Even with all the fancy drinks being consumed, there isn't an extra ounce of body fat to be seen. I almost want to strip them down just to see if they're real. In a scientific way, not a sexy way. Because the thought of actually having sex with one of these male specimens is downright horrifying. No way would I ever allow one of them to see me naked. Plus, anyone *that* into themselves is probably not a *put her pleasure above your own* -type.

    The second half of the crowd is comprised of your dad's boardroom buddies. Much like the chicken skewer guy. Old, white, suit-wearing, drinking brown liquor in low-ball glasses with comb overs that aren't fooling anyone. I'm assuming a handful of them are also City Council Members, and - for this reason alone - I hope my cousin gets the votes he needs. He can young-en things up a bit by adding some non- cholesterol-medicated blood into the veins of the city.

Even with the clashing demographics, everyone is mingling and small talking and munching on the catered food. And then there's me.

I put a decent amount of effort into getting ready. I dusted off the Little Black Dress from the back of my closet. It's classic and safe. The skirt flares out a bit and comes nearly to my knees, making sure I don't look like a street walker. Some people don't realize that when you have an ass, like - a giant handful of an ass - it makes a short dress even shorter. It takes fabric to cover up this behind, and those minidresses do not have enough material for my dimensions. I need to be able to lean over without flashing the cheeks and lady bits to everyone. I'm not like the rest of these waif-thin, waxed-to-perfection creatures, so my hourglass curves stand out a bit more than I prefer.

I'd paired the dress with my now deceased shiny black pumps, some dangly earrings, and a teal clutch, and left my light brown hair in loose waves.

I'd felt amazing until about three seconds after walking through the door, when this landscape of manscape made my extra fifteen pounds feel like fifty. But I stuck it out. I've been here for nearly two hours. Now, it's almost 10 p.m. and my pajamas are at home calling my name. My small-talk filter is wearing thin, and that second glass of wine did not help to rein me in. Then I take one magically cursed step toward some mini fruit tarts, and the heel snaps right off my shoe. If that's not a sign to GTFO, I don't know what is. So, I'm out.

Front door in sight, I start to plan the best route that'll avoid any accidental conversation when my eyes lock onto a profile I - unfortunately - would recognize anywhere. My feet stop moving.

You have got to be kidding me!

Bradley. *Bad Boyfriend Bradley*. A literal *FML* moment. I just want to leave. I want to go home. And I want to do that without having to make eye contact, or voice contact, with mother-freaking *Bradley*.

Taking in all the angles, I try to see if there's a way for me to *Beautiful Mind* my way past this situation. He's standing a few feet away from the door, talking to a few of *the young and the restless*. Looking closer, I realize that the woman next to him is with him. Like *with him*, with him. Her arm's snaked around his back, her hand playing with the collar of his dress shirt.

I take a few steps back as I try to decide what to do about Bradley and his new girl. A girl in a tight red dress, with an ass that does not nudge her obscenely short hemline into misdemeanor territory.

Nope. I'm not dealing with this. Not now, hopefully not ever. Bradley's a tool. Our relationship was short; it was over six months ago. But when I tried to break it off, he got all nasty and he turned it into *him* dumping *me*. I hold no longing for him whatsoever, but the last thing I want to do is run into him, dateless, carrying my broken heel, leaving a party early.

So, I do what any normal woman would do in this situation. I search for a place to hide.

Turning away from the front door, I look around the great room. It really is a beautiful space. Dark wood floors, tall ceilings with big windows, and oversized leather furniture. Weaving my way through bodies, I find myself on the far edge of the room. I'm seriously considering hiding behind the drapes when an escape presents itself in the form of a staircase.

I bite my lip. No one else is paying any attention to the fact that there's apparently a lower level. A glow at the bottom of the stairs beckons me closer. I cross my fingers, hoping there's an extra living room down there, and not a sex dungeon. Or - if it *is* a pleasure room - hopefully it's not in use. Either way, it's worth the risk. I need to be somewhere else while I wait for Bradley *The Ball Bag* to vacate the doorway.

Not wanting to kill myself on the descent, I slip my shoes off and carry them silently down the steps.

Reaching the bottom, I happily find that the floor is covered in a plush carpet. Wiggling my aching toes in the soft goodness, I look around the room. Blinking my eyes to adjust to the dim lighting, I grin. I've found something much better than a second living room. I've found a secret library. Or study. Or whatever rich people call it.

It's beautiful, in a masculine way. There are two pairs of large wingback chairs on opposite sides of the room. Every chair has its own side table and lamp, but just one light has been left on. It gives the room a warm, nighttime feel. Three of the walls are lined with floor-to-ceiling bookshelves. The fourth wall hosts the staircase I just came down and a closed door. Probably that damn sex room.

There are some little trinkets on the shelves; an old-fashioned set of opera glasses, a candy dish filled with little wrapped caramels... but mostly the shelves are filled with books. Lots and lots of books.

I was hoping for a hideaway space I could waste time in, but I ended up finding my real-life happy place. As a copy editor, books are literally my life. Mostly I work on romance novels and adult fiction, but I'm fascinated by all forms of the written word. I love books even more than I love snooping, so combining two of my favorite pastimes . . . *Don't mind if I do.*

I start browsing next to the candy dish. Without thinking, I pick up one of the caramels and bring the waxy wrapper to my nose. My mouth instantly waters at the smell. Feeling only a little bad about stealing, I quickly release the candy from its papery cage and pop into my mouth. A groan immediately leaves my throat. *These are homemade.*

Stuffing the empty wrapper in my pocket, I steal another caramel before shifting focus to the book titles. The collection is eclectic, and arranged in a pattern I can't quite figure out. The fingers of my right hand drag across the book spines as my left hand clutches the second caramel. I'm so caught up in reading titles that I don't hear the footsteps approach behind me.

"Find what you're looking for?"

CHAPTER TWO

KATELYN

The deep voice behind me is so unexpected that I let out a short scream, spinning around and clutching my chest. Only to find myself face-to-chest with ... a beast.

All I see is a vast expanse of man-body, covered by a black button-up that's tight enough for me to tell that this guy is *built*. With slight trepidation, my gaze traces upward, where I find the top two shirt buttons undone, exposing a bit of dark chest hair. I've never been attracted to chest hair before, but *good gods* my hands are itching to reach out and touch it. Continuing the theme of dark hair, my view reaches the bottom of his beard. It's not a long beard, but it's not trimmed close to his face, either. Maybe it's like an inch? I don't have a measuring tool on me at the moment, but - if I did - you can be damn sure it wouldn't be his beard I'm measuring. Scruffy beard or not, it doesn't hide the wide jaw with a mouth showing exactly no emotion. Not a smile or a frown, just man lips held in a firm line. Sexy. Tempting. Man lips.

I almost hesitate, but there's no turning back now. With a swallow, I drag my eyes up to meet his. They're almost eerily blue, set off by long dark lashes. Not dropping his stare, I'm able to see his hair is the same dark brown as his beard. It's unruly and longish, reaching just past his ears. A natural wave making it look both rugged and touchable.

Stick an apple in my mouth. Drop me on a platter. And ring the bell.

I'm done.

This guy is my wet dream come to life, served up in a dark secret library. I cannot imagine a single scenario where I get out of here with my dignity intact, but I am going to try. I'm going to try real hard to focus on reality, and not on climbing this man like a tree.

"Well?" he says.

Oh right. He asked me a question. The one that gave me a heart attack.

What'd he ask? *Find what you're looking for?*

"I did find it… A hideout." *Ugh.* I want to slap myself. I sound like an idiot. Clearing my throat, I try again. "So, um, I came down here to hide. What brought you to this gem of a room?"

He raises an eyebrow. "Gem of a room?"

Gah, his voice.

I don't really know what to say to this guy. His silence is making me want to fill the quiet. But I, more than most, know that oversharing is a problem in these situations. So I force myself to take a breath and glance away.

In doing this, I see that second caramel laying on the floor next to this man's foot. I must've released my grip when he scared me half to death. Not wanting to waste the delicious morsel, I quickly crouch down to retrieve it.

Straightening back up, I realize I've moved dangerously close to the stranger, so I take a large step back.

Except now he's looking at my hand. And that's when it dawns on me... This might be his place. Not only because he's huge, fit, and could for sure be a professional athlete, but also because he seems very at home down here. He knew about this room. He's not looking like this is his first time down here.

Find what you're looking for?

This is his room. His home. His homemade caramels.

Shit.

"Sorry," I say, holding the caramel out to him. "This is yours, isn't it? I didn't mean to intrude. I just wanted to get away from the crowd for a moment and got sidetracked with all your beautiful books. When I first saw the staircase leading down here, I thought there might be some sort of hidden sex chamber. You know… for going all *Fifty Shades* and shit. But a secret library is way better. And when I saw these puppies -" I indicate the caramel - "I just had to try one."

Ohmygod for the love of humanity, stop talking!
I clamp my mouth shut.
"Hmm…" is his only response.

Good lords, the sound coming from him is deep and rumbly, and I swear I feel it vibrating through my bones. But it still doesn't reveal how he feels about our situation.

I make eye contact with him, arm still extended with the caramel between us. He slowly looks down my body, assessing me, taking me in. I know what he sees. I'm cute. Cute, pretty, occasionally beautiful, but I've never been called hot. Unless you count *hot mess*.

I can feel that my hair has lost some of its curl. I'm sure my makeup is smudged. And the icing on the cake, I'm barefoot. My damaged shoes casually discarded somewhere between here and the door, along with my purse.

By the time his eyes meet mine again, my candy offering has lowered to my side. I feel small. Literally, because this man is a good foot taller than me. But also because the past two hours of being surrounded by perfect human cyborgs has dented my tough exterior. Dulled my shine. Bruised my confidence.

His voice pulls me back to the now. "I'm not really sure where to go from here. I've never found a girl like you in my place before, trying my mama's caramels, making herself at home." He pauses. "You sure you should be eating those?"

I feel my throat constrict. Isn't *that* a line I've heard too many times in my life. *Should you be eating that?*

You know what? Fuck this guy. I came down here to get away from Bashing Bradley, and then this Adonis takes all of a minute to assess me and dole out his findings. I am so over this night.

Setting the caramel down on the nearest bookshelf, I look at my toes. I'm trying to decide if I want to unleash my rant on this guy or just walk out. The last thing I'm expecting is for his large hand to come up and cup my chin, applying just enough pressure to have me looking up into his eyes.

His face shows pure puzzlement, and I'm sure he's taking in the sudden, and embarrassing, shine in my eyes.

I swat his hand away.

"I may not be the perfection that you're used to, like all the gorgeous creatures upstairs. And I may have come into your library uninvited, but that doesn't give you the right to make me feel like I'm less." I straighten my spine. "I'm sorry for disrupting your evening."

I move to step around him, knowing it's past time for me to go.

"Whoa now, hold on a second -" he reaches out and grabs my arm just above the elbow.

I pause but I don't look back over to him. Even though I don't know him, I don't feel any fear being alone with him. But I've already made a fool of myself in front of this complete stranger, and I need to get away from civilization before I punch someone in the throat.

He doesn't let go of my arm. "I have a sister I've pissed off more times than I can count. Seeing your reaction, and replaying my own words back in my mind, I think that maybe there was some miscommunication between us." He gives my arm a little tug, causing me to turn back toward him. He leans in to make sure I'm looking in his eyes before he continues. "You, my little Kitten, have some claws hidden in that enticing package. And right now, I'm looking at the only *gorgeous creature* that has captured my attention tonight.'

"I saw you upstairs earlier, so that once-over wasn't the assessment you seem to think it was. That was me taking in the details up close. Now - I'm trying to be polite - so I won't make a comment about your delicious curves in that dress. Rather I'll comment on how much I like your attitude. And when I said 'Are you sure you should be eating those,' that was in reference to you thinking I had a sex dungeon down here for - how did you put it? - *going all fifty shades and shit.* For all you know those could be laced with some sort of mood-altering sex drug. They *are* homemade, after all. But since my mama makes me those caramels, and I've eaten plenty, I'm fairly certain that there aren't any roofies in them. I can text her to ask though. If you want."

Oh. Wow.

I'm legit speechless right now. And anyone who has ever met me knows how momentous that is. I feel like I should be apologizing for thinking the worst of him, while also thanking him for his compliments.

But all that comes out is . . . "*Kitten?*"

He smirks. And freaking crap, it's adorable.

"Yeah, Kitten. You're equal parts little and fierce. It seemed appropriate." He holds out his hand. "Jackson Wilder. Pleasure to meet you."

I can't help the blush that rushes to my cheeks while I place my hand in his. He doesn't shake it, nor does he pull my hand up to kiss it like some old-timey weirdo. He just holds it. His giant palm completely consuming mine while adding just a hint of a squeeze. It's way hotter than it should be.

As he releases my hand, I find my voice. "Hi Jackson, the pleasure's mine." This brings his smirk into a full-fledged grin. "I'm Katelyn Brown."

"Hmmm. Katelyn... *Kitten...* I was pretty close. Do you go by your full name?"

I shrug. "You're the first one to change it to a feline form, but some people call me Kate or Katie or Kay. I'm pretty lax on the nickname thing." I can't help but to ball my hand into a fist. His palm was so warm against mine that the loss makes it feel almost cold. "Thank you for your hospitality tonight. I know Daniel really appreciated that you opened your home to him."

Something flashes in his eyes. "Daniel... as in - the man of the hour? Are you two close?"

It takes a moment for me to get what he's hinting at, and I can't help my snort of laughter while scrunching up my features into a grossed-out face. "Sure, we're close. Daniel's my twerp of a cousin. He's three months older than me and likes to pretend that makes him some wise old prophecy-maker rather than the giant dork that he is." I quickly add, "But you should totally vote for him. He's great."

"Copy that." The damn smirk is back. "So, if Daniel's your cousin and you're down here hiding by yourself, is it safe to assume that you're flying solo tonight?"

I do my best to control my eye roll as I reply. "That's a safe assumption."

He asks, "Care to tell me who you're hiding from?"

"I'm not dying to, no."

His response is a direct stare with a slight tilt of his head.

I sigh. I shouldn't have told him I was down here to hide. "Okay fine. If you must know, I was trying to leave. But my ex, and what I'm assuming is his new girlfriend, were chatting with some people right in front of the door. I did not feel up to dealing with that drama."

His face darkens. "Want me to go kick his ass?"

Laughing, I say, "Desperately."

Jackson turns towards the stairs, which only causes me to laugh harder. Lunging forward I grab his arm and choke out, "I was kidding!"

Jackson turns back to face me. "Well, if I can't kick his ass for you, then we'll just have to entertain ourselves down here for a while. Until we know the coast is clear."

"I really should head home," I mildly protest.

"Pets waiting for you?" he asks.

I shake my head.

"Did you drive yourself here?"

I shake my head again. "I took a Lyft."

"Sounds like you don't need to leave. And you'll just bruise my ego if you try to ditch me now." As he says this, he takes hold of my hand and starts to lead me toward the door that was closed when I got down here, but now sits partially open.

There is a blue glow coming from the room on the other side of the door.

"Umm . . ." My feet slow a bit. "Where are we going?"

Jackson looks down at me. "Let's go get freaky in my sex room."

Excuse me, what?!

Half a second later, Jackson breaks out into loud, manly laughter.

"Oh Kitten, the look on your face..." He starts laughing harder, to the point of bending over and putting his hands on his knees.

Damnit, he is way too hot to laugh like that. Surly hot men are one thing, but that same face broken into a wide smile... it should be illegal.

Narrowing my eyes at his hunched over form, I mumble to myself, "We've got Mr. Fuck Hot over here thinking he's all hilarious, cracking jokes." I don't want to admit how much my pulse skyrocketed, in a good way, when Jackson said he was taking me to his *sex room.*

"Fuck Hot?" Jackson questions.

Crap, I must've mumbled too loud.

I give him a glare. "You done?"

Chuckling, he grabs my hand again and continues our path to the doorway. At this point I'm ninety-five percent sure that there's not a sex room down here.

"Oh, wait." He drops my hand and quickly strides back to the bookshelf. Grabbing the bowl of caramels, he says, "I almost forgot these." Then he winks at me.

He fucking winks.

"Kitten, may I present to you . . . my movie dungeon." With a bow he pushes the door open.

"Har. Har," I fight a smile as I cross the threshold.

I try to act unimpressed, but I'll admit - this room is pretty awesome. Straight ahead is a giant screen mounted onto the wall. Technology is not my area of expertise, so I won't pretend to know anything other than it's large and probably expensive. There's some sort of screen saver or hold screen that is casting the room in that blue glow.

Instead of having the fancy reclining movie chairs that I've seen in some home theaters, this room just has a couch. One gigantic U-shaped couch that looks like it could easily seat a dozen Jackson-sized men.

Football players? Basketball?

I feel like I should know what sport he plays but asking him now might be insulting. I'll wait and Google him when I get home.

The couch is dark grey, and - once I get close enough to touch it - I can feel that it's a soft, almost fuzzy fabric. It might be okay for Jackson to sit on and still have his feet on the ground, but the sitting part is so deep that if I put my back against the rear cushions my feet will stick off the end like a little kid. I cannot wait to get on this couch. This is the sort of furniture you'd volunteer to sleep on.

Without waiting for further invitation, I hurry around and plop myself in the middle of the couch. I pull my knees up and to the side to keep my dress from showing too much leg.

Jackson is smiling at my reaction as he makes his way over in a much slower and more controlled fashion. He sits to the left of me, wedging his body into the corner. Maybe it's the extra corner cushions around him, or maybe it's just because he's sitting there looking divine, but his spot looks even more comfortable than mine.

"Were you watching something?" I ask, nodding towards the big screen.

"I was. Then I thought I heard a noise in my library and figured I should go corral the drunk partygoer back upstairs."

"Hmm. How'd that work for you?"

"Jury's still out. But now I have company to share a movie with, so I'm thinking it's working out okay."

"Decent answer." My cheeks feel like they've been in a constant state of blushing. "So, Jackson, what're we watching?"

"*The Godfather Part Two.*"

"Cool."

Jackson watches my reaction with suspicion. "Have you seen it?"

I shrug, "Nope."

He narrows his eyes a little. "Have you seen the first one?"

I feel like I'm failing a test, but I answer truthfully. "Also, nope."

"That settles it. We need to start at the beginning."

"I mean I've heard of it," I state, while he clicks his remote to pull up the new movie choice. "Is it a favorite of yours?"

"The original is definitely in my top-ten list. I watched it with Pops, my grandfather, when I was probably too young. Mama had a righteous fit when she found out, so it's always stuck with me for sentimental reasons."

He calls his mom mama. Melt.

I make a sound of agreement. "I can understand that. Is your pops still around?"

"Nah, he passed several years ago."

"I'm sorry. Grandparents are the best. Of course mine never let me watch racy gunslinger movies. But I did get my fair share of cookies from my grandma."

"Well, you're in for a treat." He looks at me for an extra beat. "I think my pops woulda liked you."

This guy. One little comment and just like that, *all* the bumblebees land in my stomach. Jackson saying his grandpa would like me shouldn't feel like such a big thing. I just met him. Like less than ten minutes ago. But this thing, this energy, already feels like something. Like a *start*.

I know better than to catch feelings so quickly, but he's so damn likable.

My internal buzz intensifies. People always talk about butterflies. But they're fragile, and I've never run away from a butterfly. Now, a belly full of bumblebees? Bumblebees are cute, and necessary for life, but a whole pile of them can be more than a bit terrifying. Kinda like feelings.

"Are you single?" I blurt out.

Wow, Katelyn, way to be subtle.

"Yes?" he replies. Dragging the word out, turning it into a question.

"Just wondering if there'll be any territorial women breaking through that door looking for you," I rationalize, gesturing to the now closed again door behind us.

"Not likely. I imagine at some point I'll be hunted down by the party staff to let me know the guests are leaving. But you shouldn't have to worry about pulling out your claws for that."

"Cute." I deadpan.

"And you? Any boyfriends gonna come sniffing you out?"

"Not even the slightest chance." Looking back toward the screen, I pretend our mutual single status isn't affecting me. "Are you ready, or do you want to hype it more before we start?"

With a chuckle, Jackson starts the movie. As the opening credits roll, I notice the bite to the air on my bare legs and arms. Looking around I spot a blanket draped over the back of the couch on the far side of Jackson.

"Um, can I borrow that?" I ask, pointing to the blanket.

"You cold? I can turn up the heat."

"I'd prefer the blanket actually. I like chilly rooms, so long as I can cuddle up into a blanket or something to stay warm."

He hums, pulling the blanket toward him. But instead of passing it over to me, he just lays it across his own lap. "I agree with you." Then he lifts the edge of the blanket closest to me in blatant invitation. I give him side-eye in return. "Kitten, I'm not trying to pull a fast one on you. But this is the best and softest blanket in the whole house. Trust me when I say that it, combined with me, will keep you plenty warm." He holds my gaze for a beat, then adds. "I promise to remain a perfect gentleman."

The sad part is that I totally trust he's telling the truth right now. I'm sure he will be a gentleman. I'm also sure that I really *really* don't want him to be one. But keeping our movie viewing behavior PG is the smart choice here.

Without further comment, I rise off the couch and walk the half dozen steps over to where Jackson is sitting. With him pressed all the way back into the corner I will either need to crawl, scoot, or walk across the three-foot-deep cushion to get myself properly situated into his side. I may never see this man again, so I'm going to bring my cuddle game up to Olympic levels and savor every moment of it.

Standing there, I contemplate the best approach. Scooting myself backward across the cushion toward him is a no go. Trying to crawl, in a dress, without catching myself on the hem and faceplanting into the back of the couch... hard pass. So, with my hands holding down the edges of the skirt I step up so I'm standing on the couch. The look of surprise on Jackson's face gives me a moment of smug victory as I take a step toward him, then spin around and drop into a seated position snug against his side. He wastes no time draping the blanket across me and putting his arm around my shoulders.

Since I've already decided to go big or go home, I curl myself into his side and rest my head on his chest. Relaxing into him, I almost feel like I'm in high school again. Snuggling under a blanket in the dark. Almost... because none of the boys in high school were built like Jackson.

I take a deep breath to calm my poor heart, and am forced to stifle a groan. How does a man smell this good, this late at night? I'm not sure if it's cologne, or if it's just *him*. If it *is* bottle-produced, I might need to buy some. Then I can shamefully spray it on a pillow when I'm feeling lonely and want to come back to this moment. Yikes. Just thinking that depresses me a little. Okay, whatever, I'm going to live in the now. I'm going to enjoy this feeling, watch the movie, and go home with a lovely memory of the evening that didn't turn to shit after all.

CHAPTER THREE

JACKSON

I'm not sure when my little Kitten fell asleep, but it was fairly soon after the movie started.
My Kitten. When did I become such a sap?
Even though I've seen this movie about a hundred times, I couldn't begin to tell you what's going on. I haven't been able to focus on a damn thing since my senses were overwhelmed with the scent and warmth of *her* being near me.

Guess it gives me an excuse to insist that I see her again, so we can actually watch this movie together, when we're both awake and paying attention. I should've had an early bedtime tonight, but sitting down here with a cute Kitten snuggled into my side is preferable to being alone in my bed. Plus, I'm not exactly exerting myself, and it's comfortable as hell, so I'm counting this as resting.

If - earlier this evening - someone had told me that I'd end the night curled up in my theater with a beautiful woman, watching one of my favorite movies, talking about my pops and sharing my mama's caramels, I would've said they're a fool. But now *I* feel like the fool because here Kitten is, still in my arms, and I'm already worrying about how I'm going to see her again.

When I'd first heard the noise coming from my library, I was furious. I'd been promised by the party planners that guests would stay out of my private rooms. It's not that I have anything to hide. Surely nothing as exciting as a sex room. (Though now I'm starting to think maybe having one isn't the worst idea . . .) And it's not that I dislike parties, but tonight was not my scene. I'd had my teammates pull in some favors to get the desired guest list, but that crowd was not mine. I happen to like Daniel's talking points, so - when my agent proposed hosting this party - I was happy to do so. But after an hour of shaking hands, and gently turning away women I wasn't interested in, I needed to escape.

It was then that I first saw Katelyn upstairs. She was talking with an older couple in a very animated way. All three of them were laughing, but her smile was what made me stop and watch. I was aware that I was being a bit of a creeper, but she stood out to me. Her shiny hair was catching the light every time she moved her head, causing the color to dance between shades of brown. She was stunning in that black dress. It showcased every sexy inch of her, but didn't flash flesh like so many of the other ladies' outfits. I'm no prude, but I do like a little left to the imagination. Especially once I make a woman mine. I don't need every other man with eyes taking in more than they need to. Okay, so I'm not a prude, but I'm aware I can be a bit of a caveman when it comes to the people I claim.

So, when I opened the door preparing to yell at whoever was in my library, I was stunned into silence when I realized it was the same woman. I had already been kicking myself about not approaching her upstairs. Now was my chance to make up for that mistake. And then, like the big goddamn buffoon that I am, I frightened her, insulted her, and almost scared her off. I've done some dumb things through my thirty-four years of life, but I'm not sure I've ever hated myself more than I did when I saw those tears forming in her eyes after what I said.

Like I told her, I have a sister, and a mama, so I know all about the struggles that women deal with. And I know how much the words of another can make-or-break some of those tenuous feelings. What broke my heart was not only that I said something to make her feel poorly, but that she even has those seeds of doubt in her brain to begin with. I knew it was too soon in our meeting to drop to my knees and tell her how absolutely perfect she was, and that I wouldn't change a damn thing about her.

I'm not saying those other ladies upstairs weren't beautiful. They were. But this Kitten caught my eye. And there is no denying she has some sort of special pull on me. And that ass, with those curves, on that body... I'm a big guy. I'm strong. I tend to get very *into the moment*. I need a woman who can hold her own with me. One who I don't have to worry I'll break in two. Pretty sure Kitten and I could get rough and hot and both make it through to the end.

Shit. I need to stop thinking about this. The last thing I need is her innocently waking up on my shoulder, with me sitting here sporting a hard-on that's impossible to miss.

My phone's on silent, but I can feel it vibrating in my pocket. It's on the opposite side of Kitten, so - thankfully - it's not disturbing her.

I manage to get the phone into my hand with minimal movement, seeing a text from the guy upstairs saying his party staff are cleaning up and almost done for the night. I'm not sure if I'm going to get Agreeable Katelyn or Feisty Kitten when she wakes up, so I'm thinking I should take this opportunity to get her phone number.

I text back asking if Daniel is still here. The *yes* reply is immediate, and I ask that he send Daniel down to the theater, but to please be quiet. Another instant reply confirms my request. This guy has catered parties for me before, so he can tell Daniel where to find me.

I don't have to wait long before there's a light knock on the door as it opens. I don't pause or mute the movie, since I don't want a change in atmosphere to wake the sleeping Kitten in my lap.

Daniel's eyes take a moment to scan the room before he finds me. We spoke for a while during the party setup, and I'll admit that I like the guy on a personal level. He seems down to earth, while still being professional and driven. I think he could have a long political career ahead of him, and

I respect that sort of dedication. But he's also a man, and a man that knows this firecracker better than I do. At least for now, that is. So I'm hoping he'll help me out a bit.

Lifting my hand to motion him over, I speak quietly. "Hey man, hope you had the turnout you were looking for tonight."

He steps up to the back of the couch, far enough to my right that we can make eye contact without me having to crane my neck all the way around.

"It was great! Seriously Jackson, I can't thank you enough for all you did to help make this happen. If there's ever anything that I can do for you, just let me know. This was huge!"

Smiling, I reply, "It's funny you should say that." And I nod to the sleeping woman tucked into my side.

Daniel looks down, and I can tell the second he recognizes who is sleeping next to me. His brows furrow as he raises his gaze back up to mine, a question in his eyes. Clearly this guy likes me and wants to stay true to his word, but he is also exuding caution. I'm glad to see that look on him.

"I met Katelyn earlier tonight, and we kind of hit it off. But you see"—I pause—"I'm really starting to like her, and I want to stay in touch with her. I, of course, was planning to ask for her number when she wakes up, but I'm not entirely sure that she'll give it to me."

At that, Daniel breaks out into his wide politician smile. "You sure you just met her? You've already realized that she can be a total pain in the ass." Getting more serious he says "She can be a pain, but she's an amazing person. You seem like a good guy, so I'll give you the benefit of the doubt on this one. But she's special to a whole lot of people, a whole lot of people who will get pissed at me if she gets hurt by you. So, if you're only interested in a fling, I'd kindly ask that you look elsewhere."

I nod in understanding. "I'm glad you're looking out for her. I can't predict the future to tell you where this goes, but if I was just looking for an easy lay, I wouldn't have to look that hard. This here is something else." I can't help but to look back down at the sleeping woman. When I look back up, I see that Daniel is openly watching me.

Finally, he sighs. "Give me your number. I'll share her info with you."

Taking his phone, I type my number in. Now if I mess this up, at least one of Kitten's relatives will have a way to track me down.

Seeing there is no good way to shake hands, he just smiles a little. "I'm not sure which one of you I should feel sorry for right now." Laughing under his breath he turns and walks out, closing the door behind him.

It only takes another minute before my phone buzzes with a text from Daniel. Luckily for me, Daniel went the easy route and just shared the whole contact with me. So now I have Kitten's phone number, email, and home address.

A plan starts to unfurl. With a smile pulling on my lips, I lean over and kiss the top of her pretty head.

CHAPTER FOUR

KATELYN

I can't believe I slept through the whole movie! I completely missed out on our cuddle time. Well, I mean I was obviously there for it, I just don't remember it. I'm a little mollified by the fact that, at some point, Jackson also fell asleep. When I finally awoke, the ending credits were still playing, and Jackson's head was tipped against the back of the couch, mouth shut, sleeping silently. It's not fair. He's even good-looking when he sleeps. Can't he at least pretend to be human and have his mouth wide open, with drool on his chin? I'm sure that's how I looked.

Luckily, I had my face buried so far into his body that there was no way he could have seen me. And fuck, what a body. It's a real body. Big and burly and strong and warm and big. Have I mentioned big? It took all my willpower to keep my hands still, rather than run them all over his chest.

My stirring must have woken him, because he slowly blinked his eyes open and looked down at me. It was the most adorably adorable thing I had ever witnessed. I kind of wanted to shave off one of his eyebrows just to bring him down a peg and onto a more even playing field. But he'd probably find a way to make that look good, and that would just annoy me even more.

Waking up also made me realize that I *really* had to use the bathroom. Like - if I had laughed, even a little, I would totally have peed my pants. Dress. Whatever. So, climbing off the couch I asked to use his ladies' room and he pointed me in the right direction while he shut down the stuff in the theater.

Which brings me to now. I'm still in the bathroom, fretting, and if I don't get out of here soon, he's going to think that I'm suffering from stomach problems. I like this guy. I like him a lot. I have decent self-confidence, but I'm pretty sure this guy is out of my league. And not just because he's good-looking. *And he is beyond good-looking.* But also because he's clearly loaded, and probably famous. Or at least famous to people who watch . . . whatever the hell sport it is that he plays.

Gah! What am I supposed to do? Do I ask for his number? Do I put myself out there like that?

No. No, nope, *no*. I'm leaving this in his hands. His big, strong, capable hands. Ack! Okay, I need to get over myself and get out of here.

Stepping out of Jackson's powder room, I spot him strolling across the condo in my direction.

"Thank you for sharing your movie with me. Sorry I slept through the whole thing."

"You're welcome. And even if you can't prove it, now you can tell people that you've watched it. It truly is a crime that you hadn't seen it," he smiles.

"Okay. Well, thanks again. I should really head home now." Biting my lip, I gather up my purse and shoes, and head toward the door.

I can hear Jackson walking behind me. "I wish I had a pair of shoes in your size I could give you, since you can't walk in your broken ones."

Reaching the door, I turn back toward him. "Honestly, I'm kind of glad you don't. I'm not sure if I would want to wear the shoes of some ex-girlfriend or one-night stand."

Jackson's grin is a bit devilish as he says, "I was thinking more along the lines of my sister's shoes. But I kinda like that the idea of another woman sleeping over gets your fur up. My Kitten is getting a little green, I think."

With an incredulous look I tell him, "You can be a bit of a cocky ass, you know that?"

"Mmm-hmm." Jackson steps so close I can feel the body heat radiating off him. Leaning in, he puts his lips next to my ear. "Yeah, I'm cocky all right, but I think you might like that about me. And you're a feisty little vixen, and I *know* that I like that about you."

Pulling away from me I hear the click of the door opening behind me. His long arm somehow reached back and grabbed the handle, all while he was distracting me with his words and his hot breath on my neck.

"Goodnight, Kitten. Sweet dreams."

Not trusting my mouth to say anything that wouldn't be horribly awkward, I turn and walk out Jackson's door. I don't even exhale until I'm down the hallway and hitting the button to call up the elevator. I think I hear him shut the door behind me, but I'm not willing to turn around to look. My heart couldn't take it if I locked eyes with him again. It's still going crazy, and he didn't even kiss me. He didn't kiss me. He didn't really touch me. But my body is lit up. I feel like we just had a bout of energetic foreplay and a single touch would set me off at this moment. How does he do that?

And what does it mean that he didn't try to kiss me? Did he not want to? Did he think I wouldn't approve of a kiss? How the hell am I supposed to *not* overthink this?

The elevator door dings as it slides open. Stepping in, I press the button for the lobby and sag against the wall. It's not until I'm exiting the building, phone in hand, that I realize he never asked for my number.

Well, shit.

CHAPTER FIVE

KATELYN

"No offense mom, but if you hadn't sent Daniel a thousand apology notes for being out of town last night, he probably wouldn't have even noticed you weren't there."

"I just want to make sure that he knows how much we love and support him," my mom says into the phone. "And what do you mean he wouldn't have noticed? You said you went. He would've seen that Dad and I weren't with you."

"Believe it or not, when a thirty-one-year-old woman goes to a party, it's not automatically assumed that her parents will be with her." I try to rein in the snark. I try, but I'm not successful.

"Yes, dear, I know you're an adult now."

Now? Legally I've been an adult for thirteen years. It's a good thing we're on a regular phone call and not on FaceTime, or - as Mom calls it - *FacePhone*, because then she would see just how far my eyes are rolling.

It's Saturday morning. The party was last night. I got home extremely late, and my mom woke me up with this phone call. Doing the quick math in my head, I figure I got about six hours of sleep last night. I'm not a morning person, and I'm not a function-on-less-than-eight-hours-of-sleep person either. And, unfortunately for my mom, that means my patience is thinning.

"Did you meet any nice boys at the party? If our absence could have gone unnoticed then it must have been crowded."

"*Nice boys*, Mom?"

"Well, you know what I mean. Any gentlemen?"

Of course, my mind instantly pictures Jackson's face when he said he'd remain the perfect gentleman.

Jackson! I can't believe I forgot to Google him!

A knock at the front door startles me out of my thoughts and gives me a great excuse to get my mom off the phone.

"Sorry, Mom, I gotta go. Someone's here. Love you, bye."

I hear "who is" before I hang up. I try to not hang up on my mom too often, but there are times when I can't resist the pull.

Honestly, I have no idea who could be at my door. My guess is a package delivery. It's before noon on a Saturday, and my friends don't just swing by. We aren't in college anymore, stopping by unannounced hasn't been a thing for years. Reaching the door, I glance through the peephole and don't see anyone there. My initial assumption is proved correct when I open the door and find a box on the front step.

I live in a little two-bedroom townhouse about twenty minutes outside of downtown Minneapolis. I'm currently renting, since I'm not quite ready to commit to buying a house on my own. I've added enough of my own personal touches to make it feel like home. The neighbors on both sides of me are older, to the point of being elderly, which is great because they are quiet and bring me leftover baked goods on the regular.

Setting the box down on the kitchen counter, I realize that it looks more like a present than something shipped in the mail. It's white, about the size of a large shoe box, and tied with a green ribbon. Strange. Was this sent by courier?

Pulling on the ribbon, I flip open the box to discover a folded shirt of some sort. Grabbing near the collar I pull it out and it unfurls to reveal a jersey. A really nice one that looks legit and expensive. It's blue and green, with a storm-cloud logo, and the words *Minnesota Sleet* across the front.

Turning it over I see the number *33* with *Wilder* written above.

Well, damn. Jackson Wilder, of the Minnesota Sleet. He's a hockey player. I should've guessed with the beard and unruly hair. Saying his name together with the team name sounds a little familiar, even to me. I wonder just how big of a deal this guy is.

Oh, holy shit, hold up!

This is from Jackson!

This had to have come from him. Right? And he wouldn't be sending me his jersey if he didn't like me. He must... Wait, how does he know where I live? I brush that thought away. He's rich. Rich people play by different rules, and I refuse to be creeped out by Jackson.

Looking back at the box, I see there's an envelope that had been hidden by the jersey. The outside is unadorned, but it has the texture of nice stationary.

Opening the envelope, I find a plain white card inside. When I go to read it, a ticket falls out. Reading the details, I see that it's a ticket for a Sleet game. Tonight's game. Well... *that's* interesting.

There's a note written inside of the card. The handwriting is neat and legible, but has a heavy-handed look to it.

>*Dearest Kitten,*
>*I was having a fairly dull evening last night, until you wandered into it. If you're not otherwise occupied, I would like to have you in the stands tonight at my game. Hopefully cheering me on. I got the feeling that maybe you aren't a hockey fan, so I included something for you to wear. There are usually a couple of*

people wearing my jersey, so don't worry about everyone knowing that we slept together last night just because you're wearing my name.
    Yours,
    Mr. Fuck Hot

I think I read the letter four times before I start fanning myself with the card. Even mentally hearing him say *slept together*, causes my knees to go weak and I grip the edge of the counter. Looking back at the ticket I confirm that it's for one seat. There is no plus one. No chance for me to bring a date, or even a friend as a buffer.

I don't even have to think about it. I'm going. Even if I did have plans for tonight, I would cancel them.

The game isn't until eight. I have plenty of time to pamper myself and learn everything there is to know about hockey. And Jackson.

CHAPTER SIX

KATELYN

"Okay, that's a little strange," I say to myself, looking at a life-size cutout of Jackson. He's all dressed up in his hockey gear, holding a stick, but no helmet so you can see his handsome face. There's a family waiting for their turn to take a picture, while a trio of teenage girls takes endless selfies with the fake Jackson.

I mean, I get it... he's super hot, but it's still a little weird to be watching this. I just found out who *real* Jackson is. Plus, he's got to be literally twice the age of these squealing fans. Ugh, who am I kidding... my teenage celebrity crushes knew no bounds, nor age restrictions.

This arena is huge. I did have to look that term up, since I was pretty sure it wasn't called a stadium. And being that I have no frame of reference, I have to assume that it's always this packed. Wall to wall, shoulder to shoulder, crowds of people. Everyone milling around, getting their food and beer.

The nachos look like a pile of greasy wonderfulness, but I'll be honest, I'm stupid-nervous right now. I think I'll wait to see how I'm feeling until after the first period before indulging.

See, I studied. I know there are three periods in a game.

I also learned that Jackson Wilder is a big damn deal. He plays the right wing position. He's played for a couple of teams since he went professional, and this is his fifth year playing for Minnesota. I read an interview where he said that he'd like to stay here for the remainder of his career, since he loves the team and the fans so much. That could be total bullshit, but I'm hoping he meant it.

I did limit my Jackson research to his time spent playing for the Sleet. I'm sure being in the limelight is hard, and I didn't want to read a bunch of stuff about his personal life. Especially since there's a chance it could be untrue. Just learning about his five years with the Sleet has me a little embarrassed that, as a resident of this state, I didn't know who he was.

And he was clearly being sarcastic in his note when he said that "a few people" would be wearing his jersey. I think you could tally up his fans as a percentage of this crowd. Like, a majority percentage of the people here are wearing his number.

I'm taking this as a positive sign. He must be a good player, and a decent guy, or else all these people wouldn't be spending their money buying his gear.

I fit in pretty well with my Wilder jersey, skinny jeans, and knee-high leather boots. Since the jersey is long sleeved, I put it over a long-sleeved white tee, which was warm enough that I didn't have to lug a jacket around with me.

Friendly arena staff are posted all over the place, and they help direct me towards my seat.

Shuffling past a few bodies I get to where I need to be. Dropping into the fold-down seat, I find myself right near center ice, three rows back from the glass and in the middle of the row. *Damn, this must be an expensive ticket.* I internally roll my eyes at myself for that inner monologue. The man who gave me this ticket is on the freaking team. It would've been more ridiculous if it wasn't a good seat.

There's a family to my left. The little boy in the seat next to me has his face painted with a big 33 and has an honest-to-god foam finger on his hand. As we get closer to game time, the rest of the row fills up, but the seat to my right remains empty.

Why am I so nervous?! It's not like I'm the one playing out there. And Jackson has played dozens, probably hundreds, of games by now. I'm sure me being here isn't going to make a single bit of difference to how well he performs.

A startled yelp escapes me when the pump-up music starts blasting through the speakers. When the announcer begins to introduce the team, I have to physically hold down my bouncing knees. I should have looked on YouTube for a clip of this introduction mayhem, because I was not expecting this level of theatrics. The music is vibrating the air around me. There are laser lights and projections and the announcer is still yelling out names. The whole thing is quite overwhelming.

When they announce Jackson as a starting player, the crowd - already going nuts - gets even louder. I hardly know the man, but I can't help feeling proud of him. And wow, he looks good. Hockey pads are not exactly what you'd call a sexy outfit, but - on him? - it *works*. It makes his already large frame look even more impressive and climbable.

As the teams line up for the national anthem, the crowd stands, and I lock eyes with Jackson. He's all the way across the ice, but it feels like he's right next to me. The corner of his mouth turns up in a smirk and my heart starts to beat faster. He knows I'm here. And he seems pleased. With his eyes on mine, heat starts to crawl up and down my body.

When cheers break out around me, I realize that we stared at each other for the entire anthem. Well, if lusting after one of our great nation's professional athletes isn't patriotic, I don't know what is.

The teams face off. The puck drops. And the game starts.

With my face still warm, I tell myself to calm down and pretend to be a normal person for the remainder of this game.

I'm not sure if I've ever watched an NHL game before, but I should have. These guys fly across the ice like dancers, but crash into each other like freight trains. The combination of grace and violence is fascinating. And sexy. I'm not even ashamed to admit that watching Jackson skating out there has me all sorts of hot-and-bothered. With the level of turned-on that I am, you'd think I was at home, watching porn, with my hand in my pants. Not sitting in a packed arena, watching fully clothed men crash into each other.

The first period is about halfway over when someone bumps into my elbow as they drop into the empty seat next to me.

Looking over I smile as the lady shuffles around a box of popcorn, a large beer, a bag of cotton candy, and her own foam finger sporting the number 33. She's wearing a jersey similar to the one I have on, and her short curly brown hair is streaked with grey.

"Oh my goodness, I'm sorry, dear! I just knocked right into you." She chuckles. "You'd think I'd learn that carrying all this shit at once is a dumbass idea. But I do it every time I come here."

I like this lady already. Her laugh is infectious, she curses like it's second nature, and her light blue eyes, accented with chunky purple frames, exude friendliness. Handing me her cotton candy to free a hand, she reaches over to shake mine.

"I'm Mary, and you are just the prettiest thing this side of the Mississippi."

Mary is probably in her late sixties, and I think I want to be her best friend.

Grinning I take her hand. "Aw, thank you! I'm Katelyn. And I'm thrilled that you'll be sitting next to me."

"Go on and open up that bag for me, will ya? I like to mix all my snacks while I watch. Can't stick with one flavor for too long or else I get jittery." Giving me a once-over she asks, "You refraining from eating or some such bullshit? You don't even have a drink with you."

Laughing I say, "Yeah, no, long story. I think I'm ready to snack now though." She tips her head forward and peers at me over the top of her glasses, a question clear in her eyes, so

I elaborate. "This is my first game and I was a little nervous when I got here. Or, well, a *lot* nervous. I wasn't sure I could handle eating anything. But now that it's started, and he's doing so well, I feel better."

Mary tilts her head. "You said *he*."

"Huh?"

"You said, 'he's doing so well.' Are you here for one of the players?"

"Oh, umm . . . yeah, but not like you're thinking. We just met last night. He was just being really sweet, surprising me with a jersey and a ticket for this game. We aren't like dating or anything. I don't think... No, probably not. That'd be crazy..." I trail off and Mary and I just look at each other, both blinking. Then she bursts out laughing, laying a hand on my forearm.

"Oh, honey. You are too precious. If this guy invites you to his game the very next day after meeting, I'd say it's safe to assume he's interested in being more than friends." Then she pulls on my shoulder a little bit. "Let me see who this jersey belongs to."

I lean forward so she can see the Wilder scrawled across my back.

"Well lookie here, we're wearing matching numbers!"

Sitting back up, I can see that Mary has a large and genuine smile on her face, and a twinkle in her eye. She is clearly enjoying this predicament of mine.

She gestures to my hands. "All right, you start on that cotton candy. I'm digging into this popcorn. When I say switch, you switch with me. We can share this beer until one of those handsome beer guys makes his way over here." I nod in agreement. There's no way to turn this woman down. "And while we watch this game, I want to hear all about how you met the real live Jackson Wilder."

CHAPTER SEVEN

KATELYN

Three shared beers later...

"Then the movie was ending, and I realized I'd slept through the whole thing! And instead of being cute about it, I had to run to the bathroom as soon as I woke up."

"I hear ya on that one, darling," Mary commiserates with me.

We've had our eyes on the game, but I've made it through the story of last night. The Sleet are up 2-to-1, it's the start of the third period, and Jackson assisted on the second goal. Hockey is so much more fun than I expected. Watching Jackson on the ice is a bit nerve-wracking, but Mary has done a good job of keeping me settled.

"Yeah, so, then he walked me to the door. I'd already decided that I wasn't going to ask for his number."

"Why not? Women can ask for numbers. This is the twenty-first century, Kitten." Mary dissolves into giggles.

It's hard to tell this story without mentioning the Kitten part, which she thinks is adorable. And since I didn't want to jinx this, whatever this is, I haven't told anyone else about last night yet. It's nice to finally share and get a little female feedback.

"Yeah, well, in the twenty-first century it still sucks to get rejected by big hot guys when you ask for their number and they turn you down." In my peripheral vision I can see Mary give a head nod.

"So, what happened when you left? Did he kiss you?"

I groan. "No. He leaned in like he might but instead said something all sexy into my ear and then opened the door for me to go. I believe 'Good night, Kitten. Sweet dreams' were his parting words." I say that as if I haven't replayed them over and over in my mind since then.

"And then today you get a surprise package, so you can wear his jersey and attend his game. He might be going slow on the physical side of things, but I think it's safe to say that he likes youuuuuuuuu!"

Mary starts to scream as everyone jumps to their feet to watch Jackson break away with the puck. I've joined in with the rest of the crowd, on my feet shouting, and when Jackson strikes the puck past the goalie's outstretched glove into the net, I jump up and down like a crazy person.

Somehow, I'm now wearing Mary's big foam finger, waving it above my head while the crowd starts to chant *"Jack-son, Jack-son!"*

While the arena goes wild, Jackson skates past, looks right at me, and winks. My heart stops. He's smiling, sweaty, breathing heavily, and I think I just had an orgasm.

My thighs shake and I drop down into my seat. Glancing over, I see that Mary has the popcorn box up and almost covering her face. I think it's to hide her shit-eating grin. I don't know why she is so excited about the fact that Jackson might have a thing for me. But she is just so damn maternal, I bet it's in her blood to cheer on romance.

With five minutes left in the game, a guy in a suit, who looks like he might work here, waves to get my attention from the aisle. He holds up a familiar-looking white envelope in his hand and motions it toward me. When I nod in recognition, he hands it to the person on the end of the row indicating that they should pass it down.

After hearing my story already, I'm pretty sure Mary knows exactly what this is, too. Opening the envelope, I find another card inside.

Little Kitten,

I know I've already taken up a lot of your time tonight with this game, but I'm greedy. Please come to our after-game gathering at The Den. It's a bar not too far from here. I have to arrive with the team, or else I would offer you a ride.

Your Player

CHAPTER EIGHT

KATELYN

This place is crazy! It's pretty big for a downtown bar, and it's packed full of people. The noise level is off the charts, so you need to be all up in someone's Kool-Aid just to hear them talk. It feels like an extension of the energy from the arena, and I think it's safe to say that everyone here knows that the Sleet players are on their way.

Mary has turned out to be a treasure trove of information. Apparently, she has been a hockey fan all her life, and she goes to as many hockey games as possible. Her husband passed away nearly fourteen years ago, but he had played hockey growing up and instilled his love for the sport in their whole family.

Along with rules of the game, Mary taught me that the scantily clad chicks that seem to be all over this bar are called puck bunnies. And apparently their goal is to "fuck a player and bag themselves a sugar daddy," or so Mary says. She does admit they aren't all as bad as she makes them sound, but there are a few who earn the nasty rep.

And yeah, I know Jackson's letter didn't say I could invite a friend, but Mary ended up being a bit of a godsend tonight. And when I asked if she would like to come with me, she lit up like an excited puppy. Plus, I figured it would take a while for the team to arrive, and drinking with Mary is way more fun than freaking out by myself.

As soon as we got here, she went to the bar and came back with vodka cranberries for us. She said she was done with beer, and that the juice made it a health drink. Hard to argue with that logic. I'm definitely stopping after this one, though, because a good buzz is fine, but I don't want to be shit-faced when Jackson shows up.

I'm reminding myself of that thought when a commotion at the front of the bar signals the arrival of the players.

I can't stop the smile that spreads across my face, as I turn to Mary and shout, "He's here!"

Motioning for Mary to stay put, I push forward to go find Jackson.

The size of the crowd slows my progress, but being short works in my favor as I slip between bodies. Finally, I get close enough to spot Jackson. He's showered, and his hair still looks a little damp. He's wearing black dress pants and a grey button-up shirt with the sleeves rolled up.

I give him a once-over. Twice.

Willing myself to be brave, I bite my lip and start to walk closer.

He's talking to one of his teammates, and both of them are ignoring the two women who're trying desperately to get their attention. As if he can sense my gaze on him, he looks up and locks eyes with me. With a nod to his friend, Jackson sidesteps the ladies, and strides my way.

Being large and intimidating has its perks, such as getting a crowd to part by sheer will.

A breath later, Jackson stops a foot in front of me. My heart stutters when he brings his hand up to the side of my face, swiping his thumb across my cheek.

"Kitten, you came." The look on his face is full of something warm, and sweet.

"You're a hard man to resist, Jackson Wilder." He smirks. "And apparently you're kind of okay at hockey." My straight face fails me as I grin up at him. "Congrats on your win!"

Knowing the alcohol has gone a bit to my head, but not caring enough to stop myself, I stretch onto my toes so I can wrap my arms around his neck in a hug. I have a flash of worry, but - before it can turn into panic - Jackson bends a little and hugs me back, surrounding me in his shower-fresh scent and strong arms. I can't help myself; I burrow my face into his neck and inhale.

Pulling back just a fraction, I speak into his ear. "Come with me, I have a friend I want you to meet." I'm still too close to him, so every word has my lips brushing against his skin. I can see his jaw tick and I'm not sure if it's from annoyance, or something else.

Stepping away, I take his hand and start to lead him through the crowd, toward where I left Mary. After a few steps, I glance back and see him looking up to the ceiling. The face he is making is one of those *lord give me patience* looks that I've gotten from my mother, a time or twenty. It's not a look I want to cause on anyone, especially not on Jackson.

Stopping suddenly, I release Jackson's hand, which snaps his attention back to me.

"I'm sorry... If you need to go talk to other people that's fine. I totally understand. I'm sure a lot of these people are here for you." My hands are fidgeting. I hate feeling this unsure of myself.

"What?" he questions. Then it seems to click. "Oh no, that wasn't what it looked like." He grabs my hand again, interlacing our fingers as he steps closer so I can hear him. "Trust me, you're the only person I want to talk to tonight. I wish we could go somewhere else, but Coach wanted us all to make an appearance." Jackson's eyes stay on mine. "You got me?"

I nod, believing him.

He squeezes my fingers. "Good. Now let's go find your friend."

Bolstered by his words, I continue pushing through the crowd. Spotting Mary, I drag Jackson along until we end up right behind her.

Pulling Jackson so he's standing next to me, I say, "Jackson, I'd like you to meet my new friend Mary."

Hearing her name, Mary turns to face us.

At the same time Mary says, "Jacky!" … Jackson questions, "Mama?"

CHAPTER NINE

KATELYN

I blink once. Twice.
Well. Fuck. Me.
Looking back and forth between the two of them, I squint my eyes, as if that will give me some better insight. Slowly, it becomes painfully obvious. Same light blue eyes. Same dark brown hair, with grey and a little extra curl in Mary's.

"Mama, I thought you were out of town all week?" Jackson asks, clearly still shocked to find his *Freaking! Mom!* at this afterparty.

Mary just smiles. "I came home early. I was a little late to the game, but I got to spend time talking to your Kitten."

Oh. My. Holy Hell. Please, Earth, if you're listening, swallow me whole, right now.

"Kitten?" Jackson asks, then looks over to me. "You told her that?"

I throw my hands up. "I didn't know she was your mom!" Then, turning to Mary -"Uh *hello?* You didn't think to mention that? Like, at all?"

Mary's smile doesn't falter. And then, in a totally inappropriate manner, I burst out laughing. Holding my stomach with one hand, the other hiding my face. This situation is so beyond ridiculous I don't know how to handle it. Maybe if I wasn't halfway-to-drunk, from drinking with Jackson's *mom*, I'd be able to handle this better.

Unfazed, Mary's looking more than pleased with herself, while Jackson looks part confused, and part horrified.

Choking down another laugh I say, "I'll give you two a moment." Then I turn, and bolt.

After a quick stop at the ladies' room, I venture over to the bar. I'm still not sure what to do about this pickle I've found myself in. Yeah, I for sure told Jackson's mom way more about our little meet-cute than I ever would've had I'd known she was his mom. But how the heck was I supposed to know that? And why didn't she mention it? Well, I know why she didn't mention it. She was getting unfiltered information about her son, and she was seeing hearts and wedding bells and whatever else partially insane mothers hope for.

Taking a deep breath I try to take a mental step back from the problem. Maybe this isn't that bad. Maybe we'll all be laughing about this in a few minutes.

Standing with my back against the bar, I search the crowd trying to spot the pair in question. When I do see them, my heart sinks. Jackson has his head tilted back, eyes closed, and is pinching the bridge of his nose. It's not the look of a happy man.

He just helped to win his game. He should be happy. *Very* happy. But instead, I've brought stress, via his mama, into his night. He should be celebrating, not dealing with this crap. I feel like such a jerk. This is all my fault. And he has every right to be upset with me, but I'm not sure I can deal with that right now. Jackson yelling at me, or even gently scolding me, would be too much for me to handle. I was already frazzled before this little family reunion, so I believe it's time to go.

Looking back up, I see that Jackson is staring at me, while still talking to his mom. He's giving me the look of a man constructing a plan. And that's my cue to expedite this exit strategy.

I recognize the guy at the bar next to me as the teammate Jackson walked in with. He has a partial drink in his hand and seems to be only half-listening to the pair of guys standing next to him.

Stepping forward I tap him on the shoulder.

When he turns to look at me I give him my best innocent look. "Hi there. I have a big favor to ask you."

He lets loose a toothpaste-commercial-worthy smile as he says, "Hey. Aren't you the one who greeted our boy Wilder with a hug?" He tosses a thumb over his shoulder, gesturing towards the entrance.

"Yeah, that's me." I grab the drink from his hand and toss it back in one go. Coughing a little I hand him back the glass. He chuckles as my eyes start to water. I think that was straight whiskey. I shake it off. "Long story short, I need you to stall him if he comes over this way. I'm going to make a break for it out the back, and I think there's a good chance he'll try to stop me."

I dig out a twenty from my pocket and tuck it in his hand next to the empty glass he's still holding.

The smile on this guy's face just keeps growing. "Now why would you be trying to escape?"

"So . . . turns out the friend I made at the game, who I brought with me to this party, is actually Jackson's mom." *Cue laughter from whiskey guy.* I'm talking fast now to wrap this up so I can get on my way. "I may have told her more about us than I should have. Not knowing who she was, obviously. And, understandably so, Jackson is all sorts of pissed. I don't want a scene. And I don't want to be told off in public. That twenty in your hand is payment for your troubles, and the drink I just stole." I take a breath, that extra drink did the opposite of calming me down. "So, what do you say? Will you stall him, if he comes over?"

He looks up in Jackson's direction and then back to me. "I think you're right about him being pissed. But I don't think the look on his face is about you talking to his mama. I think he's pissed about you over here talking to me."

"Huh?"

Moving closer he drops his voice. "Please don't punch me." He places a hand on my shoulder, turning my back more toward Jackson. "I am definitely going to help you, because Wilder is definitely going to follow you." He bends closer still. "And me getting close to you like this is proving my point. Based on the look he's giving me, I'd say that fucker is already planning my death." He laughs. "And I don't need your money, but this bill is going to play into the little plan I have."

With that, he straightens up, and lightly grazes his hand down my arm as he releases me.

I don't know what he's talking about, but he said he'd help me and that's all that matters.

Slipping back through the crowd, I pull out my phone and request a ride as I head toward the rear exit.

Two minutes later, I'm in a car heading home.

CHAPTER TEN

JACKSON

I did not see that coming. Seriously. What the fuck just happened? I leave Kitten alone for *one game*, and all of a sudden my mama and my girl are mostly drunk and the best of friends. And yeah, I know she's not technically my girl yet, but that's the goal.

Hindsight being 20/20, I can see how this all shook out. The team has a chunk of freebie tickets that we're allotted for home games. We each get two for every game; more, if we ask. I gave Kitten the ticket for the empty seat that my mama usually fills with one of her friends. Mama always has the ticket for the seat next to it, but she was supposed to be out of town tonight. When I spent the whole national anthem staring at Kitten, there was no one next to her. And later in the game, whenever I'd look over at her, I clearly didn't notice that Mama had arrived.

I'm kicking myself for not noticing, but I was a little busy playing hockey.

Honestly, I can't even blame Kitten for telling Mama about our evening together. Mama has this witchy way about her that gets you to spill all your best-kept secrets. She already knows pretty much all of my embarrassing stories, so there's nothing that Kitten could've told her about us that could even be close to over the line.

But seeing my mama, in this setting, being introduced to me by Kitten . . . I was totally caught off guard. And I could've handled the shock in a better manner. I'm usually a pretty smooth guy. But from the moment I entered the bar, I've been presenting a bad image to Kitten.

First, as soon as I walked in the door, chatting with my teammate Luke Anders, a pair of bunnies appeared at our sides trying to get our attention. So, by the time I saw Kitten approaching me, there was already a woman trying to plaster herself to me. Not my fault, but I'm thinking that might have been my Strike One.

Then Kitten surprises me with that glorious hug. I was not prepared for that level of contact. And feeling her warm, soft body pressed against mine had my brain going haywire. Then she goes and hums sweet nothings into my ear... or something about meeting a friend, who knows? ... because all I could focus on was the brush of her lips across my cheek as she spoke. When she grabbed my hand and started walking, she could've been leading me to my own execution. I would've followed her anywhere after a whisper from those lips.

Then as she tugged me along, I looked down. At her ass. And - sweet merciful god - what an *ass*. The only other time I've seen her, she was in a dress. I could tell she had a great ass, the type you want to caress when she kisses you and spank when she sasses you. But the dress she'd been wearing only gave a hint as to what she was hiding. But tonight, those jeans she has on? ... they fucking outline her assets in detail.

Realizing that I was staring, and that the sight was starting to turn me on in what would soon be a very obvious way, I had to get a hold of myself. When she happened to turn around, I was looking to the heavens, the furthest point from her tempting rear end, trying to mentally recite one of my mama's many lectures about respecting women. Of course - to her - I'm sure I just looked annoyed, or mad, or some other unpleasant emotion. I did my best to play it off, but I'm thinking that was my Strike Two.

With my mama's lectures still in my mind, imagine my surprise when Kitten's friend is my very own mother-freaking Mama. It doesn't take too long after that little introduction before Kitten bolts. I'm thinking she'll go spend some time at the bar to recover from her obvious panic, and when she comes back hopefully the two of us can sneak away for some alone time.

"Jacky, honey, you gotta know that I was just trying to look out for you, and that's why I didn't tell her who I was."

"I know, Mama, and I appreciate the thought. But I'm sure it didn't take the entire game to see that she's a nice girl."

"Oh, she really is. I think I'm half in love with her myself! I mean, we only got to spend a little bit of time together, but I can already tell that she would be the perfect fit for you."

"Take it easy, Mama. It's been one day."

"I know. I know. But even after two years I never felt like this about Lacy. It took a long time before we were able to see her for the icy bitch that she was, but even when she was hiding her true personality, I never did like her. Katelyn though... that beautiful girl is made of pure gold. And she's so much fun!"

"Seriously, Mama?" I ask. "Why would you even mention *her* right now?" Pinching the bridge of my nose as I close my eyes and will the Lacy-induced headache away. Talking about that vile woman is the last fucking thing I want to add to this evening.

Opening my eyes, I look over to see Kitten staring right at me. I drop my hand but I'm sure she just witnessed my nose-pinched-in-anger expression. And I'm sure she's making the wrong conclusions. Damn it. I'm thinking this is my Strike Three.

I'm only half-listening to what my mama is saying at this point, because now I'm watching Katelyn approach my buddy Luke. What the fuck? She taps his shoulder and says something to him, causing him to plaster on one of his *panty-melting smiles*, his phrase not mine.

My mouth pops open when I see her grab the drink from his hand and throw it back like a shot. Now *his* hand is on *her* shoulder, and my vision starts to narrow.

He's leaning in way too close, talking with his lips basically against her ear.

What. The. Fuck.

Luke glances at me, then as he straightens to full his height, he drags the tips of his fingers down her arm.

Seriously, what the fuck!

As she starts to walk away, I see him fold something and put it in his pocket. Luke might be one of my best friends, but tonight he's a fucking dead man.

"Mama, I'll be right back." I don't even wait to acknowledge that she heard me before I stomp off.

I watch Kitten walk toward the back of the room, but I need to deal with this Luke situation before it goes any further. I didn't fill him in on the details of how I know her, but I know he saw her hug me when we walked in the door. That should have been enough to invoke bro-code. But since it apparently wasn't, I'm about to make it crystal clear.

"Luke!" The bar is so loud I have to shout his name to get his attention.

Turning toward me, Luke gives a satisfied smirk before he says, "Hey, brother, what's up?"

Getting right in his face, I seethe, "How about you tell me. What the fuck were you doing with your filthy hands all over Katelyn? And what the fuck is in your pocket?"

"Woah, dude, chill!" Luke puts his hands up in placation. "Who the hell is Katelyn?"

"Who is . . . seriously? The woman you were just talking to. You had your greasy palms on her while you were breathing down her neck."

"Oh, you mean that brunette chick? The one with the nice ass?"

That comment forces me to take a step closer, putting us chest to chest. We're about the same height, but I have several pounds of muscle on him. This should feel like the stare down that it is.

I lean in. "If you lay so much as a finger on her ass, I will break it off, so help me god."

Luke holds my eyes for a beat before throwing an arm around my shoulder and breaking out in laughter. For not the first time tonight, I don't know how to react. I think the best course of action right now is to do nothing. So, I just stand there. Like an idiot. Wondering what the fuck is happening to my life.

With actual tears of hilarity rolling down his face, Luke gets himself together enough to form words. "Holy shit, dude, I wish I had someone recording that! Talk about going all caveman over a woman!" More laughter. "I had about ten seconds to cook up that plan, and it couldn't have worked any better. My man, you just got played so hard." Patting me on the chest, Luke shakes his head.

"What?" I ask, not hiding my confusion. "What are you talking about? Am I dreaming? Is it a full moon out tonight?"

"Naw, man, your girl there just asked me to delay you for a bit."

"Delay me? What for?"

He shrugs. "She wanted to sneak out without you stopping her."

"What the fuck! She left?" I turn to try to chase her down, but Luke stops me with a hand on my arm.

"Dude, she's gone. Sorry, but she was stressing out and just wanted to get out of here." Reaching his hand in his pocket he pulls out a twenty and unfolds it. There's nothing written on it. "She even gave me this to pay for my drink that she slammed. And to pay me for the hassle of stopping you, if you can believe that."

I take the offered twenty from him. It's clearly implied I should give it back to her. "Did she say why she was leaving?"

"She mentioned something about your mom being here, and you being pissed. And that she didn't want to be - and I quote - 'told off' in public."

Rubbing a hand down my face, I groan in frustration. "I'm such an idiot."

"Yep."

"Fuck off, man." My shoulders slump in defeat. "I wasn't pissed at her. And I'd never tell her off over any of this. I just wanted to spend time with her, but somehow I manage to mess up at every opportunity."

"Yeah, well, you are a big dumb animal." Luke yelps and jumps back as I go to punch his arm. "Kidding! Jeez! Damn, that girl has you wound up tight. I saw you watching us and knew what you'd be thinking. And I do love screwing with you, but - above all - if a woman asks me to help her leave a situation, I'll never say no."

"I wish I could be mad about that, but I think that would make me an asshole."

Luke nods his agreement. "Want to tell me who she is?"

"As much as I'd love to sit here and gossip with you, my mama's still in here somewhere. I need to go find her, then I'm calling it a night."

"What are you gonna do about your girl?"

Rubbing my thumb across my bottom lip, I think for a moment, "I have a plan."

CHAPTER ELEVEN

KATELYN

Well, it's the morning after the Mother Mary incident, and I feel like a total fool. I did not handle any of that well. First off, spilling my guts to a stranger. Not smart. Then inviting said stranger to a party before finding out she's the mother of the man I've been lusting after. Not great. Then after I stir up that proverbial hornet's nest, I ditch. Really not cool.

There's no way that Jackson will ever want to see me again. I'm pretty sure last night I became his dating horror story, and we aren't even dating. Some night in the future, he'll be out with friends and everyone will start to tell stories about bad dates they've had. Then Jackson will chime in about the time some chick got drunk with his mom and invited her to his party, only to leave him there to pick up the pieces. Yep, time for me to just roll over the edge and drop into my spinster grave. I should probably invest in a pile of cats while I'm at it.

There's a knock at the door followed by, "Open up, bitch!"

Trudging across the floor, I take a deep breath to help clear my mind.

The knock comes again and for the first time this morning, I smile.

"Patience, woman!" I call out as I flip the lock.

Opening the door, my friend Meghan whirls in, a cloud of curls and sugar-scented air surrounding her.

Meghan has a larger than life personality and a heart to match. Her long red hair reminds me of a feral princess. The large wavy mass always looks amazing, even though she claims to hate it. When she's in work-mode she's all professional, but when she's not, her inner hippie-slut comes out to play. *Her words not mine.* I've seen her in everything from tie dye hoodies to strapless dresses that leave nothing to the imagination. Meghan has the curves to match her oversized chest, and she knows how to flaunt them. Today she's dressed down in emerald leggings, a large grey knitted sweater, and her signature feather earrings. She's wide awake, exuding confidence, and she's the only reason I'm even out of bed. Today is our monthly Sunday brunch. We switch off who hosts, and today it's at my house.

I have a classic egg bake going in the oven and a large pot of coffee ready for consumption. Meghan has brought her bubbly self and what looks to be a homemade coffee cake. If I didn't love her for *her*, I'd love her for her cooking and baking skills. That girl has a gift. And she knows, better than most, that carbs cure all.

"Okay, so I gotta be honest, Katelyn - I have no idea what any of your cryptic texts meant last night. But I did bring the goods." Putting the coffee cake on the counter, she digs into her giant purse and pulls out a bottle of champagne. "So, let's fill up our plates and toast to whatever insanity you're about to rain down on me."

I can't help but grin at her preparedness. "I hate to be the downer here, but I don't think I deserve to day drink after last night. Also, I don't have any orange juice."

"Okay, so fuck mimosas. We can drink this straight up, like the ballers we are. And what do you mean you don't deserve it? Unless you spent last night drowning kittens, or replying to dick pics on Tinder, I think you're fine."

Her use of the word *Kitten* has me cringing inwardly, but her examples have me outwardly cringing. "Good gourd. I wasn't doing either of those things, obviously. And I don't even have a Tinder account."

She rolls her eyes. "I know. But you should get one."

"Why, so I can spend my nights looking at unsolicited dick pics?"

"First off, *every* dick pic is unsolicited. And secondly, you *should* get online. Maybe then you can meet someone that has a dick. And maybe you can see it in person. And if you're really lucky, maybe you can even touch it." She wiggles her eyebrows at me.

"Okay, wow. It's too early for this much dick talk." Pulling the egg bake out of the oven I decide to just go for it. "Besides, I was with a guy last night. And the night before."

"What?!" Meghan screeches so loud I have to suppress a wince. "Um hello, best friend here. When were you planning to tell me about this guy? Before the wedding or after?"

"Oh, please, dramatic much? And it wasn't like that. I met him at my cousin's political fundraising-party-thing the other night. And then . . ." I stop. I was going to say *and then I went to his game* but that's a whole big thing to explain on its own. I mean this is Meghan, we tell each other everything, I'm going to tell her about Jackson. Plus, she'll be able to help me sort out where to go from here. If there is anywhere to go. But just blurting out the whole *game* thing seems like I'm jumping ahead. Ugh. This dilemma needs coffee. I grab two mugs and pour us some of the liquid gold. Handing Meghan her mug, I look up and see she is staring at me like I stripped naked inside a grocery store.

"What?" I ask her.

Her eyes go even wider. "What the hell did I just witness?"

"Huh?"

"You stopped mid-freaking-sentence, and just stood there. And now you calmly hand me coffee as if you didn't just slip into the twilight zone. Are you okay? Did that guy hurt you or something?"

"What? No! He's great. He's really great." Running my hand up and down my face, I'm thankful we don't bother with makeup for these brunches. "It's just that the last two days are a long story."

"Okay, well, it's a good thing we have all day. You met him at the party . . ." she trails off.

"Yeah, I was about to leave for the night, but then I spotted Bradley."

"Gross! Did you go punch him in the testicles?"

That makes me smirk. "No. I hid from him. He was with some chick."

"Hid, like behind the curtains?" I can tell she's trying not to laugh. It's not working.

"No, dummy, I snuck down into the basement. Er, lower level. I was hoping there would be a room for me to hide out in."

Meghan lights up. "Ooooo, was it a sex room?"

"That's what I thought!" I'm relieved that I'm not the only person whose mind would go there. "Sadly, no sex room. But I did walk into this magical little library. I got sidetracked drooling over the books so I didn't hear it when Jackson appeared out of nowhere. He scared the shit out of me. Like - I think I screamed."

"Jackson? Is this the guy you've been with?"

"Yeah. It was his place."

"Whoa, whoa, whoa . . . his place? Didn't you say it was gonna be at some athlete's house?" Meghan gasps, answering her own question. "Wait... *Jackson?* Was it Jackson Wilder?!"

"Umm, yeah, actually. How do you know that name?"

"How do I . . . ?" Meghan's hands are in the air, waving around, as she talks. I don't know if it's excitement for me or exasperation with me that has her this riled up. "Did you NOT know who Jackson Wilder was?"

As I shake my head, she laughs so hard she has to cross her legs.

"Oh my god, girl! Go back, tell me everything."

So, I do.

CHAPTER TWELVE

KATELYN

I wasn't sure it was possible for one friend to laugh so much at the expense of the other, but Meghan proves that threshold is much higher than I imagined. I just finished telling her the entire story. No detail too small to be ignored.

"Meghan, you're supposed to be *helping* me, not laughing to tears over my dumb life."

Sighing, Meghan says, "I don't think it's actually as bad as you think it is. I mean, it's funny as shit, you drinking with his 'mama,'" (she says *mama* in her deepest man-voice.) "But you got to spend time with *the* Jackson Wilder. And you went to his game! And duh, he clearly likes you."

"Uh, I doubt that."

"You shut your pretty mouth. He's lucky to spend time with you. You're brilliant and funny and gorgeous and kind. He may be some sort of big hotshot athlete, but he seems to be smart enough to know a good thing when he finds it. I know hockey players get a bad rep for being a bunch of big muscle-headed Neanderthals, but I've always heard that Jackson was a civilized one." Shaking her head she mumbles, "I can't believe you had to Google him."

I shrug. "Well, even if he doesn't hate me for last night, I can't ask him about it. I don't have any way to reach him." I hold up a hand to stop her before she says what I'm sure she's going to say. "And I'm not just showing up at his place. That would be stalkerish. Plus, the building has security. I can't just go knock on his door."

"That's so hot." I don't know if she's talking about the fact that his building has security, or if she's just talking about Jackson himself. About ten minutes ago she started an image search on my laptop for Jackson Wilder, so she could drool over him while we talked. I can't even be mad. He is hot. I drool over him too.

Even if I don't know what to do next, I do feel better after having shared my story with Meghan. Now my experience is at least documented in the memory of one of my friends. So when I'm an old lady, and I say I almost dated a famous person, I can, sort of, prove it.

As we put away the remnants of brunch, there's a knock at my door. Looking at each other, Meghan raises her eyebrow in a *well-answer-it!* gesture. Opening the front door, I find a little white box wrapped in green ribbon. A box identical to the one I received from Jackson yesterday, only smaller.

Carrying it to the table I can feel my heart rate pick up. This has to be a positive sign. Right?

I can feel Meghan watching me, but I'm not sure I can form a sentence right now. I just stay silent and pull the ribbon off the box. Opening the lid, I find a short stack of laminated cards. Pulling out the top card, I see a photo of Mary. Flipping it over, I see that the back has been printed with *Mama—Mary Wilder*. Reaching in for the next card I find a pretty blonde and on the back it reads *Sister—Stephanie Wilder*. I don't even try to contain the stupid grin that spreads across my face. This guy. He is so many things, but right now the only word that comes to mind is *wonderful*. Jackson is wonderful.

Pulling out the rest of the stack, I find cards for his late father, his ninety-four-year-old grandmama, his best friend Luke, and his childhood dog Puck. The man has made me real-life flashcards of the important people in his life.

At the bottom of the box is another one of his white envelopes.

Sweet Kitten,

> *I'm sorry that we didn't get more of a chance to talk last night. Since extenuating circumstances keep getting in our way, I'd like to have a chance to control our environment. Please tell me you're free for dinner tomorrow night, at my place. If you're up for it, I was thinking we could give* The Godfather *another try.*
>
> *In the meantime, I thought I'd put together some study material for you. I know how much you like to read.*
> *Sincerely,*
> *Mama's Boy*

Meghan shocks me out of my daze by shouting, "Holy shit, you're totally falling for him!"

I blink. "What? No? No. That's not a thing. I barely even know him."

"Oh don't try that 'I don't even know him' bullshit on me. You are great at reading people. You slept in his arms, for shit's sake. And let's not forget that you are basically besties with his mom by now."

"Shut up!" I say, laughing. "Okay, so I like him. Who wouldn't? But we still have a lot to learn about each other."

"Yeah, like if he knows how to use his *hockey stick* in the bedroom," Meghan says with an exaggerated wink. I scoff, but she ignores me. "Seriously, if you could've seen the look on your face as you read that letter, you'd know what I'm talking about. You have it *real* bad for Jackson Wilder."

As I blush, I'm saved from responding when my text chime goes off.

Picking up my phone I see it's from a new number. Opening the message, that now familiar buzzing is back in my belly.

Hello, Kitten. I hope you slept well last night. I trust my box of study materials has arrived. If you're open to joining me for dinner tomorrow, how does 7:00 sound?

Holy shit.

"Holy shit!"

"What is it? Is it Jackson?" Meghan asks.

I hand her the phone.

"You're going." She doesn't ask it, she tells me.

"Of course, I'm going," I say. I still feel a little bit like I'm waiting for the *just kidding* part to come. Meghan is right, I feel myself falling for this guy. And it isn't because he's stupid-handsome. Well, it's not *only* because he is stupid-handsome; I do enjoy that part. I like him because he's funny, and clever, and he's sweet to his mama, and he's sweet to me, and when we're together I can sense that edge of possessiveness that I think he has.

Now look, I am a huge proponent of equality for all, women's rights, and non-gender roles. But I can't help it that I get all turned on when he gets worked up about some other guy giving me attention. Don't get me wrong, I don't want to be with some jackass who's popping off over every conversation I have with another man. But knowing how riled up Jackson got when Luke was pretending to hit on me, that was hot. And I'm not sorry to say that I thought about that scene when I got home last night. I thought about it in detail. Twice.

"Wow, Earth to Katie. Want to quit fantasizing about your man candy long enough to text him back?"

I shrug. "What can I say? You're right - he is man candy. But okay, yes. I need to reply." Tapping my fingers on the table I stare at my phone. "Wasn't this supposed to get easier as we got older? Why do I feel all awkward about telling a guy I'll have dinner with him?"

"Don't overthink it. Just do it."

Taking Meghan's advice, I pick up my phone, tap out a response and hit send.

Me: I think I can shuffle my schedule around to make room for you. Can I bring anything?

In the amount of time it takes me to save his number in my phone, he's texted back.

Jackson: Just your lovely self.

Jackson: Was that too much? Let me try again...

Jackson: I'll order something for delivery. Just bring your smile.

Me: I'm rolling my eyes so hard, I'm not sure I'll be recovered in time for dinner tomorrow.

Jackson: Hm, that can be dangerous. If it still pains you, I can kiss it and make it better.

The mental image of him kissing me *anywhere* blanks out my mind.

Shaking my head, I snap back to the present.

Me: Is there any chance I might run into one of your relatives along the way? Maybe one who isn't in my study guide?

Jackson: The threat is minimal. I'd say Defcon 5. Or 1. Whichever is the lowest risk.

Me: Copy that.

Jackson: I'll let you get back to studying. Until tomorrow, Kitten.

Looking up I glance around for Meghan, only to find her standing right behind me so she could read the messages. I didn't even notice her getting out of her chair. Her eyes are wide and she's clutching her hands in front of her chest.

"Ohmygod, you guys are so goddamn cute!"

"Glad you think so. And yeah, sure, feel free to read my messages."

She huffs, as if it would be ridiculous to wait for permission. "I expect to hear a full report back on how many bases you round tomorrow night."

Throwing my napkin at her I say, "Okay, time for you to go. Thanks for laughing at me all afternoon. Now I need to go figure out what to wear for this date. Wait, is it a date? He never said date. He said dinner."

"Obviously it's a date."

"You can't say obviously. What if he just feels bad, about me feeling bad, about the whole Mother Mary Thing."

"Ohmygod. First, that's not what this is. Second, you need to stop calling it the *Mother Mary Thing*. Third, if that guy wanted to pity fuck me, I would let him pity fuck me. All. Night. Long." Meghan sighs. "Man, I can't wait to write about this in my diary."

I roll my eyes as I stand from the table. "You and that damn diary. I swear, one of these days I'm going to find it. And I'm going to read it."

Shooing Meghan out the door I decide that I won't worry about whether it's a date or not. I've got to imagine that after the catastrophe of last night, things can only get better.

CHAPTER THIRTEEN

JACKSON

I've been in the playoffs many times throughout my career, even won the Stanley Cup once, but I don't think I've ever been as nervous as I am right now. I know Kitten likes me, likes spending time with me. Logically, I realize that we hardly know each other and that we haven't spent much actual time together, but this feels different. I mean, I've dated plenty. I've been in serious relationships before. But it's never felt like this... Sure, the other night was pretty damn weird. But it just endeared Kitten to me even more. My mama might have been playing her - in a sneaky, well-meaning way - but they still clicked. After Kitten snuck out, I drove Mama home and she talked about my girl the whole time. She had only good things to say, and I'm a little scared about what Mama'll do to me if I fuck this up. If I do fuck it up, I'll deserve whatever sort of punishment she sends my way.

I never clarified that tonight was a date. It is. But it's dinner at home, so I don't want to go overboard with dressing up. Casual seems like the best way to be ourselves. I'm wearing my favorite pair of dark-wash jeans and a grey Henley. At the risk of sounding like a douchebag, I'll admit I look good in this shirt. Hey - I make my living as an athlete; I'm proud of my body. I typically don't try to put myself on display, but - seeing as how I'm trying to impress Kitten, while also hoping she might want to put her hands on me - I'll use whatever tools I have.

It's already dark outside, and I have the lights on low in the apartment, showcasing my view of downtown. My condo has an open-plan living space, so the kitchen and large dining table have a view out the living room windows. Past the kitchen is a hallway that leads to the master bedroom, a bathroom, and a second bedroom that I've turned into an office. And, of course, on the other side of the living room is the set of stairs leading down to the library and theater. I was serious in my text to Kitten last night; I would love to watch another movie together. It's not even so much that I think she needs to watch *The Godfather*. I just want an excuse to get close to her and have her pressed against me for a few hours.

As I'm glancing around, wondering if there's anything I overlooked, my phone rings. Seeing it's the security desk downstairs calling, I answer.

"This is Jackson."

"Good evening, Mr. Wilder. Henry from downstairs, I wanted to let you know that your guest has arrived, and she's on her way up."

"Thank you, Henry. I have food coming shortly; feel free to just send it up. No need for any more calls tonight."

"As you wish, Mr. Wilder."

"Have a good night."

I gave Kitten's name to the guys at the security desk downstairs so they could send her right up when she got here, but I appreciate the heads up. Knowing she's this close has my impatience ramping up. I head to the door so I can greet her when she gets off the elevator.

I'm standing in my open doorway when the elevator dings and the doors slide apart, giving me my first view of her.

Kitten's standing there, looking down, and I can see her chest rise as she takes a deep breath before smoothing down the front of her shirt. She went the same route as I did - dressed casually, but she looks fine as hell. I can't help but give her a slow once-over, starting at her feet. A pair of black ankle boots. Tight grey jeans. Her shirt is black, and looks soft enough to touch. It's not tight, but it's clinging in all the right places with a low neckline that I'm already a fan of. Her tan jacket is hiding some of her body from me, but I know that I'm going to love the view from every angle.

She left her hair down, in glossy waves. Her pretty hair shouldn't give me dirty thoughts, but it does. It really fucking does. I want to have my fingers running through it, gripping it, pulling it just enough to tip her head back so I can—

"Hi, Jackson."

As my eyes snap to hers, I can't help the smirk that pulls at my mouth. She just caught me daydreaming about her. And I'm not the least bit sorry.

"Kitten." I extend my arm, gesturing for her to enter my condo. "Welcome back."

As she walks past me, biting her lip, I get a whiff of her delicious scent. I don't know if it's something she wears, or just a combination of hair products and soap, or whatever it is that women lather themselves in. Either way, she smells divine. Like spring flowers and sex.

Stepping in behind her, I close the door and realize I missed my opportunity to get a hello hug. So I adapt.

Placing my hand on her back I ask, "Can I take your jacket?"

She flicks a glance over her shoulder at me before nodding. "Please."

Stepping closer, I slide my hands over her shoulders, across her collarbones, and grab the lapels of her jacket. Slowly, I pull them aside, letting the backs of my fingers drag across the soft material of her shirt before sliding the coat down her arms.

Taking a woman's coat off should not be this sexy. I feel like I'm a fourteen again, and a pretty girl just brushed against me in class. Walking her jacket over to the entryway closet, I take the moment to compose myself. No need to embarrass us both with my immediate lack of control.

Turning back, I find her standing at the windows looking out at the city.

"It was so crowded when I was here before, I don't think I even noticed your view. It's stunning."

Approaching, I make a noise of agreement as I try to focus on what she sees, not just looking at her reflection in the glass.

She leans closer to the glass. "Do you ever just stand here and watch the people down at street level? It's like having your own little ant farm."

The comment makes me smile. "It kinda is. I haven't always lived in a big city, so I find the bustle entertaining. I'm just glad to be up high enough that I don't hear the traffic noise too much."

"Hmmm. I can understand that."

We stand in silence for a moment, both looking down at the world below us.

But I can't help myself. I reach over and touch the back of her arm. "I'm really glad you came tonight. I was a little worried that my mama's attempts at being 007 would've scared you off."

Chuckling a little, she turns to face me. "I am so sorry about all of that. I can't believe I didn't realize who she was! And then I invited her along... Seriously, I'm sorry." Katelyn shakes her head at herself.

"There isn't a thing for you to be sorry about, Kitten. My mama is a wily one, and she would've found a way to tag-along with- or without an invite. I, of course, told her that she shouldn't have tricked you like that. And she, of course, told me that it's a mama's job to pry." I give her a crooked smile. "I definitely wasn't upset with you, and - try as I might - I can never be upset with my mama."

Kitten sighs. "She is kind of fantastic. And unapologetically in your face. She had me eating cotton candy within five minutes of meeting her. I don't think I've had that stuff since I was in grade school."

"That sounds like Mama. She's good at being motherly, but she can also be a damn bulldozer."

Looking at me with mischief, Kitten says, "I bet you have some good stories about getting in trouble when you were little."

"That I do. But before you get me spilling all my childhood mess-ups, would you like a drink? I have the usual suspects. Oh, and are you okay with sushi?" Inwardly, I wince; I should've asked that the moment she arrived, since I already ordered it. "We can get something else if you'd like, it's no trouble."

"Sushi sounds great! I love it, but for whatever reason I never seem to eat it as often as I'd like."

"If that's the case, then you're welcome. This will be your new favorite restaurant. One of the security guys downstairs has a cousin who owns the joint. He introduced it to me one night when I walked past his desk and caught sight of his dinner."

"That's quite the hard sell. It'd better live up to the expectation."

The smile she gives me hits me deep. *I am so screwed with this girl.*

"I promise to live up to your expectations." I give her a little wink and - to my undying enjoyment - she blushes. "I believe I offered you a drink?"

"Water is fine, thank you. I was debating about bringing a bottle of wine, but I wasn't sure if you can drink during the season. I mean I know we were at a bar the other night, and that drink I took from Luke was definitely alcohol..."

Laughing I say, "Yeah, that was a pretty clever ploy you laid out with Luke. You'll be happy to know it worked, even if I did almost punch that smug fucker."

"What!" Kitten giggles and covers her mouth. "Why would you want to punch him?"

"He was saying shit about your ass." I give her my steely glare.

"He doesn't like my ass?" she asks like she's confused.

Stepping closer to her I feel myself growl. Like a damn animal. "He was very complimentary."

Kitten glances back behind herself, pretending to look at her ass. "Well, that was nice of him. Can you give me his number? I'd like to thank him personally."

As I step closer, putting me in touching range, there's a knock at the door.

Kitten laughs as I stride away, and I hear her mumble, "Saved by the bell."

-

Standing side by side, we look down at the array of sushi and side dishes that I've spread across the kitchen table.

Giving me a little side-eye, Kitten says, "So is the rest of your team coming over for dinner?"

I can't really blame her for questioning my sanity. This is a stupid amount of food for two people. "I may have gotten carried away."

"May have?"

"Okay, I did. I most definitely got carried away. But everything is so good, and I wanted you to try all my favorites, and I didn't know what you'd like. So, yeah . . ." I shrug.

I gesture to a seat at the end. The table is a large oval of heavy dark wood with seating for ten. Putting Kitten at the end means I can take the spot next to her without being like those strange people who sit side by side in a booth.

Taking my seat, I ask, "You sure you're fine with just water? I have some wine, but unfortunately no sake."

"Thanks, but I'm good with this. I honestly don't drink too often, and between your mother and Meghan I could use a night of hydration."

Using chopsticks, I start to put some of everything on our plates. "Meghan? Oh, and to answer your earlier question - I try to limit my alcohol during the season. When we have team outings like we did the other night most of us will have a drink or two, so long as there isn't a game the next day.

Like you said, hydration is important, so we can't drink a bunch the night before a game."

She nods. "That makes sense."

I can't help but stare as she works her chopsticks around a roll and brings it to her mouth. Some of these rolls are fairly large, and it's a bit pornographic watching her open her mouth wide enough to take one in whole. Then she closes her eyes and releases a moan. A moan I feel low in my body.

Her eyes open, and I'm sure I look slack-jawed and lust-filled, because I am.

Katelyn brings her hand up to cover her full mouth. "This is so freaking good."

Getting control of my face, I grin. "Told you."

"You were right. I can see why you ordered an army's worth." Selecting the next one she wants to try, she answers my previous question. "Meghan is my best friend. We met in middle school, bonded over being book nerds, and have been besties ever since. She was at my place for brunch yesterday and brought some champagne with her. She's a whirlwind, and I love her."

Imagining how it might have played out, I ask, "Was she there when your gift arrived?"

"Oh, she was there all right. But I'd already laid out the whole embarrassing series of events, so - sorry to burst your bubble - but you didn't get to out me."

"That's a shame."

"Uh huh." She moans around another bite of sushi.

"So, you were a book nerd even back then?"

I listen in rapt attention while Kitten tells me about how her love of stories started when she was a kid. She met Meghan in the library after school one day. They were both reading *Goosebumps*, and they decided to become best friends. Listening to her recount the story, and their subsequent friendship, I find myself drawn into her world. Kitten has such a way with words, pulling me into her story so that I feel invested. I want to hear her talk about everything. *Anything.* All her thoughts are so lit up with emotion, it's nearly exhausting just to witness.

She tells me she went to college for writing, and how she's now a copy editor for a local book publisher. I gather that it might not be the road to riches, but she seems to be doing well for herself, and she loves it.

I like the idea of her working from home, curled up on the couch with her laptop. During the off season, I could stop over and distract her from work. Or just sit next to her, reading something of my own.

Whoa, buddy, way to jump ahead! This is our first actual date and I'm already planning out our afternoons 5 months from now. Somehow she's turned me into a pussy-whipped glob of putty, and I haven't even felt her lips on mine yet.

We've been steady in conversation, neither of us focusing on food, with the exception of Kitten's intermittent moans when she tries something new. So we've hardly made a dent in the pile of sushi.

Kitten surprises me once again, telling me that she didn't read about me online, that she'd rather learn about me in person. She admits that - the morning after we met - she Googled my name to learn what sport I played. It's adorable how embarrassed she looks telling me this. But, apparently - after reading an article about me - she felt like a stalker, so she closed down the browser. I can't even express how much I appreciate that. And honestly, I don't care that she didn't know who I was. I really like the idea that I'll be the one who gets to teach her about hockey.

Kitten breaks into my thoughts, "Tell me about your sister. According to my flashcard, she's quite beautiful."

That makes me roll my eyes. "Yes, Stephanie is beautiful, and that's been a thorn in my side since I hit puberty. She's two years younger than me, and all of my friends liked to talk about how hot they thought she was. Then I'd have to punch them. Then I'd get in trouble with my mama, or get detention. And then the cycle would start all over again."

Kitten fights back a smile as I continue, "Steph was never a troublemaker, just the opposite. And as we got older, she became more and more of a busybody... getting involved in my life, trying to set me up with 'a nice girl,' or trying to decorate my apartments. I swear she becomes more like Mama every damn day." I'm sure my exasperation is apparent in my tone. I love my sister. I do. But she can be a total pain in the ass. "How about you? You mentioned a brother. Do you guys get along?"

She scoffs. "Our situations are flipped on this one. My brother, Alex, is three years older than I am. And he's a total pest. When we were little, he'd do his best to torture me with bugs and rigged faucets, and just pranks in general."

"Pranks, like what?"

Katelyn leans back in her chair. "Like the time when I was ten and he poured water on my bed while I was sleeping, and then convinced me that I peed myself. I was mortified. I secretly washed my bedding that day because I was too embarrassed to tell my parents. It was years, literal *years*, before he told me he did that! *Ugh. He* is the *worst*. And now he's a fourth grade teacher, if you can believe that. He's actually great at it, but I'm pretty sure that's because he stopped maturing when he was that age, so he relates well to his students."

I can't help but laugh. "I wonder if I could try that bed-wetting scheme on my sister now."

Smacking my arm, Kitten scolds me, "Don't you dare!"

I grin like a fool. The girl I like just touched me.

Katelyn's expression freezes. "I didn't even think about my brother."

My brows furrow. "What do you mean?"

"I mean, he's a huge Sleet fan! I never really paid attention to his hockey rants, but I know he watches all the games. I've seen him wearing jerseys on several occasions. I think he has more than one. Oh god, what if he has your jersey! If he finds out that we're ... well ... you know ..."

Looking to me for help, she sees me grinning at her expense. Smacking my arm again, she says, "Oh *shut up*. When he finds out that I know you, he's going to hassle me nonstop until I introduce you guys. So, remember how you're laughing now when he shows up on your doorstep with a tattoo of your face across his back."

My grin has turned smug. "I can handle your brother, Kitten."

There's a knock at the front door.

The food is already here; I'm not expecting anyone. Damnit, when I told Henry he didn't have to call up again, I was referring to the food delivery. I forget how literal he can be sometimes.

I push my chair back from the table. "Sorry for the interruption, I can't imagine why someone is here. But while I'm up, I can refill our waters."

"No, you get the door, I'll top off the glasses." Kitten stands at the same time.

Eager to get back to our conversation, I stride to the door and pull it open. And find Luke standing in front of me.

When he goes to step past me to come inside, I put my hand up on the door frame, my other hand still holding the handle, well-aware this is probably the least subtle way to keep him out of my condo.

"Uh, *hey*, Jackson. Whatcha doin in there?" Luke says, craning his neck to try to see what I'm hiding.

"Luke. This is unexpected."

"You know normal people would start with 'Hello' and 'want to come inside?' ... I might have to give your mama a call to ask where she went wrong raising you."

I'm not trying to hide Kitten from Luke for any reason other than wanting him to leave. "Sorry, but now is not a good time. Can we catch up tomorrow?"

"No-can-do, buddy. Coach is on his way over." His smile turns into a grin. "Now."

"Seriously? What the fuck?" I drop my hand from the frame, and Luke wastes no time pushing past me.

Spotting Kitten standing in the kitchen he stops in his tracks. "Katelyn! How nice to see you." He slowly turns back to give me a raised eyebrow look of surprise.

She gives him a little wave. "Hi, Luke."

"Did Jackson here give you back your twenty yet?" He laughs.

Kitten glances at me before replying. "That was payment for your services. I don't want it back."

I make a mental note to tuck the bill into one of her pockets sometime tonight. "This is a lovely little reunion and all, but - Luke - care to tell me why Coach is on his way over?"

"He called me and said he wanted us to go over some footage for the game against Winnipeg this week. He just said he'd meet me here. Seeing as you never do anything fun. With anyone. Ever." He winks over at Kitten. "I didn't think I'd need to give you a heads-up. I can call and try to get him to push it back to tomorrow morning."

Kitten jumps into the conversation. "Don't do that! Really Jackson, I can entertain myself while you guys do your thing. Or we can just continue this another night. I don't want to interfere with your team work."

Just when I think this girl can't get any better, she talks about it like playing hockey is an actual job and not just me goofing around. It takes a lot of work to be on a professional team, but a lot of people view it as just showing up for games and having fun.

"Don't leave. Please." I walk up to Kitten and bring my hand to the side of her neck. "We won't be long."

"Less than an hour, for sure," Luke chimes in.

"Okay," her voice comes out as a whisper, and she's looking at me in a way that has me tightening my grip on her. I want to close the distance between us. I want to press my lips to hers. I want to feel her melt into me. I want us to be alone. She breaks into my thoughts with a question. "Why is it only you two watching these videos with your coach?"

"Hmm?" My brain takes a second to reset. "Oh, Luke and I are the captains."

Her eyes open wider in shock. "Really?"

"Geez, don't sound so surprised," Luke says. "I know he's a knucklehead, but Jackson's a decent hockey player."

Speaking over my shoulder, I say to Luke, "You're an idiot." Releasing my grip on Kitten, I walk toward the hall. "I'll get the office set up so we can get this started and over as quickly as possible." Walking away, I hear another knock at the door. That must be Coach. "Luke, grab the door!" I shout before entering my office.

It only takes a couple of minutes to get everything ready, clearing off the guest chairs and powering up my computer and wall screen. I expected Luke to bring Coach straight back when he got here, but they must still be out there talking to Kitten.

This is the last fucking thing I wanted to happen tonight. I've been enjoying Katelyn's company. I want to spend more time together, learning everything about her. Exhaling my frustration, I promise myself that I won't let this derail our evening.

Walking back down the hallway, I call out, "Hey, what's the hold up?"

Expecting to see Luke and Coach standing in the kitchen, it takes me a moment to orient myself to the new scene. Luke is sitting at the dining table with Kitten. And my sister. And my mama.

Stopping dead in my tracks, I scold myself for my previous thought. This. *This* is the last fucking thing I wanted to happen tonight.

CHAPTER FOURTEEN

KATELYN

Looking equal parts shocked and furious, Jackson stares at his now half-full dining table.

"What in the ever-loving hell is going on?"

To be fair, I was equally shocked when Mary and Stephanie walked in the front door. And it's all thanks to Jackson's flashcards that I was even able to recognize the pretty blonde, in jeans and a cream blouse, as his sister.

When Jackson went to the office and hollered for Luke to answer the knock at the door, I think we all assumed it was his coach. But as our insanely ridiculous luck would have it, Jackson's mama and sister appeared. I have a sneaking suspicion they stopped by so Stephanie could question Jackson about me, since the very first thing out of her mouth was, "Oh my god! Are you *Kitten*?"

I think I turned bright red. Scratch that, I know I did. Luke was still greeting Mary at the door, so Stephanie was the first one to see me. At Stephanie's exclamation, Mary whipped her head over, and the smile that spread across her face was instantaneous. Before I could even respond, Mary somehow teleported to my location and wrapped me in a hug.

"Oh honey, it's so good to see you!" She pulled back but still had her hands on my upper arms, examining me like it'd been years, not a matter of hours, since we last saw each other. "Katelyn, this is my daughter Stephanie. I told her all about you, and she was so hoping to get to meet you someday. This couldn't have worked out better!"

Stepping into my space, Stephanie also pulls me into a hug. "It's so great to meet you! I can't wait to tell you all the embarrassing stories I have about Jackson. He was such a little shit growing up!"

I still hadn't uttered a word by that point. I wasn't sure if I should start by clarifying that this was just a casual dinner, not the serious relationship their words were implying, or if I should just act chill and pretend this was all normal. Thankfully, Luke cut off what was sure to be awkward silence by ushering us all to the table.

He was grinning. "Come on, sit down! Oh man, this is going to be priceless! Jackson will be back out here any moment, and I want him to find us all sitting here, eating his food."

I did my best not to laugh. I really didn't want to cause Jackson more stress, but what options did I really have?

Taking back my original seat, Stephanie and Mary sat in the open spots next to me, and Luke took the seat on the other side of Jackson's plate.

Finally finding my voice, I turned to Stephanie. "Stephanie! It's so great to meet you. Jackson was actually just telling me about you. All flattering, I promise." I smile and glance at the others. "And he clearly went way overboard when he ordered our dinner, so please help yourselves. We'll never finish all of this."

"Please, call me Steph." She beams.

It's at this point, when everyone is filling their plates with food, that Jackson walks in.

"What in the ever-loving hell is going on?"

Mary's not fazed by Jackson's outburst. She simply smiles up at him. "Hello, Jacky dear. Your sister and I thought we'd stop by to see if you'd like to join us for dinner. But now with Katelyn's invitation to join you, we can all just stay in tonight."

I cringe a little at her wording. I see Jackson's jaw tick as he quickly glances at me. I shrug. Because really, what the hell was I supposed to do. Ask them to leave? I don't think so.

Ignoring his mom's comment, Jackson strides over and grabs the tray of sushi rolls that Luke was reaching for and slides them all onto his own plate.

Looking offended, Luke pouts, "Hey, those are the best ones!"

Jackson drops into his chair. "I know. Get your own."

Then he slides a few of the treasured rolls off his plate and onto mine, with a wink. *Gah, that wink! So many bumblebees!*

"Hi, brother. It's so nice to see you too! I've been fine, thanks for asking. Care to introduce me to your beautiful dinner guest?" Stephanie's sarcasm rivals that of a teenage girl.

Sighing, Jackson visibly slumps a little before responding. "Hey, Steph. How are things? You look lovely. Please let me introduce you to Katelyn. You're right, she is beautiful. And we *were* having a very nice evening. Alone. Until Luke showed up." As if just remembering why Luke showed up, he shakes his head a little. "And Coach should be here any minute now for an impromptu tape viewing."

This obviously isn't what we had planned for our night, and Jackson looks so disappointed. Wanting to reassure him, I slide my hand over to the top of his thigh and gently squeeze. And - sweet holy muscles - what is this man made of? I give his leg a second squeeze before I realize, A: what I am doing, and B: that it looks like I'm staring at his crotch.

Quickly looking up, I lock eyes with Jackson. I don't have time to be mortified before he places his hand over mine. Securing its place on his thigh.

Clearly seeing Coach's pending arrival as an opportunity, Mary perks up. "Oh well, don't worry about us. We can keep Katelyn company while you boys go do your hockey thing!"

"That'll be perfect!" agrees Stephanie. "See, aren't you glad we showed up tonight?"

Jackson lets out a half laugh, half guffaw. "Oh yes, I'm *so* glad."

I roll my eyes at him then turn to Steph. "That'd actually be great. If you guys weren't here to entertain me, I'm positive I'd get bored and go snooping through all of Jackson's stuff. Then I'd probably end up feeling guilty about it, and wrestle over whether or not I should tell him what I did. And what if I found something that was a red flag? I mean what do I do then? Confront him or just sneak out the door and block his number?" I raise my eyebrows. "So you see, it's a good thing you're here."

The girls' laughter is drowned out when Jackson smirks at me. "I've already found you sneaking around once before, so you know where my dungeon is. Just what do you think you might find otherwise?"

I'm saved from answering by another knock at the door. Luke jumps up. "I've got it!"

He circles the table, darts his hand over Jackson's shoulder, and steals one of the rolls Jackson took away from him. Jumping back out of Jackson's reach, Luke pops it in his mouth and makes a big show of chewing and moaning and being entirely obnoxious as he heads for the door.

"Jackass!" Jackson calls after him. Then he leans closer, so only I can hear him. "Seriously, Kitten, I'll find a way for us to have an entire evening alone together. But please, I beg you, don't run away while I'm back in the office. I promise we won't take long, and when we're done I'll kick my mama and Steph out so we can enjoy the rest of our night."

I can't stop staring into his perfect blue eyes. He seems so concerned that I'll let this whole debacle scare me off, when really - this craziness is right on par for us. Before I can respond, we hear new voices entering the condo. Jackson glances to the door, and a beat later I see him straighten his back.

At first, I think it's because his coach is here and he's being respectful, but then I see the small look of annoyance cross his face. I look toward the door and see Luke talking to an older man, dressed casually, with a full head of grey hair and a serious-but-friendly look to him. And a woman. The woman looks to be in her mid twenties, maybe thirty. Blonde, perfectly curvy, and gorgeous. She's not dressed nearly as casual as the man she came in with. Wearing a mustard-yellow wrap dress and a pair of heeled boots, she looks like an on-air news reporter.

"Well, this just keeps getting better," Jackson mumbles. "Isabelle is here."

At that, Mary furrows her eyebrows in a disapproving manner, and my curiosity piques. But that curiosity quickly turns into dread, laced with jealousy, as this Isabelle character locks onto Jackson's location and beelines toward him.

In an act that I assume to be in deference to the coach, and not to the approaching blonde, the entire Wilder family stands from their seats. Rising with them, I'm able to watch the slow-moving collision on both sides of the table. Jackson's coach walks up to Mary and Steph, greeting them both with a hug. Isabelle doesn't stop until she's right in front of Jackson. And I mean *right* in front, like - if she took a deep breath her boobs would brush against his chest. And since she came around the far side of the table, Jackson had to turn towards her, leaving me standing behind him. Hidden by his mass. From here, all I can see are her arms as they move around him in a hug.

"Jackson Wilder, it's been too long! I feel like I never see you." Her voice is sweet enough, but she sounds a little fake. Like she's trying way too hard.

I know he's not mine, not technically, but I still feel the little green tendrils taking hold. I don't want to make a scene, but at the very least I need to announce my presence. Clearly the fact that his mother and sister are in the room isn't enough to deter this girl from basically throwing herself at Jackson. Maybe a little competition will do her good.

Stepping around to Jackson's side, I watch him delicately extract himself from her grip and step back.

Still not seeming to notice me, a living-breathing-human two paces away, Isabelle continues. "Daddy and I are going to dinner tonight. When he said he was stopping by here first, I figured I'd come with and save him the trouble of picking me up after. Would you be able to join us? I'd love to spend some time with you."

Daddy? This is the coach's daughter? Interesting.

"I appreciate the invite, but I have plans tonight," Jackson says in a practiced manner. This doesn't seem to be the first time he has had to let this girl down. Seeing that she's his coach's daughter, I'm sure he knows to tread lightly.

"Oh, that's a shame." She frowns. "It seems our schedules never line up."

Taking the tiny silence that follows as my opportunity, I extend my hand. "Hi! I'm Katelyn, I don't think we've met before."

Looking a little stunned, she takes my hand. "Hello, I'm Isabelle." She glances over to the rest of the group, trying to figure out where I fit between Jackson, his family, and Luke.

Wanting to keep her talking, to someone other than Jackson, I continue, "I just love that dress! Fall is my favorite season, for so many reasons, but mostly because those rich jewel tones are in style. Of course, I don't have the coloring you do to pull off that yellow. Not that it stops me from trying the color on when I see it. But it never fails, I always end up looking a sickly shade of pink and I have to put it right back on the rack."

Isabelle blinks at me for a moment, then grins. "Oh, you're too kind! This old thing is just too comfortable to give up. And I know what you mean about fall colors, they're just the best. It's the spring colors that always wash me out. Until I'm able to get a tan."

I smile back. Well, look at that. Project distract-the-new-girl is working out perfectly.

Jackson sets his hand on my shoulder, which Isabelle instantly notices with widening eyes. "Katelyn, I'd like to introduce you to Coach."

Turning, I am now face-to-face with the infamous *Coach*.

He holds his hand out. "Hello, dear. The name's Don Thorpe."

Shaking his hand, I smile. "It's great to meet you, Mr. Thorpe. Whenever Jackson talks about you it sounds like he's speaking about a mythical creature."

"Oh please, call me Don, or Coach. And I'm sure Jackson sounds that way out of fear, not awe." He chuckles, slapping Jackson on the back. "These boys know I'm liable to make them skate 'til they puke if they step outta line."

Luke groans from the other side of the room.

Jackson bends down and talks in a stage whisper, "Luke got into trouble a few weeks back, so Coach had him skating Killers. Luke was one short of finishing when he hurled. Coach gave him ten minutes in the lockers, then made him start all over again."

Coach barks out a laugh. "Served the boy right! Now let's get to these tapes and get this over with."

With that, the three men stroll off down the hall. Leaving us women to fend for ourselves.

CHAPTER FIFTEEN

KATELYN

Facing the newly formed group of ladies, Isabelle included, I wonder what the hell we're gonna do to pass the time. We all look around at each other for a moment before I put my hands on my hips. "I think this night calls for a drink."

I know that I just told Jackson I was good with water tonight, and that was true when I said it. But then his mama, his sister, and his coach's daughter - who seems to have the hots for him - ended up being my evening's company. Things have changed.

I head into the kitchen with the rest of the women trailing behind. "Jackson mentioned that he had a bottle of wine in here somewhere."

Steph chuckles, "Oh, I have all sorts of booze stashed in this place. Just because he's Mr. Athlete doesn't mean I'm going to stay sober every time I visit." Pulling one of the island stools over to the cupboard, Steph climbs up, opens the top door above the fridge, and does Vanna White hands to showcase the nearly dozen bottles of liquor she has hidden up there.

"Holy crap!" I say at the same time Mary says, "Why didn't you show me this sooner?"

Isabelle stays quiet as she takes a seat at the island. Steph starts to hand me down a few of the bottles. There's a Merlot, a Cabernet, a bottle of tequila, and even a bottle of unopened margarita mixer that looks far more high-end than anything I've ever purchased. Climbing off the stool and looking at the selection she chose, she asks, "What should we open first?"

Isabelle clears her throat then looks to me, "Are you dating Jackson?"

Unsure how exactly to answer, I give a one-shoulder shrug.

But Mary interjects, "She's his girlfriend. And they're just so damn cute together."

At that Isabelle slumps down on her seat and looks to Steph. "Tequila, please."

"Hot damn, girl. I knew I liked you!" Steph's a little overly happy with her delivery, but it does coax a small smile out of Isabelle. "Mama, find us some glasses that will work for margaritas. Katelyn, can you dig around and see if Jackson has any limes?" Steph glances around the kitchen then slaps her hands down on the counter. "And where the hell is his salt? What sort of person doesn't leave it out sitting out?"

Finding two limes in the fridge, I place them on the counter along with the glasses and the now-found salt. Seeing that Steph has the rest in hand, I take a seat next to Isabelle. Side by side, we watch the drinking making magic happen.

With her perky façade gone, Isabelle asks, "How long have you and Jackson been dating?"

Feeling a little bad for ruining whatever fantasy she had, I decide to be honest. "I think tonight was actually our first real date."

At that she looks over at me, then over to Steph and Mary. "He invited his family over on your first date?"

"What? Oh, yeah, no. I can see how it would look that way." Shaking my head, I think about when I really did meet his mom for the first time. Catching my eye, Mary must be thinking the same thing because she bursts out laughing. Looking back to Isabelle, I tell her, "Tonight was just supposed to be the two of us for dinner, but then Luke showed up saying that your dad was on the way for the tape stuff. While we were waiting for Coach to show up, Mary and Steph arrived. Unannounced." I shoot a fake glare over at them. "So, by the time you and your dad got here, our party of two had already turned into a party of five."

Isabelle's cheeks get a little pink. "I'm so sorry... I wish we'd known. I would've told Daddy to reschedule. And I definitely would *not* have come along."

"No worries. Like I said, you guys were hardly the first ones to interrupt our evening."

"But still... I asked him to dinner, right in front of you!" Isabelle puts her face in her hands, shaking her head back and forth.

Mary comes over and pats her back. "There, there, dear. No need to be embarrassed."

"I'm so sorry. If I'd known he was in a relationship I never would've even *hinted* that I was interested. Please forgive me. I would never interfere with what someone else has. I only wish the best for Jackson." When she turns to me, I see sadness on her face I wasn't expecting. Sensing that her strong feelings might be coming from past experience, I soften even more to this girl.

Placing my hand over hers on the counter I tell her, "Seriously, no apologies are necessary. But yes, of course, you're forgiven. Hell, he's a great guy! If you're single and *not* hitting on him, I'd think there's something wrong with you."

Isabelle's mouth pulls into a little smile. "Honestly, I've tried asking him out a few times. I don't know him well, but everything I've heard about him says he's a good guy. I've dealt with a lot of jerks in the past, so I figured I would try my hand with a nice guy for once. He has always been so kind when turning me down. I thought maybe he was just being gentlemanly and taking it slow, but I don't think he was ever really attracted to me."

"Isabelle"—my tone is flat—"have you ever looked into a reflective surface? Of course, he, and every other male in a hundred-mile radius, is attracted to you. Shit, *I'm* attracted to you. But you're the coach's daughter."

She cocks her head, not understanding the point that I think is obvious. The point I realized about ten seconds into her interaction with Jackson.

Sighing, I elaborate. "All of the guys that play for your dad clearly respect him. They also fear him. Now imagine he finds out that one of them is dating his daughter. That one of the big, sweaty, men that he coaches, has had big sweaty sex with his little baby girl. Do you think that would go over well?"

Isabelle's cheeks color and she gives a small shake of her head.

I continue. "Now imagine you and this guy break up. Say you got serious and he breaks your heart. What do you think would happen to him?" I don't give her a chance to answer. "I'll tell you what would happen. Along with making the jerkhole player skate until he pukes every day, your dad would trade his ass off the team in a heartbeat. Hopefully before he breaks the guy's kneecaps in the locker room when no one is looking. Does that sound about right?"

Isabelle locks eyes with me before responding. "Well, fuck."

CHAPTER SIXTEEN

KATELYN

For being another night that got totally jacked up by unforeseen events, I'm having a ton of fun. After Isabelle accepted that professional hockey players were no longer available to her, Steph poured a round of very strong margaritas.

We've moved our party down to the theater room. We can be as loud as we want down here, and it's the perfect excuse to get back on this amazingly-comfortable couch. We have the lights on low, and Steph somehow finds a way to sync up her phone to play YouTube kitten videos on the big screen.

I divulge the story of how Jackson and I met, the subsequent game, and the Mother Mary incident. Isabelle finds it all highly amusing, but I think Steph is going to hyperventilate, she's laughing so hard. Which is ridiculous because I *know* she heard the story from Mary already. But perhaps the margaritas make it funnier. And it *is* funny. Now that it's over.

Wiggling my shoulders, I bury myself further into the corner of the couch. The same spot I shared with Jackson. Mary and Steph are seated together in the middle and Isabelle is opposite me on the far length of the couch.

Looking to Isabelle I ask, "So, what's your story? Have you always lived in Minnesota?"

"Me?" Her eyebrows pop up at my question. "There's not much to tell. I've kind of lived all over. We moved a lot growing up since Daddy's job would take us to different towns every couple of years. It was just him and me, so - aside from switching schools - it wasn't hard to pick up and move."

Mary gives her a look of motherly sympathy. "Oh honey, I know how hard it can be to start new schools. That must have been difficult."

Sighing, Isabelle admits, "It wasn't always sunshine and rainbows, but I knew how important Daddy's career was. He was busy, but always found plenty of time for me. And he made sure I had the best of everything.

"We spent several years in Iowa, but I finished up high school in New York. I liked it out there, and I stayed for college, but when Daddy took this job a few years ago I decided to move back. The Midwest always felt like home, and I missed living near him."

"It is pretty great here," I nod. "I've been here my whole life, aside from travel. Did you say you went to college in New York City?"

"Not quite, I went to Cornell, so more in the middle of the state."

"Damn, girl!" My eyes widen; I had definitely misjudged her as a ditzy blonde.

"Yeah," Steph agrees. "That's impressive."

Isabelle just shrugs.

"What did you study?" I ask.

"Oh, um, I just majored in finance, and economics."

Laughing I say, " 'Just?' Like, 'I'm just a flipping math whiz,' no big deal."

She glances away. "I'm an insurance underwriter right now, nothing really exciting."

It's hard to tell in the dim lighting, but I think she's blushing. This makes me grin. "Shit, Izzy, you're a nerd!"

Isabelle straightens up and locks eyes with me for a moment before turning away. I must have offended her. I thought she would know I was kidding. "Sorry, I didn't mean nerd in a bad way. It was meant to be a compliment. I wish I was great at math, it's just not my thing."

When she replies, there's a little tremor in her voice. "No, it's not that." She pauses. "You called me *Izzy*."

"Oh, uh, sorry. It's just a nickname. If you don't -"

She cuts me off. "I like it. It's just no one has ever given me a nickname before. I mean other than my daddy." As she reaches up to quick brush her hand against her cheek, I feel a mirrored tightness in my chest. "I don't have many girlfriends."

"Well, you have a few more now," I say. Izzy looks up at all three of us, and I see Mary and Steph both nodding their heads.

Steph cuts the tension by raising her glass. "Cheers to that! The more bitches the more merrier!"

"Hear, hear!" cheers Mary.

Izzy and I both silently raise our glasses and tip them toward each other.

After taking a sip, I hum as an idea starts to form. "The players might be off limits to you for dating, but - with brains like yours - you could work for them. Your education added with the real-life knowledge that you have, you could start your own business. Be a financial planner, or investment guru, or whatever it's called, to the stars of hockey. And aside from having the smarts to do it, you have the next and possibly hardest step done, access to the players."

Steph is practically bouncing off her seat by the time I finish. "Holy crap that's a brilliant idea! Izzy you have *got* to do that! You'd be perfect!"

Izzy looks back and forth between us, biting her lip. "I don't know, do you think they'd take me seriously?"

Mary scoffs. "Of course they would. And these girls are right, that's a great idea. Those boys don't know the first thing about what to do with their money. Most of them blow it all away on strippers and stupid cars."

"Mom!" Steph exclaims while laughing.

"Well, not my Jacky boy." Mary looks at me. "He would never do that."

"No ma'am," I agree, trying to keep a straight face.

"You know what, you're right. It's a great idea!" Izzy grins. "I've always wanted to be my own boss. But... I don't know the first thing about starting my own business."

"I do!" I slap a hand over my mouth, I didn't mean to shout that. I'm getting *way* too into this. Lowering my voice to a normal volume, I continue, "Well, not me, but my best friend has her own business. She's an event planner, here in the Twin Cities, so she's had to do the whole registering a business thing, and taxes, and blah blah blah *nerd stuff*. Which I'm sure you'd enjoy." I wink at Izzy. "Her name is Meghan. She's an absolute terror of a friend, but she's a savvy businesswoman. I'll have to introduce you to her."

Izzy nods. "That'd be so great."

I picture their meeting and grin. "Ohmygod, Meghan is going to love you! But - fair warning - she'll help you set up your business, and then she'll get all up in your personal business. She seriously doesn't understand boundaries. She'll critique your dating profiles, and will definitely ask you detailed questions about your sex life."

Steph laughs. "I like her already. Invite her over right now!"

I chuckle.

Izzy grimaces a little. "I don't have any dating profiles."

"Please, do yourself a favor, and at least make up a fake Tinder account or something to show her. If you don't, she will literally force you into one."

Steph leans forward. "Since you won't be able to date hockey players, especially if you're working with them, then you totally need to get online!"

"Really? You think I should do online dating?" Izzy asks.

"Dating, going out for drinks, fucking for fun, whatever." Steph shrugs.

"It's not as bad as it sounds. I'm on Silver Singles," Mary says.

Steph looks at her. "Seriously? Are you dating someone?" It's hard to read the look on her face. It's definitely shock, but it's hard to tell if it's the good kind or the bad kind.

"I've been on dates, but there's no one special yet." Mary puts her hand on Steph's lap. "I'll always love your father. He was my perfect pairing, but life chose to be a bitch and took him too young. *Stupid giant heart of his*. Me dating has nothing to do with me loving him any less. But your father always told me that if anything ever happened to him, he wanted me to keep living my life. So, I'm doing what he said." Mary pauses. "And if I'm gonna hook myself a sugar daddy, I've gotta do it while I'm still hot."

I have no idea what to say to this, and clearly neither does Izzy. We wait another beat before Steph throws her arms around Mary. There's a sound like a laugh, mixed with some jumbled words. Mary pats Steph on the back saying, "There, there, quit making a fool of yourself."

I feel like such an intruder right now. This is clearly something that's meant to be a private conversation. But I feel like getting up to leave would be just as inappropriate as listening, so I wait it out.

Steph chokes out a "Mom, I understand," then, "I'm so happy for you."

Clearing her throat, Mary pats Steph on the back. "Enough of this emotional mumbo jumbo. Let's make Izzy a Tinder account, so she can go get laid!"

I think under any other circumstance, Izzy would have fought the idea. But coming on the tails of Mary's declaration, she gives in. And that's how we spend the next hour - drinking margaritas, and creating a sexy new dating profile under the name *Izzy*.

CHAPTER SEVENTEEN

JACKSON

I rub my eyes in frustration. "We need to rethink our entire strategy for this."

Nodding, Coach agrees. "Let's call it a night and meet before practice in the morning to flesh out a plan. It's already getting too late to deal with this crap anymore tonight."

At that, I look over at the clock on my desk. "Shit! Has it really been two hours?" I jump out of my seat.

Both Luke and Coach look at me in sympathy.

"Sorry, brother," Luke apologizes, cringing a little.

Standing, Coach pats me on the back. "If it's any consolation, they must be having a good time. Not a single one of them has come back here to check on us."

"Or they all left," Luke helpfully states.

Glaring at Luke, I pull open the office door.

Walking down the hall, I expect to hear them. But it's oddly quiet. Glancing around the main room, I see that the dinner leftovers have been put away, but the makings of… margaritas?... are on the counter. *Steph.* I knew she had a hidden stash here. I can't help but smile to myself as I walk toward the stairs leading to the theater. Now that I'm closer, I can hear voices. Whatever's happening down there, they sound like they're having fun.

Knowing that Luke and Coach are following, I make my way down the stairs and through the open door of the theater. I pause to take it in, and the guys come to stand beside me.

In the corner of the couch, where we shared our first evening together, is Kitten. She's curled up with that same soft blanket and has her head thrown back in a laugh. The laugh causes her hair to trail down the back of the couch, exposing the soft skin of her neck. My eyes linger on her pulse point for several heartbeats before I take in the rest of the room.

Crammed up right next to Kitten is Isabelle. Steph is crammed right up next to her, and Mama is crammed right up next to *her*. It's like they forgot this is the largest piece of furniture in the house and had to sit as close together as possible. Then I see that Isabelle and Steph are both hunched over what I'm guessing is a phone, as Steph reads off of it.

" *'Looking for a woman who can enjoy an evening in, as much as an evening out. And who loves to cuddle.'* " Whatever it is, she read it in her male-impersonation voice before making a gagging sound. "Ugh, yeah, pass. This just means the guy is broke, won't take you out, and has probably never gone down on a girl."

Uh, wow. What the Hell did we just walk in on? Looking over at Coach, I see his eyes are wide in either shock or embarrassment, and beside him Luke is holding back a laugh. Before I'm forced to hear anything else out of my sister's mouth, I clear my throat and enter the room.

Kitten, apparently the most sober, hears me right away. She quickly turns her head in my direction, and some of that shiny hair falls over her face. Her welcoming smile causes my heart to beat a little faster. I silently mouth, "Hi, Kitten." To which she bites her lower lip. Oh, how I wish I were that lip right now.

Coach has circled around the other side of the couch to stand in front of the women. He has a look akin to pride on his face as he takes in Isabelle squished in between Kitten and Steph.

"Hey Peanut, we're all wrapped up for the evening. Did you ladies have a fun night?"

I can hear the smile in her voice. "Hi, Daddy! We had such a great time! Oh, and before I forget, can I please have four tickets to the next home game? Katelyn has a friend who's hopefully going to help me with a little project. I'd like to bring her to the game with us."

Coach looks at the four of them together on the couch. "Won't you need five tickets?" he asks.

"Oh, no need, Don. I plan to sit in my usual spot," Mama says. "It's my lucky seat and I already have a friend planning to join me. It'll just be these three troublemakers and a girl named Meghan."

Coach nods. "Your wish is my command. Remind me tomorrow and I'll square those away for you. Now - if you don't mind - I'm starving. We'll have to switch our dinner to something quick. We have an early morning tomorrow, since we have more strategy work to do."

As Isabelle stands, Steph and my mama get up too. Kitten follows and gives them all hugs goodbye. Apparently, everyone has shared phone numbers as there are a lot of "text me later" and "talk to you soon." I even hear Kitten call Isabelle "Izzy." Strange. As I go to hug my mama goodbye, she stops me, telling me to walk her out.

Turning to Kitten I say, "You stay right here." I point to where she had been sitting, in the corner of the U-shaped couch. "You sit in our spot, and I'll be right back."

She doesn't say anything, but she plops back down and shimmies up into the corner. With the intention of getting back to her as quickly as possible, I herd the rest of the group up to the front door.

Once everyone has made their way to the elevator bank, Mama grabs me by both hands and forces me to look her in the eye.

"Jacky boy, that girl down there is special. I think she already means a great deal to you, and I can tell you that you mean a great deal to her. But you, you need to make your intentions clear." She gives me her pointed Mama glare as she says this. "When Isabelle asked her if you two were dating, she didn't know what to say. If you want her, you need to make sure she knows that." Pulling me down further, she kisses my cheek. Then she cuffs me upside the head. "Goodnight, Jacky. I love you."

CHAPTER EIGHTEEN

KATELYN

Waiting for Jackson to come back is torture. From what Coach said, I'm thinking we'll need to cut tonight short so he can go in early tomorrow morning. But if that's the case, I don't know why he wouldn't have let me leave with the rest of the group. Okay, so I can understand him maybe wanting to have a few private words, but why ask me to stay down here? Surely we won't have time to watch a movie.

My thoughts are stopped by the sound of Jackson entering the room. I stay silent as he circles the couch and comes to sit by my feet. Since I'm in the corner, there's a stretch that extends out right in front of me, where I have my legs stretched out. It's a little strange that he chose to sit at my feet and not up by my side, but I guess this way we can see each other better.

With his large hands, Jackson grabs ahold of my ankles, scoots closer, and sets my feet on his lap.

Leaning back, he looks to the ceiling and sighs. "Kitten, tonight went a little... off script." I'm trying to ignore the feeling of his warm palms so I can listen to him. But I can feel the heat of them through my jeans. That heat spreads when he starts to slowly rub his hand up and down my shin. Just a few inches. Up and down. "I'm really sorry. I didn't want anything to interrupt our evening. Least of all an entire group of meddlers."

I can't help but to smile at his description. "Jackson, I had a great time tonight." He looks over to meet my eyes, and I hope he can see the truth in my words. "Of *course* I'm a little disappointed that our time together was cut into, but - the time we did share was wonderful, and I really did enjoy myself with the girls. I already adored your mom. Your sister is super sweet, and Izzy is a great girl. A little misunderstood, but I think she might become a good friend."

"Hmmmm."

Gods. I don't know what it is about that rumbling sound coming from him, but it goes straight to the center of my being.

I grin. "And now you owe me a makeup dinner. So, it's really a win-win for me."

"Is that right?" Jackson asks, though it doesn't sound like he's asking.

My grin dims. "It sounds like you have an early morning tomorrow."

To this, Jackson nods.

Letting out a breath I say, "Then I should head home. We can try for a normal evening next time."

Jackson stands and I think he's going to help me up. Only instead of reaching for my hands, he grips my ankles again, and pulls.

With way too much ease, he drags me down the length of the couch he had been sitting on, until I'm flat on my back.

Releasing his grip, steps up to my side. Slowly, he leans over and places one hand next to my head, then the other. He shifts his weight onto his hands and brings one knee between my legs while the other goes to the outside of my hip, on the edge of the couch. I don't know when I spread my legs apart, but I'm sure it was a normal biological reaction to having a man like this climb on top of me.

He lowers himself, an inch at a time, until there's only a breath of space left between us.

This is closer than we've ever been and my heart is working it's hardest to thump out of my chest.

Still looking me right in the eye, he says, "I was told that I need to make my intentions clear. So, this is me, being clear. This is me making sure you understand *exactly* what I want."

He lowers another inch, putting his face to the side of mine so he's speaking directly into my ear. "I *will* make you my girl, Kitten. I promise you that. But I'm going to take my time in doing so. I'm going to wait until you're ready for me." His cheek brushes against mine.

Oh. My. Fuck.

"What if I don't want you to wait? What if I'm ready now?" My words are breathy, and sound just as lustful as I feel.

In answer, Jackson lowers himself the rest of the way onto me. I can tell he hasn't put his full weight down, probably for fear of crushing me, but I can feel every inch of his body pressed into every inch of mine. I can feel his heat seeping into me, the rise and fall of his chest as his breathing quickens to match my own. And, holy crap, I can feel the impressively hard length of him pressed against my thigh. It takes everything I have to hold still and to not grind myself up against him.

Testing me, Jackson gives me the lightest nip on my ear lobe. And I can't help it, I moan. With a heavy exhale, Jackson applies a tiny bit more pressure with his thigh, that is now pressed between my legs. This small movement sends a pulse from my core to the tips of my toes.

Jackson's rough whisper fills the air around me. "Oh, Kitten, you're not ready for me yet. I'm a lot to handle. And once we start this thing between us, I won't be able to hold back. But fuck, woman, make no mistake, you're mine."

And with that, his weight is off me.

He grabs my hand, helps me up, and intertwining our fingers, he leads me upstairs.

I'm at an absolute loss for words. I'm more turned on than I think I've ever been in my whole life. There is nothing in this world that compares to the sexual energy this man exudes.

Still silent, I grab my purse and slip on my shoes. With his hand on my lower back Jackson walks me to the door. Once it's open and I've walked through, I finally turn and meet his eye.

Jackson brings his palm up against my cheek, holding me still as he slowly closes the distance between us. His mouth is so close to mine I can feel his breath on my lips.

"Dream of me tonight, sweet Kitten." His words are barely a whisper. Leaning a hair closer to me, he brushes his lips against mine, so lightly, I'm not even sure it really happened.

I don't even realize my eyes have closed until he steps back, the loss of his warmth causing my eyes to reopen.

Looking up and into his gaze, I say the only thing I can manage. "Goodnight, Jackson."

CHAPTER NINETEEN

KATELYN

Groaning, I pretend to throw my laptop across my living room before gently setting it down on the couch next to me. I'm trying to work, but I've reread the same paragraph four times now, and I still can't tell if it's a run-on sentence, incorrect use of a semicolon, or written in Klingon. *Ugh!* Last night with Jackson has officially fried my mind. What's left of my brain has crawled out of my head, down my spine, and is currently residing somewhere near my ovaries.

I don't even know how I managed to walk out of his building last night, let alone find my way home and put myself to bed. Scratch that, I know exactly how I put myself to bed last night. Let's just say it involved a lot of memory recall and I woke up with my sleep shorts on the floor. That beast of a man is totally screwing with my sanity. Which is why I am now sitting here having absolutely zero luck concentrating.

I haven't talked, texted, messaged, or whatever, with Jackson today. He most definitely "made his intentions clear" last night, so I'm at least pretty sure that we're dating now. Fairly sure. I mean, I know he wants me. He didn't come out with a sheet of paper and a *Do you want to be my girlfriend check Yes or No* note. But he did climb on top of me, pressing his hard *everything* against my everything, so... yeah, still no idea what we are.

What I do know is that I need more coffee. It's past lunchtime, but coffee is my drug of choice, day or night. If anything can help to sharpen my focus, it's the sweet nectar of the caffeine gods. Deciding this calls for the big guns, I take out my French press and start the process.

I'm tapping my foot, waiting for the grinds to soak, when my phone rings. Glancing at the screen before answering, I grin.

"Hey, Izzy! How's it going?"

"Hey! It's going great! How was the rest of your evening?"

"Oh, uh, good. Yep, it was good." I sound like an idiot.

There's a beat of silence before I hear Izzy giggling on her end of the line. "Oh, it was good, was it?" she asks.

"Okay, not like that! I mean it was good, but I left just a few minutes after you guys."

"Oh really?" Izzy sounds genuinely sad, which is sweet since just yesterday she was still hoping for a chance to date Jackson herself.

"Yeah, well with the early meeting they were having this morning we had to call it a night."

Izzy hums a little. "I feel like you're leaving something out... but maybe you can tell me over dinner Thursday evening? I talked to Daddy and he got us some great seats for the home game Friday night. I thought it might be nice if we could do dinner the night before, so I can meet your friend Meghan. That is, if she's even interested." Her tone turns uncertain. "She seriously can say no; I'll totally understand. And she can of course come to the game even if she doesn't want to help me with this business stuff."

"Okay, hold up, Iz," I interrupt her. "She's totally in, so quit your rambling. I texted her already and gave her the super high-level overview. But she's all about women owning their own businesses, so she's jacked about helping you get set up."

Izzy lets out a relieved sigh at this news. "Oh, thank god. I know we just talked about this last night, but I'm so excited already! Having someone point me in the right direction is going to be such a big help."

"Just don't praise her too much. That shit will go right to her head."

"Deal," Izzy replies with a laugh.

"Should I see if Steph is available for dinner, too?" I ask

"Yes, please!"

"Perfect. I'll start a group text when we hang up and then we can figure out a central location to meet."

"Thanks, Katelyn. I know we just met, but I can't thank you enough for all you've done for me already. I owe you."

"Oh hush, it's what friends do. Plus you're totally getting us all seats for the game. And I'm positive I don't want to know how much those tickets cost."

"Well, that's the perk of *knowing a guy,* I guess. Okay, I'll hang up now so you can start the group text. Bye, Katelyn!"

As it turns out, everyone's open for dinner Thursday, and we settle on meeting at the Mall of America. This should work out great, since I'd like to pick up some more Sleet clothing to surprise Jackson with, anyway. Obviously, I love the jersey he gave me, but if this thing with us is going to last for at least a few more games, I'd like to have some outfit options.

I've finally gotten myself settled back on the couch, laptop on my lap, cup of now nearly-too-cool coffee on the side table, when my phone chirps with a text. Resigned to the distraction, I pick up my phone, only to have my heart rate spike when I see it's from Jackson.

Jackson: Kitten, I find that you have been very distracting today.

Melt.

I was hoping that he was at least *partially* as frazzled as I've been after last night, so this is a good sign.

Me: Is that so? I can't possibly think of why.

Jackson: Do you need a reminder?

Me: Oh, I think I know exactly what you're talking about. That sushi last night was to die for. I'm still thinking about it today too!

Jackson: Kitten, don't make me come over there and drag you around by your feet. Again.

Damn. Is it hot in here? I feel like it's hot in here. I should check to make sure that my thermostat is working.

Me: It's coming back to me now. I do recall a declaration or two. But I'll be honest, I'm not sure I heard much after that ear bite.

Jackson: Let's call it a nibble. Saying I bit your ear sounds a little too Mike Tyson. (He's from a different sport, FYI.)

Me: Wait, what? You're not a boxer? Guess I'll just call this whole thing off now. We had a good run.

Jackson: You're lucky that you aren't here with me. That comment would get you a smack on that fine ass of yours.

Me: Oh really? Then I'll make sure to repeat it next time I see you.

Did I really just say that?!

Jackson: Fucking hell, Kitten. If I wasn't about to get on a plane, I'd be at your door already.

Me: That's right, you're heading to Canada, eh? Get everything squared away this morning?

Jackson: Yes and Yes. (Or I should say Yeah sure, Yeah sure.) The game is tomorrow night.

Just knowing that he'll be out of town makes me feel a little sad.

Me: I hope you don't mind, I just talked to Izzy and she has tickets for us to attend your Friday game at home.

Jackson: Damn right I don't mind. I need my Kitten cheering me on and purring when I score.

Jackson: Wink, wink.

Me: I don't know if I should laugh or groan at that one.

Jackson: No groaning, sweet Kitten. Only moaning for you. (Like you did when I bit your ear.)

Me: Nibbled. And this is exactly why I haven't gotten any work done today.

Jackson: I knew it! You tried to play it all cool, but - see? You've even distracted yourself.

Me: Yep, it's all me. All my fault.

Jackson: Okay, I gotta go. Time to take off.

Me: Safe travels!

Jackson: Watch my game tomorrow?

Me: Of course.

Setting my phone down, I realize that my cheeks hurt. Touching my face, I don't know why I'm surprised to find it stuck in the biggest grin ever. I'm glad Jackson can't see me right now. I'm sure I look like such a dummy. But I can't help it. He's so sweet. And funny. And hot. And he uses proper grammar when he texts!

Okay, I need to snap out of it. Jackson's on a plane, and I have work to do.

Distractedly taking a sip of coffee, I grimace. It's now completely cold. Damn it.

CHAPTER TWENTY

KATELYN

I'm either a genius, or a lunatic that should be locked away from society. We just sat down at the Northern Grill in the Mall of America. We basically all showed up at the same time, from different directions, so the introductions have just finished. Meghan is the only new one in the bunch, but she is such a firecracker that she immediately fits right in.

I'm not at all worried about Izzy and Meghan working together; they'll be a dream team of beautiful nerds. Meghan and Steph though, together they might be the perfect storm. They're both so energetic, I almost wonder how long they could keep each other going.

The conversation is easygoing. The level of excitement radiating off our table is drawing some added attention, but I think we have a fierce enough vibe going on that the couple guys at the bar who keep eyeing us should stay away. Seeing as there's not a single wedding ring at this table, we need to send out *Back Off* energy, because tonight is about bonding, not about boys.

Boys. Boy, I can*not* stop thinking about Jackson. Last night, for the first time ever, I sat in my house and watched a hockey game on TV. And it was just as stressful as when I went in person. I'll never admit this to anyone, but I wore his jersey while I watched. Not out of any superstition, just because I wanted to. I also found myself tempted to call Mary so she could calm me down with her chattering, just like she did before I knew she was his mama. I didn't call though. It seemed a touch too stalker-y to be calling my maybe-boyfriend's mom this soon in our maybe-relationship.

Just as before, I had nothing to worry about. The Sleet won their game, and Jackson played amazingly. I know this because it looked like he was playing well, and because the announcers kept saying his name and praising *this move* or *that pass*. Also as before, I found myself proud of him. I'm still waiting for the part of Jackson that will make him more human. Push him back towards the mortal side of the spectrum. He just seems a little too perfect. Like there has to be something I'm missing.

Not sure how busy he would be right after the game, I shot him a text about an hour after it finished, congratulating his win. To my surprise, and stuttering pulse, his response was to call me. I will be forever grateful that it was a regular call and not FaceTime, because I blushed the second I heard his voice. Plus, I was already in my pajamas. Meaning no bra, no makeup, and messy hair.

Our call was brief; since Jackson was just about to hop on the bus to head back to the plane to come home. He said he called since it's safer than walking and texting, and because he wanted to hear my voice. I swooned. I swooned hard enough that I couldn't think of a single goddamn thing to say in response to that, to which Jackson cracked a joke about needing me to actually *speak* if he was going to get to hear my voice. That brought me out of it enough to have a conversation.

I don't know what he's doing tonight, but he said his mama already told him that I'd be out with the girls and that he needed to leave me alone. I'm desperate to see him again, but I'm thankful he didn't try to interfere with our girls' night. I don't know if I would've been able to resist him if he tried to steal me away, and this time with my friends is important.

"And this is what I like to call Catatonic Katelyn," I hear Meghan say.

"Huh?" I realize I've been zoning out and find all three girls staring at me. Meghan is looking particularly smug, so I direct my false confidence at her. "I wasn't being catatonic anything. I'm here in the now. Super Zen."

Meghan rolls her eyes. "You're not even fooling these newbies here with that line of bullshit. Pretty sure even grandpa over there, with his hearing aid turned off to drown out his daughter-in-law, can hear how full of shit you are."

I can't help it. I turn to look at the table in the corner. Sure enough, there's a large group and the old man looks so focused on his meal that he doesn't even bat an eye at the flailing hands of the younger woman who's talking loudly next to him. There's no way for Meghan to prove her hearing-aid theory, but I wouldn't bet against her.

I shake my head and see I'm not the only one who looked. Izzy seems legitimately concerned about grandpa.

"*Any*ways..." Meghan draws the word out, "You were obviously daydreaming about Jackson." Shooting a look at Steph, Meghan says, "Is it going to gross you out to hear about your brother as a love interest?"

Steph makes a face. " 'Love interest?' Okay, Grandma."

Meghan laughs. "You know what I mean. A *sexual being*."

"It doesn't bother me, unless you refer to him again as *a sexual being*," Steph shudders, then turns to me. "I mean, if you guys blow each other, I sure as fuck don't want the details, but you can say 'we had sex.' I can deal with that."

Meghan smirks.

Izzy giggles.

I blush.

I shake my head. "You guys are whacked in the thinker. And no, we haven't *blown* each other. Or had sex. We haven't even really kissed."

That gets a reaction. There's a chorus of "wait, what?" "really," and "how is that possible?!"

I slouch back in my chair. "Honestly, he's being a real fucking tease. If he doesn't put out soon, I'm going to end up with blue balls. Blue uterus. Whatever." I glance over. "Sorry, Steph."

She shrugs. "Don't apologize to me. Hell, I feel like I should be apologizing on behalf of the Wilder family. What's his hold up?"

"Yeah, what the hell?" grumbles Meghan.

"It's obvious he likes you," Izzy adds in, sounding like she's trying to cheer me up. "With the way he is around you, you can just tell."

Meghan hums, "So what happened after these guys left his place the other night? Izzy said you stayed behind."

I look at Izzy, wondering when she told them, causing Meghan to laugh. "I called it! Told you you were going all Catatonic Katelyn earlier. If you had been listening, you'd have heard Izzy tell us."

"Okay, okay. Yes, I stayed down in the theater while Jackson walked everyone out. When he came back, we sat for a moment and we talked about yet another night going haywire on us." I pause for a moment, not quite sure how to explain what happened, especially in front of Steph.

"Spit it out, woman!" Meghan leans forward across the table, clearly impatient with my stalling.

"Right, so... he kinda pulled me down."

"Pulled you down?" Izzy asks.

Gah, why does she have to look so innocent while she asks that?

"Yeah."

Steph bursts out laughing. "Oh my god, just explain what the hell happened. Your blushing and over-thinking is making my imagination go wild! We know you didn't even kiss, so - out with it!"

"Fine! Okay!" I decide keeping my gaze on the table and talking fast is the best way though this. "He got up like to leave, but then he grabbed my ankles and pulled me so I was flat on my back on the couch. Then he climbed on top of me and while I was pinned beneath him, he started whispering in my ear about how he wanted to make his intentions clear. And that he would make me *his,* but that I wasn't ready for him yet because he's a lot to handle."

Crickets.

Raising my eyes, I find all three of them staring at me. Mouths slightly open.

Meghan's the first to talk. "Holy fuck, that's hot."

Izzy clears her throat.

"I want to be grossed out by that, but I gotta admit it was a pretty great move on his part," Steph says, begrudgingly.

"That's not the first time he's gotten close to me. But it was the first time he freaking climbed on top of me."

"Steph, close your ears," Meghan says, and I just dread whatever question is going to come out of her mouth next. Steph does not cover her ears, and Meghan carries on anyway. "So, did you get a feel of his equipment?" She follows the question with an eyebrow bob.

Steph puts her hands over her face, laughing, and I just blush harder.

"That's a yes." Meghan beams. "I'll skip the follow-up questions, given the company, but don't think I won't be asking about this later."

"Can't wait," I say in a tone that implies I really can.

We both know I'll tell her all the details. Men don't seem to understand that women tell each other everything. Like, *everything.* Guys might brag about a sexual act in big-picture terms: I hit that, she blew me. But women, we describe in detail. Vivid, accurate, detail. I have a pretty good mental image of basically every dick Meghan has ever seen, and vice versa. So yeah, I'll give Meghan more details later, but I won't give those details in front of Steph. Some familial lines should not be crossed.

"We've texted and talked on the phone since then." I sigh. "I'm hoping I'll get a chance to see him after the game tomorrow night. Maybe I can get that kiss then. I mean, he did - kind of - give me a kiss when I left his place. But it was such a light little peck that it hardly counts." I tell them. "That's all the update I have for now. But I promise to fill you guys in if something big happens." I'm hoping I can push the conversation past Jackson and on to something else for the remainder of the evening.

My plan works, and the rest of dinner is focused on other topics. As we wrap up, I mention that I want to check out what sort of Sleet gear they have at the mall, and Izzy says she knows the perfect shop.

We walk down the wide hallway in a little cluster, talking amongst ourselves.

Steph is next to me so I hear her say, "Oh fuck," just before a voice ahead of us calls out: "Steph, is that you?"

Following the voice, I find myself looking at a stunning redhead. Seriously, she looks like she came from a photoshoot. She's model-tall, and even more so since she's wearing stilettos. *Who the hell wears stilettos to the mall?* Her strawberry hair is perfectly straight, around a perfectly done-up face, on top of a painfully thin body, with tits that have got to be man-made. She's a total knockout. If you go for the red-headed Barbie look.

"So nice to see you," the mystery woman coos to Steph. "How's Jackson doing?"

And just like that, I hate her.

The fact that Mattel Ginger over here knows Jackson makes my bitchy-sense tingle.

"Hi, Lacy." I don't even have to look at Steph to know that she's wearing a blatantly fake smile. "Jackson is doing really, really great. This is his girlfriend, Katelyn." She gestures to me.

I try to look as nonchalant as possible, even though I want to simultaneously cower and claw this girl's eyes out. Lacy gives me a very obvious once-over as her smile turns into a sneer. She does *not* look impressed. Shit, I'm not really impressed with myself either, standing in her vicinity.

"Nice running into you, we have to go." Steph is already walking, pulling me along with her.

We all allow the following silence to go on for a few minutes until we reach the store we were looking for.

Once inside I halt Steph, "Umm, care to explain what that was all about?"

"Yeah," Meghan says, "Who's the plastic bitch?"

I have to smile; she went to the same place I did with that insult.

Steph grits her teeth for a moment. "That plastic bitch is Lacy. She's Jackson's ex. She's awful. We all hate her. End of story."

His ex. She said she was Jackson's ex, not *one of* his exes. There's significance in that. But - just like how I don't want to read about Jackson's life online - nor do I want to hear about it from his family, either. I decide to focus on the fact that this Lacy person is his ex and not his current. She might be built like a sex doll, but she doesn't have him now.

"Okay," I nod.

"Okay?" Steph asks, not believing that I won't press for more details.

"Yeah. And thank you for calling me his girlfriend. That might not be technically true, but it was great to see the look of horror on her face."

Steph grins. "The only thing that would've made that better would be if I'd've punched her in the boob after saying that. Or at the very least beat her with one of those ridiculous shoes."

Even Izzy comments on that. "Those were pretty impractical shoes for walking at the mall."

"Yeah, but I bet they're great for skewering baby bunnies and roasting them over a fire." Steph makes a face at her own comment. "All right, I'm done now. Lacy is getting no more of my brain space tonight. She's a stupid whore and I'm sorry you had to meet her. Now let's shop."

Finally taking in the store, I smile. I'll definitely find a few things to buy here.

As we venture toward the Sleet section, I vow to put Lacy out of my mind. It's hard to deny that we couldn't be more different if we tried. But they aren't together anymore.

And Jackson promised he'd make his move on me soon.

CHAPTER TWENTY-ONE

KATELYN

"Izzy, you are *so* my favorite person right now, these are the best tickets ever!" I don't even try to play it cool as I drop into my seat.

"I'm choosing to not take offense to that," Meghan shimmies her shoulders, "since I got the best spot out of the four of us."

The seats Izzy got us are directly behind the Sleet home bench. Dugout? No, *bench*. Pretty sure it's called a bench. I'll ask Jackson later. With this view, I have to vow to myself that I'll watch the game, and not just stare at the back of his helmet if he's sitting on the bench. *Yeah, that sounds right, it's a bench.* Anyway, that in itself is super cool, but - to top it off - we have the four end seats in the row that butt up to the hallway-ramp-thingy that the players walk down when they're coming on and off the ice.

Since this is Meghan's first game, and presumably I'll be coming to more, we all agreed to let her have the end spot by the railing so she could - and I quote - "Get all the fucking high fives from all the fucking hot guys." She's including both teams on this. According to Meghan, hotness knows no geographical bounds, and she will not limit herself based on our misguided American fanaticism. What Meghan doesn't seem to know is that only our team will be going past her; apparently the other team has their own ramp thing.

So, Meghan has the seat on the end, Izzy's next to her, then Steph, and I'm on the end of our little foursome. On my right side is a group of rowdy college-aged guys all decked out in Sleet gear and face paint. They look ready to drink their way through the game, and will probably be that group that cheers and boos for every moment of action. It should be entertaining.

We're three rows up again. The height gives us a good view of the ice, while still being close enough to the players to see the sweat on their faces. Izzy told us about these seats last night, so when Jackson texted me this morning, I told him where to look for us.

When he does spot me, I hope he's happy with my new outfit and not upset that I didn't wear his jersey. The shirt I'm wearing tonight is a fitted long-sleeve heather grey shirt with *Wilder* written across the back and the Sleet storm-cloud logo on the chest. It has a deep V-neck that, if I do say so myself, makes my cleavage look amazing. My favorite part of this shirt is that it has those sleeves that go all the way to the back of your hands with the little thumb holes. That's a fun feature in general, but it's especially great tonight since I also bought a pair of totally adorable knitted Sleet mittens. They are blue and green with *Sleet* stitched on one hand and *MN* on the other. With my thumbs through the holes, I can easily tuck my sleeves into my mittens. My hair's down again, since I was debating if I should wear the Sleet pom pom hat that matches the mittens too. After way too much internal debate, I decided to leave the hat at home.

What you can't see are the pair of Sleet-branded "Biggest Fan" undies that I'm wearing under my jeans. Meghan found those, and - when I refused to buy them - she bought them, making me promise to wear them tonight. I have no doubt that they'll go unseen, but thinking about them makes me feel a little scandalous.

In what I'm recognizing to be my new thing, I am totally freaking out right now. I don't know how all the family members deal with the wait before these games, because it's killing me. I've been stress tugging on a loose string inside one of my mittens, and if I don't stop soon, the whole thing will probably unravel. Thankfully, the lights drop, and the opening craziness begins. I was completely taken off guard during that first game when I was sitting alone for this part, so it's nice to have some friends with me.

The music, light show, and nutjob announcer make it impossible to not get pumped up. If I were a player there's no way I'd be able to focus after all this build up, but I guess they're used to it.

We're on our feet cheering when the Sleet players start coming down the ramp toward the ice. I'm only four spots in from the railing, but - with everyone standing - I have no real view of who's going past. What I can see is Meghan's ass, since she's leaning over the rail hoping to get her sought-after hot-guy high-fives. I may have mentioned Meghan's high-five fetish to Jackson this morning, so I shouldn't be surprised when I see that almost the entire team flies past hitting her hand as they go. I'm not sure if what she's doing constitutes cheering, or if it's just screaming at this point. Either way, Meghan is most definitely enjoying herself.

As the last player passes, hitting her hand, she yells, "I LOVE YOU JACKSON WILDER!"

I know—because I saw him the second he hit the ice—that Jackson was not the last person in line. But Meghan seems to have figured out that his influence is what got her all the hand action. She would *really* love him if he could hook her up with some actual hand action after the game. I snort to myself. It's almost as if she hears my thoughts, because Meghan catches my attention and gives me two thumbs up to go with her massive grin.

The guys on my right are proving to be the intensely loud group I'd pegged them for. Things settle down a bit when the anthem plays through. And as the teams gather for a final word before the start of the game, Jackson looks up and directly into my eyes.

I can't help the smile that spreads across my face. Without overthinking it, I blow him a kiss.

He grins.

I melt.

CHAPTER TWENTY-TWO

KATELYN

It's the start of the second period, and the teams are tied 1-1. Jackson is, of course, playing brilliantly. I do my best not to drool on myself every time he skates by. I know it should be gross to see the sweat dripping down his face when he comes off the ice, but it's not gross. It's the opposite of gross. It's sexy-as-fuck because I know he earned that sweat through hard work and talent. And thinking of him working his muscles makes me think of the last time I was with him, and how he put all those muscles all over me.

Steph squeals next to me a moment before Jackson slams an opponent against the glass not far from where we're sitting.

The crowd breaks out in cheers as he steals the puck and passes it to Luke. Luke's already breaking off toward the goal, and it brings us all to our feet. Jackson is following Luke down the ice, and another Sleet player has come to fill out the arrow. Luke passes it to the guy I don't know, who then fakes a shot while passing the puck to Jackson so fast I didn't even see it.

In the blink of an eye, Jackson is on the goal and slipping the puck past the goalie's skate, into the corner of the net.

I lose my shit. Steph loses her shit. The guy next to me loses his shit. Pretty much the whole arena loses its collective shit.

The roar of the fans is unreal, and I feel honest-to-god tears pricking my eyes. I'm so happy for Jackson right now. I know the actual amount of time we've spent together can be measured in hours, not weeks or even days, but I feel like I know him. I feel like I know the person that Jackson is inside, and that person is a man who puts family and responsibilities at the top of his priority list. He's funny, kind, charming, sexy-as-sin, and - to my absolute delight - he has a bit of a mouth on him. He just also happens to be a very talented professional hockey player, who is adored by thousands upon thousands of fans. I can't even imagine what it feels like to be him in these moments. But he's earned it.

I turn to Steph just as she's turning to me, and we embrace in a bouncing hug. I don't feel quite so foolish anymore, since I can see tears in her eyes as well. She gives me a knowing smile and then squeezes me tighter.

As the crowd settles down, the teams take a moment to reconvene and do whatever it is they do when they group together. While we wait, the big screen comes to life with my favorite thing - the Kiss Cam. My dad dragged me to many a baseball game throughout my life, and I would always look forward to this part. I don't know what it is that makes me love it so much. I've never been on it. It's just so much fun to see the couples blush, or the dads kiss their little kids, or the old couples full-on making out.

Smiling up at the screen, I watch what must be a five-year-old boy kiss his little sister on the cheek. The crowd releases a synchronized "Aww" before the cam moves on to another couple. They kiss, for a very long time, before the cam switches to another couple. Only this couple doesn't start kissing. They're just staring up at the screen.

Oh, wait... That's me!

It takes me an embarrassingly long time to realize that the cam is focused on me and the loud frat boy next to me. I've always wondered how people who were watching the screen could take forever to react when they saw themselves up there. I get it now.

In the image looking back at me, I can see that the frat boy is looking at me hopefully. With a deer-in-the-headlights look, I quickly glance at him only to look back at the screen and shake my head. I can hear a few laughs in the crowd, but thankfully the screen cuts away from us as the ref drops the puck back into play.

I chance another look over to Frat Boy, and he's full on smiling at me now. His friends are all laughing and the one next to him is patting his back as if to console him.

"I'm trying not to take it personal," he places a hand on his chest, "but you didn't need to look so terrified of kissing me."

"I'm sorry." *I'm not.* "I always wondered what would happen if they put two strangers up there together. Now I know."

"Well, if they put us up there together again, we can pretend we aren't strangers." He attempts a smirk.

"Uh, thanks, but I don't think we have to worry about that."

"I promise not to bite. Even if that's your thing, it's not really Kiss Cam appropriate."

I know he's trying to be funny. But he's just being a creep. I can smell the beer on his breath, and he might be cute, but he's no Jackson Wilder. Even if I wasn't here for another man, there's no way I would makeout with this guy on the Kiss Cam. That shit stays on the internet forever. *Ugh*, my denial of him will be on the internet forever too. Whatever, it's still better than letting him put his beer-infused tongue in my mouth. Barf. I give him a halfhearted smile and turn back to the game.

A few minutes have gone by, and the teams are once again on pause for a timeout. To my now dread, not glee, the big screen lights up with the Kiss Cam again. And it starts out zoomed in right on me and Frat Boy.

Fuck.

Again, I shake my head and mouth "I don't know him" using a thumb to point to Frat Boy, in case there was any question as to who I was referring to. The camera gives up and finds another couple to target. Frat Boy leans in.

"Aw, come on. Do you have a boyfriend or something?"

"Yes." I'm only pretty sure that I do, but let's just go with *yes*.

"Well, lucky for me he sent you out with the girls tonight. He'll never know."

"Dude!" Now I'm glaring at him. For fuck's sake. If you need to try to convince someone to kiss you, then you need to give up. Like, immediately. But this drunk idiot doesn't realize this is a battle he won't win.

The Kiss Cam comes back to us.

Double fuck.

A mix of embarrassment and anger fills me while I look up at the screen, seeing Frat Boy aiming his puckered lips at me.

Before I can think of how to get out of this situation, a loud crash startles everyone in our section.

My eyes jerk towards the noise.

Jackson is right in front of us, at the back wall behind the bench, helmet in hand, still where he slammed against the glass, giving Frat Boy a death stare.

I can almost hear the words as I read them off his lips: "Back. The. Fuck. Off!"

Frat Boy is suddenly sitting ramrod straight with his back against the seat as if he'd just been shoved. The color has drained out of his face, and his mouth is no longer in a kissy pout. Rather, it's hanging open like a caught fish.

Jackson turns his sights on me. He holds my gaze for a beat, then winks, and turns to get back on the ice. Be still my belly full of bumblebees.

I'm so zoned-in to our little moment that I'm not sure what the cameras caught, or how the crowd is reacting. But after a few seconds of silence, Frat Boy's friends all nearly fall out of their seats from laughter. And I have to bite my lip in order to keep my smile somewhat in check.

"Holy shit, that was hot!" Meghan shouts before she leans over to look past the other girls so she can see me. "Sorry doll, but I totally just got turned on by your man."

A lady in the row ahead of us turns around. "Me too." Meghan high-fives her.

"Oh. Um…" Seriously, what the hell am I supposed to say to that.

Frat Boy seems to have recovered some of his braveness, along with the blood in his face, because he taps me on the shoulder.

"Wow… so, you're dating Jackson Wilder?" The look he's giving me is full of awe.

"Yeah." The look I'm giving him is full of *you're-a-jackass*.

"I guess your boyfriend would have known. If you kissed me."

"Yes, well, regardless, if a girl tells you she doesn't want to kiss you, you need to respect that."

A look of regret finally makes an appearance. "You're right. I'm sorry."

I sigh. I should probably press this issue further, but he seems chastised. "Just don't do it again."

"Agreed. But it would have been kind of cool to say that I got punched by Jackson Wilder."

I scoff. "If you'd actually tried to kiss me, *I* would've been the one punching you."

He grimaces.

"And *then* Jackson would've punched you." I smile, and bat my eyes.

"You're absolutely right. I apologize for the entire thing." He nods vigorously.

One of Frat Boy's friends leans over to talk to him, "If it's any consolation, I'm pretty sure that shit's going to replay on ESPN all week!" Laughing he smacks Frat Boy's knee. "Dude, you looked like you were going to piss yourself!"

Oh joy, I guess *this* is going to be my fifteen minutes.

With the puck back in play, my attention is back on the game. Jackson keeps sneaking looks this way. I'm assuming he's trying to make sure that Frat Boy hasn't tried to grope me in the last five minutes. I roll my eyes to myself. It's sweet, but a little overkill. Especially since he's playing a game and there's not much he could do about it.

Thankfully, I feel like I'm starting to understand the rules of hockey. I know I'm missing a lot but I'm getting the basics figured out. Like - the puck goes in the net, the crowd freaks out. Goalie stops the puck, the crowd freaks out. The players do pretty much anything, the crowd freaks out. I know that goalie helmets are cool, but I have no idea what *offside* means. I think it's bad. And apparently the term *icing* does not refer to the delicious stuff you put on a cake.

One of my favorite parts is the constant face-offs, puck-drops, whatever they're called. Some of the time Jackson is the one going up against a guy from the other team. Watching his intensity when he does that is hot. Like, clench my thighs together hot.

As if thinking about it made it true, I watch as Jackson skates up for another face-off. Like always, the two opposing players stop just a few feet from each other. They should be crouching down to get into position, but it looks like the other player is saying something to Jackson.

I can see Jackson's head tilt a little, like he just heard something he didn't like. Before I have time to ask Steph what's happening, Jackson drops his stick and punches the other guy right in the face.

The guy nearly falls but catches himself, and goes after Jackson. The ref and several players are suddenly swarming around the fighting pair. I assumed they were coming to break up the fight, but I see more punches flying from players on both sides. *Ohmygod, is this normal?*

I jump up to stand, as if that'll give me a better idea about what the hell is happening. I can't even pick Jackson out of the growing mass of bodies anymore.

My hands are at my mouth, and I think I'm holding my breath. I can sense that everyone around me is also standing but I can't tear my eyes away. The crowd seems to be . . .

cheering? What the hell! How can they cheer right now? This is terrifying!

The rest of the refs and players are starting to wade in to pull everyone apart. The ice is littered with helmets and gloves and hockey sticks. The crowd is still making noise, but I feel like I'm on the verge of all-out crying.

Finally, I'm able to pick Jackson out of the herd. He has a scowl on his face, and the exposed part of his cheek above his beard on one side looks red, but I don't see any blood.

Wait, scratch that. His gloves are off and his knuckles are bloody. I inhale.

The ref leads Jackson across the rink to the penalty box and the rest of the players gather their scattered gear. I'm pretty sure I can pick out the guy Jackson was fighting, since he's the only one having his face tended to. It looks like he might have a split lip. Maybe that's where the blood on Jackson's hand came from, which would mean it isn't his own.

I can't believe Jackson just started a massive fight in the middle of a game! Even being a hockey novice, I know that fighting on the ice is kind of a thing. But I was not at all prepared for that level of brawling. Especially since Jackson started it!

The penalty box is directly across from our seats so I watch as the door is shut behind him before he turns and sits. Knowing right where to look, his eyes rise and meet mine.

I'm still standing, still have my hands over my mouth, and I'm sure my eyes are crazed. Seeing this, the corner of Jackson's mouth tips up, into a half smile.

That snaps me out of it. If he's smiling, then clearly he's fine. I drop my hands, shake my head, and collapse into my seat. Steph puts her arm around my shoulders and tugs me into her side.

"Hot damn, that was intense." She whispers.

My mouth feels dry, so I just nod in response.

"In all the years Jackson has played hockey, I've only seen him get in a couple of fights." Steph almost sounds like she is talking to herself, though her arm is still around me. "But I've *never* seen him throw the first punch. I wonder what that other player said to him."

Taking a sip of water, I find my voice. "What's going to happen to him?"

I can feel Steph shrug. "He'll get a five-minute penalty, but that's about it."

"Okay." Exhaling, I straighten up in my seat as Steph takes her arm back.

Hearing what sounds like a prayer, I look over and see Frat Boy crossing himself.

CHAPTER TWENTY-THREE

KATELYN

The rest of the game has gone by in a blur. There is only a minute left in the third period, and both teams have managed to score, keeping us up by 1. Steph has been texting with her mom, and they're going to meet up after the game to grab a drink. I've been invited, but I'm just going to head home tonight. After the stress of this game I need a good night's sleep. And probably a fucking Xanax. Not that I have any.

Meghan and Izzy have become fast friends in the past twenty-four hours. I've overheard some of their conversations, and it sounds like they'll be getting together this weekend to talk business stuff. I'm super excited to have Izzy and Steph as a part of our girl squad. I know it's kinda weird to be friends with a guy's sister when you've only just met, but it's not like anything else we've done has been normal. And considering I already met his mama, hanging with his sister seems hardly noteworthy. Obviously, I have high hopes for Jackson and me, but - even if we don't work in the long run - I hope Steph and I can stay friends.

With plans set for us all to catch up next week, the final buzzer sounds and the game is over.

Once again, we're standing and cheering as the players start to file off the ice and down the ramp past Meghan, heading towards the locker room.

I track Jackson's progress, watching as he steps past the glass wall and onto the solid ground of the walkway. The standing crowd blocks some of my view, but as he approaches space miraculously clears, and I can see him. And he's staring right at me.

Slowing, Jackson hands his hockey stick off to a little boy in the first row. Even from my bad angle, I can tell the kid is ecstatic with this sudden gift. Never breaking eye contact with me, Jackson drops his gloves to the ground and ruffles the kid's hair.

Taking another step forward, Jackson removes his helmet and drops that to the ground as well.

I don't know how to read the expression he's giving me, but my heart is beating wildly.

Another step and he's reached our row.

Jackson reaches up, puts a hand up on the railing next to Meghan, jams his skate onto a support bar below, and pulls himself up.

And then he's there. Standing on the outside of the railing, at the end of our row, staring at me.

"Get over here, Kitten."

His voice is full of barely restrained intensity.

The girls all press back against their seats making room for me to pass. With shaky steps and a galloping pulse, I inch closer.

I'm still a foot away from Jackson when he grows impatient, growling, "Closer."

I step closer.

He keeps a grip on the railing with his right hand, but his left hand reaches out and curls around the back of my neck.

Tugging me toward him, Jackson whispers, "Closer."

I step up to the rail.

Jackson closes the distance, pressing his lips to mine. Firmly.

My body shudders at the contact, and his grip on my neck tightens. Without my asking them to, my hands come up and grab the front of his jersey, pulling him further into me.

He deepens the kiss.

I tilt my head.

His tongue brushes my lips.

I die.

The crowd goes wild.

Breaking our kiss, Jackson pulls back just enough for his gaze to meet mine. "In case there was any question as to who you should be kissing." He smirks. "Meet me behind the locker room. Isabelle can show you the way."

And then he's gone. Dropped down to ground level and out of sight before I can even remember to breathe.

"Oh. My. Holy hot-guy gods!" Meghan shouts, startling me out of my daze. "That was the sexiest fucking thing I have ever witnessed." She fans herself. "That was better than porn. Fuck it, I'm going to be watching that replay *as* porn."

Izzy giggles. Steph groans.

CHAPTER TWENTY-FOUR

JACKSON

I am in so much trouble with this girl. I finally got my lips firmly pressed to hers, for all of about five seconds, and it was more intense than I had imagined. I didn't even get a chance to properly taste her, but the feel of her lips will forever be burned into my memory.

I wish I could've drawn that kiss into more than just a moment, but I knew the cameras would be all over us. And dammit, I should've at least warned her about the potential fanfare that dating me would stir up. But it's not like I had expected tonight to go the way it did.

Would it bother her to have a video of us kissing go viral? *Shit.* Well, at the very least - if she wasn't sure about my intentions before - they should be crystal fucking clear now. And if I'm lucky enough to convince her to be my girlfriend, then she'll eventually end up on an ESPN clip or photographed in some gossip rag. Either way, I'll apologize. Not for kissing her, but for making a spectacle about it. And even though I'll apologize, I still wouldn't change what I did.

Earlier in the game, during one of our time-outs, Luke nudged me and gestured up to the screen. I wasn't sure what to expect, but when I looked up and saw *my* Kitten paired up with some dumb-fuck kid my blood went hot. She was shaking her head and saying something, obviously distressed with the situation, before the camera panned away. I'd stopped listening to Coach and instead watched to see if the jackasses behind the camera would come back to my girl. Sure enough, a few moments later they were back on screen. And Dumb Fuck had his lips puckered up at Kitten.

That simmering anger flipped to molten. I was off the ice and ripping my helmet off in a single raging heartbeat. If they'd have been in the front row, there's a good chance I would have hopped the glass and strangled the poor bastard. But even without the bodily violence, I think Dumb Fuck got the message. He looked about a moment away from puking after I slammed my helmet into the glass just a few feet in front of him.

I don't usually relish being a *big scary dude*. But in that moment, I relished.

When I broke my glare to look at Kitten, her pretty face was covered in this expression of astonishment and innocence. Like she couldn't believe any of that had happened, and it sunk her tiny claws a little bit deeper into my chest. Since I couldn't do any of the things that I wanted to do to her, I winked. As I'd hoped, it snapped her out of her trance, and the next time I glanced over she seemed to be scolding Dumb Fuck. Good girl.

Then Montgomery happened. I've been playing against him for nearly as long as I can remember. We're the same age, we played against each other in college, and he's always been a dick. I'm a pretty chill guy. Usually. I get along with almost everyone. But I hate Jeffrey Montgomery. He's always trying to start fights and is constantly trash-talking on the ice. But in the past he's never really had anything he could use to get to me riled up, making him easy to ignore. Tonight though, he saw what went down with the Kiss Cam and saw his opportunity.

We lined up for the face-off, I was focused on the game, like a fucking professional, when I heard the tail end of something he'd said. Something along the lines of "pretty mouth on her."

So I asked, "What was that?"

To which he replied, "Your girl there has a pretty mouth. Bet it'd look extra nice if she were on her knees with my di—"

That's how far he got. That was far enough. That prick deserved every one of the many punches I landed on his stupid face.

I'm not even worried about Coach. Before the third period I gave him the ten-second rundown on what happened, and he just patted me on the back. He's met Katelyn, and he has a daughter. He's perfectly fine with how I handled that, and I'm sure he'll never bring it up again. My team though, they're going to give me a hard time for-fucking-ever. Not about punching Montgomery, everyone hates him, they'll give me a hard time about liking a girl. *Bunch of dumbasses.* But those dumbasses didn't waste a second wading in on my behalf. Usually a fight on the ice stays between the two guys who started it. But since I don't think I've *ever* swung first, my team didn't hesitate to back me up. They can definitely be exasperating at times, but my teammates have my back.

I'll deal with their ribbing tomorrow. Now, I'm showered, dressed, and ready to see Kitten. I told her to have Isabelle bring her down here. Isabelle knows every inch of this place, so I'm assuming she'll know to bring her to the rear hallway that's saved for nonpublic exits. I don't want Kitten around any press or the other players. I want it to be just her and me.

Stepping through the door, I find Kitten right where I'd hoped.

She's leaning against the wall a few feet down the empty hallway, still wearing those cute mittens I saw her with earlier. And that low-cut shirt... But it's her face, and her lips, that have me captivated. Just the sight of her, here, alone, makes my pulse pick up.

The sound of the door closing behind her pulls her attention towards me. And I swear, every time our eyes meet, I feel like I know her a little bit more.

Not looking away, I stride towards her.

She hasn't said anything. She isn't smiling. She's just looking right at me. Just like I'm looking at her.

No more waiting.

I barely slow down when I reach her. With a quick squat, I can grab the back of each of her thighs, just below that perfect ass.

Standing to my full height, I bring her with me. Instinct, or need, has her looping her legs around my waist. And pure animal lust has me taking one more step, pinning her back against the wall. I'm strong. I could hold her up. But her pressed between me and this wall is exactly where I want her.

Her small mitten-clad hands come up to hold the sides of my face. Her chest is rising and falling against mine, her quick breaths skimming my cheeks. We lock eyes for one more heartbeat, then we both move in at the same time.

Our lips crash together in a way that's nearly violent. I won't settle for sweet. Not this time. This time I need to taste her.

I sweep my tongue against her lips, and she opens for me. The soft texture of her mittens drags down my neck before leaving me completely. A moment later, I feel her fingers scrape their way up the back of my head. I groan and press my body harder into hers. I don't know what happened to her mittens but her bare hands send lightning bolts down my spine.

Kitten tightens her grip in my hair and pulls as she deepens the kiss. And I let her.

With her pinned firmly against the wall, I'm able to take one of my hands and slide it slowly, and firmly, up her side. I think she likes it since I feel her tighten her legs around me as she rocks her hips.

"Fuck, Kitten," I growl. "Do that again."

She does.

I drag my hand back down to her hip so I can pull her tighter against me, even though she's already as close as she can possibly be.

I think I might have flipped a switch on my sweet little Kitten, because the whimpering sounds coming out of her are entirely unintelligible. And I want more.

I rock my hips into her, and she moans.

Goddamn. I catch the sounds leaving her mouth with my own.

It should be no surprise that I'm hard as steel by now. If we don't stop soon, I'm going to blow in my pants from dry-humping like some teenage virgin. But I don't care.

I grind against her. She groans.

We're perfectly aligned, and even through two layers of clothing, I can feel the heat from her core. And through it all, our lips never cease their touching.

I rotate my hips into hers.

Kitten's hands leave my hair to circle around my neck. She seems to be hanging on for dear life, even though I'm pressing her against the wall hard enough that we could both raise our hands and she wouldn't go anywhere.

Then I hear it.

"More."

Her words come out as a panting whisper between kisses. "Jackson. Please."

Fucking hell, this is not helping me to stay in check.

"Kitten," I growl in warning.

"I need more. Just a little more."

"Go out with me."

"Hmmm, what?"

I pull my lips away from hers, enough to look into her eyes. "Go on a date with me, Kitten." I rock my hips against her again. She tips her head back and closes her eyes. Leaning in I drag my teeth across her throat. "Say yes, and I'll give you what you want."

"Okay," she whispers before pressing her lips against mine again.

I keep my lips brushing against hers as I demand, "Say. Yes."

She gives me a small nod as she finally agrees. "Yes."

Loosening my grip on Kitten, I take a step back from the wall, causing her to slide down my body. I want to make it slow. Tortuous. But not tonight. I don't have the patience, or willpower, for that tonight.

The second her feet hit the ground I grab her shoulders and turn her around.

"Hands on the wall," I order.

She obeys.

I band my left arm around her ribcage, right below her breasts, as I lean over and place my lips at the spot where her neck meets her shoulder. Her arms straight out, fingers splayed across the cold hard surface of the hallway.

"I'm not going to fuck you, Kitten. Not here, not like this." While I speak, I slide my right hand down to the top of her jeans. "But there's no chance that I'm letting you walk away from me when you're this worked up." I flip the button open. "So we're gonna do it like this. And I'll have you coming on my fingers in just a moment. We can get to the sex part another time." I pull down her zipper. "I promise to take it slow with you then, but right now... Right now, we're gonna go fast."

My fingers find the top band of her panties. Keeping true to my word, I waste no time in sliding my hand down the front of her. Greeted with warm, smooth skin, my fingers venture further until they find what they're looking for. My Kitten's pussy is hot and slick and so fucking perfect. The moment I make contact with her clit she loses her control.

"Oh... shit... Jackson..."

Kitten arches her back, pressing her ass into my aching cock.

I bite her neck. I want *her* coming tonight, not me. With the way she was reacting to me in our earlier position, I'm positive I could've gotten her off just by rubbing myself against her. But as much as I'm dying here, I don't actually want to come in my pants. And I would have. This is the only way for me to get my Kitten what she needs without embarrassing myself. Or fucking her in a hallway.

Pulling my hips back slightly, I increase the pressure of my fingers, circling her sweet spot. My left hand shifts up until I get a handful of one of her perfect tits. Even through her shirt and bra I can feel her nipple straining for attention. When I pinch it, Kitten releases a sound that tells me she's close.

Using my foot, I kick her feet a little farther apart. She's unsteady, and the sounds of our ragged breathing are filling the hallway.

Her jeans are too constricting, but I keep pressing down until I'm slipping my middle finger inside her. There's not enough room to move my hand around the way I want to, so I just bury my finger deeper, feeling her tightness surround me.

With a sound that's almost pained, she tosses her head back. It thumps against my shoulder and stays there.

Twisting a little, I'm able to catch her mouth with mine. And Kitten kisses me back with a fierceness I wouldn't have thought her capable of in this state. Without removing my finger, I use my thumb to press against her clit. And that's all it takes.

Her kisses cease.

Her entire body tenses.

Her pussy clenches around my finger as my Kitten comes undone.

I keep the pressure up until I feel her body go limp in my arms. I'm still breathing heavy, and even without contact I was dangerously close to finishing right along with her. Slowly I drag my hand out of her panties. I button her jeans and pull up the zipper. Then, with her gaze on me, I bring my fingers up to my mouth. Kitten still looks drugged, but her eyes widen as she watches me taste her for the first time. And fuck, she tastes like kryptonite.

Turning to face me, Kitten slumps against the wall.

I grin. "You gonna be alright, Kitten?"

She just blink, blink, blinks at me. It's fucking cute.

I give her a quick kiss, then I adjust myself in my pants.

She looks down at the bulge straining against the fabric. "Umm, did you want . . ."

"Oh, Kitten, I fucking want." I release a large exhale. "But not tonight."

She cocks her head at me like she's trying to *read between the lines*. Smiling, I bend down, grab her discarded mittens, grab her hand, and lead her down the hallway.

"I'm driving you home."

She doesn't argue.

CHAPTER TWENTY-FIVE

KATELYN

*O*h. My. Fingering. Gods.
I cannot believe that just happened. One minute I'm waiting for Jackson in some weird back hallway, then suddenly I'm wrapped around him like a baby koala. Kissing him like the meaning of life is hiding inside his mouth. Then before I even know what hit me, he's talking dirty, sliding his hand inside my Biggest Fan undies, and getting me off like it's his damn job. *And holy amazing orgasms, he did a damn fine job.* I should probably be embarrassed at how quickly I came, but I'll just let that be a compliment to his skills.

It's a freaking wonder that I'm even able to walk right now. I think I'm still shaking. And Jackson's just walking beside me, leading the way to his car, like nothing completely insane just happened. To be fair, our bar for normal is set at a different height than most couples.

But, are we a couple? I mean he did just have his hand in my pants, and he kissed me in front of a whole arena full of people. But… Nope, not going there right now. My brain still hasn't recovered.

Looking down at me, because he's tall and we are side by side, Jackson catches me eyeing him.

He raises his brows in question.

"Is there anything you aren't good at?" My tone is admittedly a little irritated.

"I'm pretty bad at drawing." He smirks.

I scowl.

He grins. "Kitten, are you annoyed that I'm good with my fingers?"

"No." I roll my eyes. "I'm pleased. Literally. I'm just annoyed that you seem to have the Midas touch with literally everything you do. It's not fair to us mere mortals."

"Are you saying that I just turned your pussy into gold?"

I laugh, even though I try not to. "Wow, so humble."

Jackson lets go of my hand, but before I can protest, he wraps his arm around my shoulder.

Stopping to pull open a door, he kisses the top of my head.

Swoon.

It appears he's led me to some sort of hidden garage where the players park.

I'm not sure what I expected Jackson to drive, but I'm pleasantly surprised to see that it's a nice, but not overtly flashy, SUV. It's all black, windows and wheels included, and it kind of looks like a cop car. It's probably very expensive, but it's subtle. Acting like a true gentleman, if we disregard the hallway scene from a few minutes ago, Jackson walks me to the passenger side and opens my door. It's a rather tall vehicle, and Jackson doesn't miss the opportunity to put his hand on my ass, guiding me into my seat.

Gently closing my door, he circles around the hood and climbs into the driver's side. Before putting the car in drive, I watch him pull up a contact on his phone and select the address. It must be mine since he's bringing me home.

As Jackson pulls out of the parking spot, I finally ask him what I've been wondering. "How did you get all my contact stuff?"

"Hmm? Oh, from Daniel."

"Daniel?" It takes me a moment. "My cousin?"

"That's the one."

"But how?"

He shrugs. "I had some compromising photos of him. I said I'd trade the photos for your number."

"Like blackmail!" I say, shocked, before Jackson laughs. "Oh, har har. You're full of shit."

Jackson smiles at me before pulling into traffic. "I'm full of shit. But I did get it from Daniel."

"During the party? But I didn't meet you until the end."

"When the party staff texted to tell me they were wrapping up, I had them send Daniel down to the theater. I figured since you two were family, he would probably have your phone number."

"Oh. Huh." I watch his silhouette. "Why didn't you just ask me?"

"That was originally my plan. But then you were sleeping, and the Daniel opportunity presented itself. Plus, I wasn't completely sure that you *would* give me your number. I didn't want to chance it."

I think this over. He might not be wrong. Jackson's stupidly good looking, and the night we met he was kind, and funny, and sweet. Not to mention the fact that I knew he was some sort of professional athlete living in an impressive home. Adding up all these details, I decide there's a good chance I would've freaked out and not given him my number.

When I look up, Jackson is side-eyeing me.

"You're thinking about it right now, aren't you? You would've turned me down."

"Well, I . . . I don't know. I mean, I liked you right away," I hedge, "but you're just so... everything."

"That feels like it should be a compliment, but you kinda made it sound like a bad thing."

I sigh. "It's not a bad thing. It's a really good thing. *You're* a really good thing."

Jackson reaches over the center console placing his hand on top of mine, keeping them both on my thigh.

Deciding to be honest, I admit - "The more I got to know you that first night I met you, the more I was completely swept away. But I was also thinking that you were out of my league." Thinking about my run-in with Lacy at the mall, I realize that my initial assumptions were right: tall perfect models were his type. Or at least they had been. I shake my head against the past. "But, I find that as time goes on, I don't care. I like you and I'm greedy, so there."

I flex my fingers a little since Jackson's grip has tightened to the point of almost painful.

Pulling up to a stop sign, Jackson glances at me. "Mama always told me not to say these words to a girl I liked, but here it goes. *You're wrong*." A huff of laughter gets caught in my throat when I see that Jackson is serious. "I sat and watched you earlier, during that party. And, yeah, that sounds way creepier than I mean it to. But you were talking to some older folks and you were all laughing. They were smiling at what you were saying, and your hands were flying around as you talked. You looked so beautiful, and full of life, that I wanted to walk over and snatch you up, right then and there."

I'm more than a little stunned by his admission. "Why didn't you?"

"Because I didn't know who you were. I didn't know if you were there with someone, but I figured you were." He shrugs. "I wasn't a part of that crowd. I was only there because it was my home. In certain circles, being Jackson Wilder is a big deal, but being a hockey player doesn't really mean much to those Mensa types. Basically, I figured *you* were out of *my* league." It's my turn to squeeze his hand. "When I was downstairs watching that movie, I was thinking about you. Mentally kicking myself for being a giant coward. Then I found you snooping around in my sex dungeon."

I scoff. "Oh, please. I was browsing."

He ignores me. "So then I found you, caught you, and dragged you away to my couch. When you were sleeping there, all adorable, I knew I wanted the chance to spend more time with you. I also know that wild cats can be unpredictable. So, when the guys messaged saying they were done, I made a split second decision to ask Daniel for your number. He did seem a bit shocked to see you sleeping with me."

"Oh gross, don't word it like that!" I reach across and smack his arm.

"He told me that if I wanted a fling, I should look somewhere else. I told him that I thought you were more than that." Jackson looks at me. "You *are* more than that."

I bite my lip for lack of a response. This guy.

With his eyes on the road, I can still see his smirk. "Luckily for me, Daniel just shared your whole contact to my phone, so now I have everything he has. I haven't seen a need to use it yet, but I even have your email. Maybe now that we've opened Pandora's box, so to speak, I can send you filthy emails to disrupt your day."

Skipping over all the stuff that has my stomach flipping, I focus on his last statement. "I'll be honest, dirty emails are a distraction I could get behind. But all is fair, and I've worked on some pretty racy novels, so I'm pretty sure I could out Not-Safe-For-Work you. Now if you want to record yourself reading those dirty emails..."

Jackson chuckles. "Quit trying to derail me. I had a point. Oh, right, ipso facto, you were wrong."

"You have quite the way of putting a girl in her place."

"Well, I'm sure it won't happen often, so I gotta drag it out when I can."

Jackson slows the vehicle, and I look up to see we're nearing my house. It's dark out, so rather than making him read house numbers, I point out which driveway is mine and he pulls in.

Turning off the car, Jackson holds up a hand, silently asking me to wait. So I stay put while he circles around, opens the door and helps me down. With my hand in his, we walk up the sidewalk to my front door.

We slow to a stop, turning to face each other. Before I can say anything, like invite him inside, Jackson holds up a hand, palm out, stopping me.

"I'll pick you up tomorrow at noon."

That's not at all what I was expecting him to say. And I find myself staring at him.

He tips his head down. "For the date you agreed to."

"Oh, right." It comes back to me. "I'm pretty sure anything agreed to under duress can't be expected to hold up in court."

Jackson takes a step forward, closing the space between us.

"Do you have other plans, Kitten?"

I smile and shake my head.

"I'll pick you up tomorrow. At noon."

"Okay, big guy. I'll be ready."

Narrowing his eyes, he says, "See that you are. Dress casual, but warm. And bring those mittens. They look good on you."

"Yes, sir."

"Hmmm, I like that." Jackson grabs my face with both hands, holding my head still, while he bends down to place a single kiss on my lips. "Sweet dreams, Kitten." Releasing me, he steps back. "I want to hear that door lock before I leave."

At a loss for words, again, I let myself into my house before looking back. "Goodnight, Jackson."

Then I close and lock the door behind me.

CHAPTER TWENTY-SIX

KATELYN

Groaning, I roll over in my bed and slap my hand around the nightstand until I connect with my buzzing phone.

The phone stops buzzing. I roll over.

The phone starts buzzing again.

"Damn it, who the hell is calling me!" I shout at no one, since I'm at home, alone. But really - who the hell *is* calling me on a Saturday morning?

Flipping the covers back, I sit up and rub my hands over my face to help myself wake up.

Grabbing my phone, I see Meghan's name and I answer with the grumpiest tone I can manage. "What?"

"Good morning, sunshine! How was the rest of your night?" She sounds way too cheerful.

I'm about to say nothing happened, exhibit A: me home alone, but then I'm jolted back to our exploits in the hallway behind the locker room. I'm glad Meghan can't see me, since I can feel the insta-blush that just crept up my face.

And just like that, my entire body wakes up, and I'm left thinking about how talented Jackson is with his hands. And his mouth. And his whole sexy body. Gah, the way he had me pinned against that wall...

Suddenly, my phone is ringing in my hand. What the hell?

It's Meghan. Again.

"Hello?" I answer.

I can hear her laughing before she says, "Okay, space cadet, I need details."

"What are you talking about?"

"Oh gee, I don't know. Maybe about how I asked how your night went and then you spaced the fuck out. Bitch, I was yelling your name. I had to hang up and call back just to get your attention. Clearly, you were reliving something, and I want to hear all about it."

"Well, we didn't have sex last night if that's what you're thinking. I'm at home, alone, and still in bed. Fuck you very much for waking me up."

She ignores my tone. "Hmmm? Okay, so there's something you aren't telling me here. But before we get into that, I was calling to warn you. Give you a heads-up. Whatever."

Well shit, that doesn't sound good.

"Okay..." I say tentatively. "What's up?"

"Nothing bad, I promise! But you're semi-famous after those videos posted from last night. Didn't take long for them to spread like head lice at a daycare."

"Ew."

Meghan keeps talking. "People *love* it. And the internet did not disappoint. There are some great edits out there!"

"What are you talking about? What videos?" I ask cautiously.

"Uh, duh, the one from the Kiss Cam with Jackson practically breaking the glass. And then Jackson climbing up the motherfucking railing to kiss you after the game! Hello! Do you not remember what happened last night?"

I breathe a sigh of relief. For a moment there I was thinking that maybe someone had video from the hallway. I would really love to get through life without ever having a sex tape made public. Even if it wasn't exactly sex last night. No one needs to see that. Except me. I would very much enjoy watching a replay of that.

"Katelyn!"

"Huh?"

"If you don't start talking, out loud, in words, I'm going to come over there and drag the details out of you!"

"Yikes, okay." Yeah, I'm distracted.

"Okay. So. What happened after the game?"

Flopping back on the bed, I think about how much of it I want to tell Meghan.

"Don't you dare leave out the good stuff," she scolds, knowing me too well.

"Fine, fine." I chuckle. "Like Jackson asked, I had Izzy bring me down to that private hallway, or whatever it was. Anyways, when Jackson came out, we were all alone, so we kissed. For a while."

"You kissed." She doesn't word it like a question. She words it like she's bored.

"Made out." I pause. "Oh, and he had me pinned to the wall. With his body."

She squeals. "All right. *That's* more like it!"

Taking a deep inhale, I talk fast to get the rest out in one breath. "Ohmygod it was so fucking hot. He lifted me like I weighed nothing, and kept me trapped between him and the wall. He was grinding against me, and kissing me, and I couldn't handle how turned on I was getting. I think I begged him for more and he made me agree to a date before he would give me what I wanted. Then he set me down, turned me around, told me to "put my hands on the wall" and shoved his hand down my pants. It was insane and he got me off in like record-breaking time."

Silence on the other line.

"And then he drove me home."

Still silence.

"And he's coming to pick me up for a date today at noon."

Silence.

I look at my phone to make sure we didn't get disconnected.

"Meghan? You there?"

"Uh. Yeah." She quiet for another beat. "Can you go back through that, slower, and using a thousand percent more detail?"

"You are such a perv." I laugh. "It was incredibly hot. You should totally be jealous."

"I am so far past jealous. I completely hate you right now."

"Aww, thanks."

"Ugh, you're such a lucky whore." She sighs. "Oh, wait! What was his dick like?"

"Um, I didn't see his dick. Also, *rude* much?"

"Like you haven't told me that stuff before." She had a point. "And when you say you didn't see it..."

"I mean, I didn't see it. It didn't make an appearance. I asked if he wanted... something. But he cut me off before I could make an offer."

"And he just said *No thanks, I prefer blue balls*?"

"I believe his exact words were 'Oh, I fucking want. But not tonight.' And he'd made a comment before the whole hand-in-my-pants thing about how he wasn't going to fuck me in a hallway. Honestly, I would've gone for it. I'm pretty sure that man could convince me to do all sorts of things I should not be doing."

"Fair." Meghan agrees before gasping.

"What?" I ask, startled.

"Were you wearing your Biggest Fan underwear last night?"

I pause for a beat before we both burst into laughter.

"Seriously, Katelyn, that man's got it bad for you. I know you don't want to do any internet snooping about his personal life, so I won't give you any spoilers, but he doesn't seem to be a player. Like, not at all. I think the fact that he kissed you in public like that, knowing cameras would be all over him, says something."

"What does it say?" I'll admit that I'm excited about the idea that Jackson might really be interested in me.

"I don't know exactly, but I don't think he was just doing that to get in your pants. Especially if he literally turned down an offer to get his rocks off."

I mull it over. "I don't want to get too ahead of myself with him. I know what you're getting at, and I find myself wanting to agree with you. But I need to lower my expectations. All of our interactions have been intense, fraught with sexual tension, and we've had a lot of interruptions. We really haven't spent that much time one-on-one. But even with all that, I feel close to him. Closer to him than I have with any other guy. And it's freaking me out a bit."

"You're falling in love with him, aren't you?"

"It feels that way," I whisper. "But it's way too soon. I mean, that's crazy, right?"

"That's the definition of a whirlwind romance. And love *is* crazy. There's no way to control when and where it hits."

I swallow against my worry. "But what if it doesn't work? He's so different from anyone I've been with before. And not just him personally, but his lifestyle. He's like a literal celebrity."

"He's just a guy. A super fucking hot guy, but just a guy. Don't let any of that other bullshit intimidate you. You are Katelyn Brown. You're a wonderful soul with a beautiful face. That hunk of man might be a lot of things, but he'd be lucky as fuck to have you."

"Thanks, Meghan. I adore you."

"Duh, bitch. I'm the best."

Smiling, I sit up again and climb off my bed. It's time for coffee.

Measuring out the grounds, I prompt Meghan, "So, about these videos..."

Meghan instantly starts laughing. "I'll send you the links now! They haven't identified you yet, but I'm sure it'll happen soon. And obviously anyone who knows you will recognize you."

I'm back to groaning. "Well, at least it will be limited to hockey fans. I don't know too many of those."

"Um, yeah, no. This shit is gold. It's already all over Facebook and Twitter."

"What?!"

"Hello? Hot professional hockey player kisses some chick in the stands? It's every girl's dream. Plus, you add in the whole alpha-male thing when he smashed into the glass to keep that other guy from kissing you. Panties all over the country are combusting."

"That's quite the visual."

"You look great in the video, by the way. Super pretty and adorable. But you also look like a normal girl, so to speak, getting kissed by *the* Jackson Wilder. I'm sure there'll be some trolls, just like with everything, but the public loves you."

"I should probably double-check that my security settings are locked down on all my social media accounts."

"Not a bad idea. Okay, I'm hanging up, then sending you the links. Oh, wait. What are you guys doing for your date today?"

"I'm not sure. He said to dress casual and warm. He's picking me up at noon."

"Interesting..." she drags the word out. "Give me a call later, and I want way more details next time!"

"Yeah, yeah. Bye!"

Hanging up, I stare at my phone for a moment. Do I try to search for these videos on my own? No, I need patience. Meghan will send them over in a moment.

My coffee maker alerts me with a beep, telling me the pot is ready. Filling a mug, I take a seat at the kitchen island. My phone chimes with a text from Meghan. Then another. Then another. Opening the text screen, I see that she has sent several YouTube links and put a little caption under each one.

The first video says *open first*; the title is *Jackson Wilder Interrupts Kiss Cam*. I click on the link. It's a mini montage of the three times Frat Boy and I were paired up on screen.

You can see me shaking my head, then mouthing *I don't know him*, then his stupid pouty lips. The camera stays on us while we're startled into looking away from the big screen. I just look stunned. Frat Boy looks horrified. It's exactly as I remember. Then the video switches to a view that must have been shot from someone's phone. It's of Jackson, up against the glass, staring down Frat Boy, mouthing *Back the fuck off*. Followed by Jackson shifting his gaze and winking, before going back onto the ice. The video ends.

The next link Meghan sent says *open second*; the title is *Jackson Wilder kisses fangirl*. Fangirl? Sure. Clicking on it, I'm brought back to YouTube. This one is short, but it looks like it was taken by one of the actual TV cameras from the game. It starts out showing the backs of the players as they walk down the ramp away from the ice. As soon as Jackson steps off the ice, you can see him start to strip off his gear. From this angle I can see the front of the little boy who got Jackson's game stick. The kid's wearing a Wilder shirt and looks like he's going to blow a gasket with how excited the gift made him. The camera had already started to zoom in for the cute-kid moment, but it follows Jackson as he hoists himself up on the railing. Everyone in the crowd was already standing, and the other fans near our row were all leaning toward him. I didn't notice that when it was happening. You can see his mouth move but it's in profile, so there's no way to read his lips. I've been so distracted watching Jackson in the video that I didn't even look for myself yet. But there I am, walking toward the handsome sweating man. Then he's reaching out, wrapping his hand around my neck, and pulling my mouth to his for a kiss I'll never forget. It only lasts for a few seconds, but I'm breathless just watching it on my phone screen. The kiss stops but he doesn't let go right away. A second later he releases me and drops back to the ground. The camera stays on me for a moment. Standing there, looking after Jackson, one hand up, fingers touching my lips. Yep, that about captured it. I think I'm still a little stunned.

The next and final video sent by Meghan says *open last, this is the bomb, I love the internet*. The title of the video is *Jackson Wilder's Kiss Cam Remix*. Oh boy. Clicking the link, I see it already has over 150,000 views. *"Oh shit"* doesn't cut it. This is either going to be great or horrible. Hitting play, I hold my breath.

The video starts with a fade-in to Jackson at some event where he's all dressed up and looking hot as fuck. It takes me a few beats to realize that I recognize the song playing along with the video: it's "Candyman" by Christina Aguilera. I burst out laughing. The video continues with a series of clips of Jackson looking sexy, in interviews, working out, laughing with a teammate. Then it cuts to the Kiss Cam clips. The short clips are switching and stuttering to the beat of the song. Then Jackson is smashing into the glass with his helmet. Whoever did this video found several different camera angles to choose from for this glass-smashing scene, since it's replayed in quick succession from all sorts of views. It goes to split screen and has pissed-off Jackson on one side and terrified Frat Boy on the other. Through the magic of editing, Jackson's face goes red with smoke coming out of his ears, and Frat Boy goes all the way pale until he's in black and white. Hitting the refrain of the song, the scene changes to the teams facing off on the ice. Oh god, I know what's coming next.

Right on cue, Jackson punches the guy across from him. Then the remix goes into high gear and replays the initial punch a bunch of times with special effects. Pale-looking Frat Boy is cut into the clip like subliminal messaging. The view zooms out to get the full brawl. And suddenly I'm popping up on screen, standing amongst the cheering crowd, hands covering the bottom half of my face. The massive fight matched to the song is actually pretty amazing. As the song builds up for the final verse, the scene switches to the view from the last video. Jackson stripping his gear, climbing on the railing, and pulling me in for a kiss. As Christina hits her high notes, the action of Jackson pulling me into him is played on a boomerang, so it looks like a dozen kisses. The final bars of the song are matched with Jackson walking away and me pressing my fingers to my mouth.

By the time it's done, I'm grinning.

I watch it a second time.

CHAPTER TWENTY-SEVEN

KATELYN

It's 11:45 and I'm trying my very hardest to not freak out. I'm so excited to see Jackson again. I really like spending time with him, and this date - whatever it is - should be no exception. But the last time I saw him, he had his hand in my pants. I'm trying to be an adult about this, but somehow this scenario seems even more awkward than if we'd had actual sex. At least with sex we'd both have gotten off. Now I just feel guilty about being the only satisfied party. And I definitely don't feel like I'm doing my best to show him I'd be a good girlfriend.

My worry-fest is interrupted with a knock.

It'll be fine. Don't be weird.

I'm out of excuses to delay, so I pull on my coat and open the door.

Jackson's standing right there. I knew he would be, obviously, but he's closer than I expected and it startles me. He takes me in for a moment, his gaze starting at the top of my head, trailing down to the tips of my boots. As his gaze travels, his smile grows.

Jackson told me to dress casual and warm. I took his word for it. I'm wearing my favorite emerald green sweater. It's snug where it needs to be and only shows a hint of cleavage. I've matched it up with dark jeans that fit my ass like a glove and are tucked into knee-high brown riding boots. I have on my tan hip-length jacket. The finishing touch of my ensemble; the matching pair of Sleet mittens and pompom hat, which I've pulled on over my straightened hair.

I prop a hand on my waist and pop out my hip.

"Hey, Candyman. Am I dressed alright for this mystery date?"

Jackson takes a step forward and I swear I hear him growl. "Kitten, you look good enough to eat."

Without warning, he takes hold of my face with both of his giant man hands and presses a kiss to my lips. But before I'm able to react, and by *react* I mean shove my tongue down his throat, he's stepping away and asking if I'm ready.

Nodding, I take his hand and let him lead me to his car.

After helping me into the passenger side, Jackson carefully shuts my door. I work on calming my nerves while I watch his masculine stride as he heads to his side of the car. We're dressed somewhat similarly. He has on a grey sweater that's stretched across his muscular chest. And his jeans might now be my favorite thing in the world, with the way they fit his firm, oversized thighs. To top it off, he's got on a worn but expensive looking black leather jacket, and black leather boots. He looks like a damn model. And not one of those pretty-boy slender models. More like a rip your dress right down the front and toss you over his shoulder models.

The knowing smirk on Jackson's face when he settles in his seat tells me he saw my ogling.

I smirk back. "You look very handsome today. But I suppose you hear that from women all the time."

"Hmmm. And yet coming out of your pretty mouth, it sounds entirely different."

"Different *good*, I hope."

"Oh Kitten, I'm pretty sure everything about you is *different good*." Jackson starts the car, then reaches over and takes hold of my mitten-clad fingers.

The warmth travels up my arm and I try to suppress a blush. "So, where're you taking me today?"

"Well, we're starting with lunch."

I arch a brow. "Starting with?"

"Yep." Jackson shoots me a quick glance as he pulls out into the street. I think he's enjoying the secrecy. "You were asking about my diet the other night, so I thought I'd take you to one of my favorite lunch spots. I'm enough of a regular that the owner and I have become friends. There are way more health-conscious places now than when I first started my career. Back then most of my food was made at home. But even with all the options, this place is still at the top of my list."

"Well color me intrigued." And just like that, all my nerves have evaporated. I don't know what I was worried about; Jackson's always been easy to talk to. "So does that mean you cook?"

Jackson chuckles. "Not well. Truthfully, my mama made a lot of my food, even as an adult. And if she wasn't available to cook for me, she'd give me detailed instructions."

"That's sweet. Even before I knew she was your mom, she exuded motherliness. You can tell she really cares about you and Steph." Jackson squeezes my hand as he nods. "Has she always lived near you? You've played for a few teams, right? So you've lived in different states?"

"Short answer, yes."

I smile. "Pretty sure we have time for the long answer."

Jackson nods. "True. So, when we were young, mama stayed home to raise us. My dad was a principal at the middle school in our little town. We lived not too far outside of Springfield, Illinois, but you wouldn't know the town unless you were from there. Anyways, once Steph and I were both in school full-time, mama got bored, so she got a job as a lunch lady at our elementary school. Said she could keep an eye on us that way."

I laugh. "She meant an eye on *you*."

"Oh, don't I know it. She stayed there for a few years even once we were out of that school, then she went to work in food service at a hospital. Said she didn't want to just follow us to middle school and have Dad as her boss. Said it would confuse things too much, since she was the boss at home." He sighs. "They were quite the pair."

My heart aches for him. I can't imagine what it would be like if my dad wasn't around anymore. It seems like his family was close, even before his dad passed away.

He seems to notice the prolonged silence and cuts it off with a huff of breath and a smile. "Sorry, Kitten. I didn't mean to get lost in thought like that."

"Don't apologize. I was just thinking about how lovely your family is. I'm really sorry about your dad. I can't even pretend to know how hard losing him must have been."

"It wasn't fun. He died of a heart attack while I was in college. It took all of us by surprise. I mean he was on meds and stuff, but you never really think something like that will happen. I wanted to move back home to help take care of Mama, but when I brought it up, she read me the damn riot act. The only bright side was - I think her anger at me for daring to give up on school and hockey gave her something to do other than be sad about my dad."

I squeeze his fingers like he had done to me. "It's good to have something to focus on."

A big smile spreads over his face, clearly remembering something fondly. "She called me every freakin night, and made me give the phone to my roommate so she could make sure I was going to class and practice. My dad was the one who got me into playing hockey, since he played some growing up. So, when I started playing for the University of Michigan they would come to as many games as they could afford. We didn't get all the good free tickets like I do now. They often ended up in the nosebleed seats, but they never complained. Dad would bring along these dorky old opera glasses claiming they helped him to see the puck from way up there. They were just happy to be at my games, and I was just happy to have family there cheering for me. Dad had a decent life insurance policy, so once he was gone Mama did her best to make it to all my college games. I had some pro teams sniffing around, but she made me promise to finish out my degree."

"What did you study?"

"Business management. Nothing too exciting, but hopefully I can figure out something to do with it when I retire from the game."

"Sounds like a smart choice. So, you waited to go pro?"

"Yep. It was the right call, and as soon as I graduated I got drafted by Philadelphia."

"I bet that was an amazing feeling. Was that your goal all along, to get into the NHL?"

"It was. And when it finally happened it was exciting, and terrifying, and humbling. I know a lot of pro athletes can be cocky, but for me it felt tenuous for the first couple of years. College was a big deal, sure. Bigger than high school. But college to pro, that was a huge change. I was always waiting for someone to come take my jersey away and tell me that the gig was up. I mean, I knew I was good, but a lot of guys are good." Flipping on his blinker, Jackson shakes his head. "My mama's always been talented at getting information out of people, so it didn't take her long to find out how freaked out I was."

"Oh, I lived it. I get it." I can't help but shake my head at myself, thinking about all the stuff I told her before knowing who she was.

"Yeah, you know exactly what I mean. Now imagine having her on the phone with you every single day. No secrets were safe."

"I bet hanging up on her doesn't work, does it?"

Jackson barks out a laugh. "I've never been brave enough to try."

"Okay, so you're in Philly and Mary has your secrets..."

"Yeah, so then I did what every man would do after getting his big break. I asked my mama to move in with me."

"You did not!"

"I did. And I didn't so much ask as beg. I begged her to move out to Philly, and live with me, and cook for me, and help guide me through the mayhem of life."

This man. When I think he can't possibly be more adorable he tells me this story. "I take it she did what you asked."

We're at a stop light, and Jackson turns a bit to look at me with a mischievous grin on his face. "Not exactly. After I got finished begging her over the phone, she said - and I'll never forget this - she said 'Jacky boy, I love you. I'll do anything for you. But you have got to be fucking kidding me. I'll move to Philly and help you in every way I can. But our days of living under the same roof have passed. You're a big stinky man now, and I don't ever want to touch your dirty underwear again.'"

"Shut up! Seriously?" I'm laughing now.

"Dead serious. But she came out the very next week. Sold her house, quit her job, and moved to Philly to help her grown-ass son. She and Dad owned the house outright, so she used that money to find a little place to rent. Since I wasn't making a ton my first few years, she wouldn't let me help with much. But she came to every game, Home- and Away."

"That's so wonderful."

"She really is. We spent four years in Philly getting our routine set. When I was traded to Denver, I nervously asked mama if she'd follow me again. She knocked me upside the head, saying 'Duh.' That was it. *Duh.* She still didn't want to live together, and by then I was more than okay with that. But I had started to make a name for myself, so I insisted on paying for her rent. She was a stubborn shit about it, but I pulled in Steph as backup and we convinced her to consider herself retired. Steph, of course, threw in some jabs about me finally being worth all the trouble."

I laugh again. "That sounds like Steph. Where was she during all of this? Did she move with you guys?"

"Naw, she went to college in Chicago - for architecture - and found a job there when she graduated. She also tried to move home after our dad died, but I believe Mama gave her the same tough-love treatment that I got. I was just the bigger, needier baby, so I got to keep her with me."

"It's a big thing to admit when you need help. Too many people don't know how to do that. Plus, your arrangement clearly paid off. You never got your jersey taken away."

Jackson smiles. "Sure didn't."

"Did you come here from Denver, or was there another stop along the way?"

Jackson pulls over and puts the vehicle in park. Glancing around, I see we're on a side street. I'm not sure where, but our lunch destination must be close.

Propping a forearm on the steering wheel, Jackson turns to face me. "No other teams, I was traded off Denver to Minnesota. As before, Mama came along for the ride. I got us rental apartments, just like we had in the other cities, but after about a year I decided that this would probably be it for me. I feel like I have a few good years of playing left in me, but I know I'm on the back end of my career. And this place"—he gestures out the front window—"just feels like home. So, without telling mama, I bought myself that condo and bought her a house just outside of Saint Paul. She had a righteous fit when I gave her the key, but I knew she was ready to settle down too."

"Jackson..." This time I use both of my hands to squeeze his. "That was very kind of you."

He shrugs and looks a little embarrassed. "It was the least I could do. I still owe her so much."

"Wait, does Steph still live in Chicago? Was she only here visiting?" The idea that she doesn't live here instantly bums me out.

"Nope, she moved up here around the same time that I bought Mama's house. Steph helped me with the house search, since I didn't want to mess it up by buying something mama hated. Over the years, Steph would travel to us for certain games and holidays. And then in the off season we'd go to her. It didn't take her long to fall in love with

Minnesota. When she first hinted that she might want to move up here to be by us, Mama made me buy her a house too."

I can't help the laugh that slips out, not only at Jackson's statement, but because he rolled his eyes while he said it. "Did you really buy Steph's house for her?"

"Yeah." He shrugs. "I hogged most of mama's time over the past several years. And now she's not allowed to complain about it anymore. That was the deal."

"Your mom was right. You really didn't waste all your money on strippers and cars."

Jackson jerks back a little, "She said what?"

Laughing, I pat his hand. "She said you *didn't,* so don't worry. She's not spreading rumors." I wave it off. "It's an Izzy thing, never mind."

"Ah." He smirks a little. "Mama did tell me about your plans to get her into the business of helping players with their money. It's a good idea. She also told me that, thanks to you, I don't have to worry about fending off Isabelle anymore. Sorry, I mean Izzy."

"Well, I'm sure the practice of fighting women off will come in handy if I'm going to stick around."

Jackson watches me for a moment and looks like he's trying to decide if he should say what he's thinking.

I'm curious to ask about his ex, Lacy, and when she fell into this timeline. But that doesn't seem like first-date material. Or is this our second date? The sushi night should maybe count as date one. Does the hallway, hands in the pants thing, count as date two? Can it really be a date if all you did was fool around? Okay... wow... I can't think about that right now.

Jackson snaps me out of my spiral when he leans forward, kisses me on the forehead, and whispers, "You're fucking adorable."

Then he's getting out of the car and walking around to my door.

I'm. Melting.

His lips didn't even touch my skin, they touched my hat. But I'm still melting, and my stomach is full of bumblebees again.

CHAPTER TWENTY-EIGHT

JACKSON

"Squeeze Me?"
Kitten is reading the sign above the door I'm leading her toward. Her head is slightly tilted and there's a small smile on her lips. I'm momentarily distracted by the things I want to do to those lips. But then her eyes connect with mine and I'm brought back to the present.

I focus on her question. "They have the best fresh-squeezed juice here, among other things. So... *Squeeze Me.*"

"If you say so."

I stop to pull open the door for Kitten, but - before I reach the handle - she startles me by throwing her arms around my waist and squeezing me in a hug. And just like that, time stops. This is just a hug. It shouldn't feel so intimate. I've had my fingers inside of her, yet this - this hug - feels so much more personal. And when I wrap my arms around her upper back, squeezing in return, I feel my heart crack a little.

I have been so cautious of women over the past two years, ever since Lacy fucked with my head. I haven't let anyone in. I haven't been celibate, but there haven't been any *girlfriends*. No one that I've taken to lunch. Definitely no one who's gotten me talking about my dad dying and my mama helping me through life. Tipping my head down, I rest my cheek next to the pompom on the top of Kitten's head.

"I think you might have the same witchy powers that my mama has. Here I am spilling my secrets to you and we haven't even had lunch yet."

It's not lost on me that I haven't let go of her. We've been standing here, blocking the front door, for over a minute already.

"Thank you for sharing." Her voice is muffled a bit by my body. "My life's not nearly as exciting, but I promise to tell you whatever details you want to know."

I squeeze her a little harder before letting go and opening the door.

The restaurant is small, so it's not a shock that both of the workers behind the counter are staring at us, wide-eyed, having witnessed our little hug-a-thon.

"Jackson! What a wonderful surprise! I didn't realize that was you out there." The older woman comes shuffling around the counter as she talks. She has on a white-and-lavender apron that makes her look a little like Mrs. Potts. As always, she grabs my cheeks to pull me down for air kisses. Stepping back, she looks at Kitten. "And who is this beautiful young woman?" Without waiting for an answer she's pulling Kitten in for the same treatment.

Kitten is not tall, so Marcy having to pull her down shows just how short the woman is.

"Marcy, this is Katelyn. Katelyn, this is Marcy. She owns Squeeze Me. She's brilliant, and talented, and second only to my mama."

Marcy beams. "Oh hush. You save your sweet-talking for your sweet girl here." Waving back behind the counter, she shouts, "Brandon, get over here!"

A boy I haven't met before comes toward us. He looks high school aged, thin as a whip, and a little bit scared. When he gets within reach, Marcy grabs him by the arm and introduces him to us.

"This is Brandon. Brandon, this is Jackson and Katelyn. If they're ever in here when I'm not around, make sure to give them the best service possible."

"Marcy, that's hardly necessary."

Kitten perks up. "Speak for yourself. I'll gladly take the VIP treatment." She winks at the older woman, gaining her a grin. And a blush from Brandon. My Kitten knows how to work a room.

Brandon reaches out a shaky hand to me. "It's an honor to meet you, Mr. Wilder."

"Thanks, Brandon. If you do a good job working for Marcy here, I'll drop off some tickets so you and your friends can come to a game."

His eyes nearly pop out of his head, but before he can say anything Marcy shoos him away. "Enough chit chat, let's get you two lovebirds fed."

We follow her to a table and she hands Kitten a menu. "Jackson, I'm assuming you'll have your usual." I nod. "Now sweetie, if you aren't stuck to eating the same things as our big handsome boy here, I will recommend our blueberry and hazelnut waffles. They're served with real maple syrup and a dark chocolate drizzle. Some of my regulars say they're better than sex." Then she winks. "But those old biddies aren't dating Jackson Wilder."

"Marcy!" I feel an actual fucking blush creep up my neck.

She just snorts out a laugh and walks away.

CHAPTER TWENTY-NINE

JACKSON

Coming here may have been a mistake. Sitting with Kitten, watching her slowly eat her dripping waffles, moaning over nearly every bite, licking syrup off her lips... is horrible, glorious torture. I'm gonna need a cold shower. Or just an ice pack to set on my junk so I can walk out of here without tenting my pants. Seriously, this girl has me feeling like I'm fifteen years old again. I'm going to have to fight off an erection every time I come here to eat. It'll be impossible for me to enjoy my oatmeal when I'm picturing Kitten's erotic waffle play.

Who am I kidding, it's entirely worth it.

Lunch was a great break after the heavy family talk we had in the car. We've mostly discussed our favorite foods and the best restaurants in the Cities. Kitten is like me and will eat just about anything, only she's actually allowed to eat the good stuff all year 'round. I'll just have to live vicariously through her, watching her savor my favorite things while I sit, aroused, on the other side of the table. Poor, poor, me.

As much as I want to ask her to order seconds, just so I can keep perving at her, we need to get going to our next destination. Rising, I take Kitten's coat off the back of her chair and help her into it. Plucking her hat out of her pocket, I pull it down onto her head, giving it a little wiggle to make sure it's on tight.

She laughs and swats at my hands. "I think you got it."

"Just making sure. You're going to need it for our next stop."

She quirks an eyebrow at me. "Oh yeah? And just how many stops are there today?"

"Hmmm, I'm not sure."

"Uh-huh." She's not buying it.

We both wave goodbye to Marcy as she calls out for Kitten to return anytime. Back in the car, I turn the engine on and pull away from the curb. I make a mental note to keep my attention on the road and not on the pretty woman sitting next to me.

"We have about twenty minutes before we hit our destination. Think you can spill your entire life story, like I did, in that amount of time?"

Kitten chuckles and then bobs her head side to side as if she's calculating the answer. I hope she does tell me, and that she finds me as easy to talk to as I find her.

I'm beginning to wonder if maybe I pushed her too much by asking, but then she starts. "I've been really lucky. I haven't had many hardships in my life. I've always lived in Minnesota. Grew up in a suburb, just north of the Cities. My parents still live in the house I grew up in. I'm sure they'll eventually sell and downsize, but I enjoy the nostalgia when I visit."

"Is your room still the same as it was when you moved out?"

She chuckles. "I wish. My childhood crap is packed away in boxes somewhere. Once I rented a place of my own after college, my parents turned the kids' bedrooms into guest rooms. Mine had been fairly tame, but I bet my brother's room needed to be steam cleaned in order to get that nasty boy smell out."

"We are a gross breed," I hum.

"Truth," she agrees.

"My dad's an electrician. By the time I was in high school, he had his own company. Now it's mostly just him, doing odd jobs for his long-time customers. He loves it and it keeps him busy. My mom's an English professor at the

University of Minnesota. She was a student there, and I think she started working there right after graduating. So, of course, that's where I went to school."

"For writing, right?"

"Yeah, creative writing. Even though our house was only about thirty minutes away, I still opted for the full college experience of living on campus. Meghan went to the U as well, but we agreed to have random dorm roommates our first year, just to see what would happen. Needless to say, by our second year we decided to rent a house with some friends. I worked at a cute little coffee shop near campus; it was fun and gave me some spending money. Alex went to a school a few hours south. Even though he was following in our mom's footsteps, wanting to be a teacher, he wanted a little more distance between himself and parental supervision."

"Do you two get along pretty well? I know he tormented you some in your youth, but now that you're both adults, and mature, are you friends?"

"Saying Alex is mature is a stretch. But yes, aside from his barbarism at a young age, we've always gotten along. When I needed someone to talk to, he would be there for me, and vice versa. He's back in the area now, teaching, so I see him for family stuff. Occasionally we'll grab a drink together when we both have a free night. He's still a bit of a player, or at least as much of a player as a fourth-grade teacher can be, so he stays busy. I think once he meets *a nice girl,* as my mom would put it, I'll see more of him."

"I have a feeling I'm going to like Alex."

"I've warned you about his Sleet obsession. Honestly, I'm a bit surprised he hasn't called me yet, freaking out about those videos."

I feel myself wince.. "I'm sorry about that. I know you didn't ask for any of this to happen and I've just kinda thrust you into the limelight."

"Apology not accepted." Her words make me dart a glance her way, but I can see that she's smiling. "As in, apology not necessary. You couldn't have known I'd end up on the Kiss Cam with some douchebag."

"Fair. But I didn't have to make such a scene scaring him away from you."

"But I'm glad you did."

"But I didn't have to make such a scene kissing you after the game."

Kitten reaches over and puts her hand on my forearm. "But I'm glad you did." Giving my arm a little squeeze before she pulls away. "Jackson, there's nothing I regret about last night." Her breath hitches a little and I look over again. This time I find her staring back at me. Biting her bottom lip.

"Me neither, Kitten. Me neither." I'm sure we're both thinking about the same thing. And it's the one thing that wasn't caught on camera last night.

We're both quiet for a bit and I wonder if I should turn on the radio, only now realizing that it's been off since I picked her up earlier today. I can't remember the last time I didn't try to drown the silence with background noise. Or the last time that it wasn't needed.

Kitten breaks the silence. "Meghan woke me up this morning, blowing up my phone, so she could question me about last night and send over the videos. I gotta admit, the music one is really well done." She starts to hum the beat for "Candyman." I don't need to look at her to know she's smiling.

I shake my head. "Yeah, well, easy for you to say. You look amazing in it. I look like a big dumb caveman."

Kitten laughs. "I beg to differ. You look like a big, *hot* caveman. I'll admit to watching it more than once. It's catchy. But I'm forcing myself to not look at the comments. I know how awful people can be online, and I don't want to get sucked down that rabbit hole of depression. I don't know how you handle all the attention."

"Eh, you get used to it. And sure, some people know who I am, but it's not like I'm a rock star who gets mobbed every time I show my face in public. I don't lead a flashy life, *no strippers or fancy cars*, so the paparazzi got bored of me pretty quickly. This"—I cringe saying the word—"'*Candyman*' thing will probably boost my screen time for a while. But it'll pass."

I can feel Kitten hesitating before she asks, "Care to tell me what that other player said to you before you punched him in the face?"

I don't even have to think about it. "No."

"I figured you'd say that. Well, if it had anything to do with me, I'm sorry for the trouble I caused."

I'm just pulling into the parking lot of our destination, so I wait until I put the gear in park before turning to Kitten. "Don't you dare apologize for anything. That piece of shit was way overdue for a punch to the face. He's been a pain in my ass, egging me on for years, and I finally gave him what he asked for. So, take any guilty thoughts out of your pretty little head." I give her a pointed look. "You hear me, Kitten?"

She nods, fighting a smile. "I hear you."

"Good. Because we're here."

Kitten looks around for a moment before she spots the sign. Turning back to me she has a huge grin on her face. "We're going ice-skating?"

CHAPTER THIRTY

KATELYN

Walking into the little community arena, I can feel how excited Jackson is about this part of our date. When I saw the sign and asked if we were skating, the look on his face was pure adorableness. He nodded his head, biting the side of his lip in an attempt to keep his grin in check. I could tell he was a little nervous about what I'd think of this idea. But I'm pretty sure bouncing in my seat and clapping was enough of a hint that I was excited too.

"Have you ever ice-skated before?"

I scoff. "Uh, yeah, in like middle school. I fancied myself as decent back then. But I also thought I was a superstar rollerblader. I tried that again in college and wiped out so bad that I needed to call Meghan for a ride home."

"Ouch. Any lasting scars?"

"Just to my ego. I was scraped up, but not so bad I couldn't have made it back if I tried. The real problem was that when I fell, I skidded a little on my side and tore my pants right down that outside seam. It was still connected at the top and bottom, but if I got any momentum the wind would have opened it up like a sail. And I didn't really feel like sailing around campus with my pink undies on display."

Jackson chuckles as he opens the front door for me. "I promise to keep your panties safe."

Snorting, I walk past him and mutter to myself, "I doubt that."

Once inside, Jackson takes a black knit cap out of his jacket pocket and pulls it on over his head. Ugh, how does that make him even sexier? The leather jacket, and the handsome face, and the scruffy beard, and the hair sticking out of his hat... I can't even handle it.

"I'm trying to be incognito," he says in way of explaining the hat to me.

I'm not looking at him like this because I'm questioning the hat. I'm looking at him like this because I think my underwear just disintegrated.

"I'm not sure it's working," I tell him truthfully. But when he reaches for his hat, assumedly to pull it off, I lunge for him and grab a hold of his arm. "Don't you dare!"

He keeps his arm up, hand still halfway to his head, as I cling to it. "I thought you said it wasn't working."

"Yeah, at making you incognito. It doesn't exactly cover your face. But it does somehow make you even sexier."

He smirks. "You think I'm sexy?"

"Oh, shut it. Of course I do. Everyone does. But that's beside the point. Leave the hat on. You look like a mysterious man of danger, not the famously nice hockey player."

" 'Famously nice?' I don't think that's a thing."

"If it's not, it should be." Exasperated at being questioned, I give Jackson a look. "So are you going to take me skating today? Or..."

"Yes, Kitten." He flicks my pompom. "Now quit distracting me."

Rolling my eyes, I follow him to the rental counter. Jackson brought his own skates but insists on paying for mine. The kid behind the counter looks so bored I think he might be one long blink from falling asleep. He pays zero attention to us, just hands over the skates and takes the cash. Even if he's a hockey fan, he didn't look at our faces long enough to notice Jackson.

Taking a seat on a bench in the corner of the room, we swap our shoes for skates. I catch myself watching Jackson as he laces his up. His hands dance over the ties, pulling them tight, sliding them through his fingers.

Jackson clears his throat. "You need some help with those?"

"Huh?" Damn it, I was ogling again. "No. Nope. Fairly certain I learned how to tie my shoes a while ago." I hurry up and finish with my skates.

It's not until we are standing at the threshold to the ice that my nerves hit me. Jackson is already holding my hand, but now I grip his back even tighter.

"Promise you won't laugh too hard when I fall?"

"Kitten, I'm not going to let you fall."

Giving him side-eye, I say, "There's no way you can promise that."

Jackson steps so our fronts are nearly touching. "I *can* promise that. I'll be right next to you, holding your hand. And if you're feeling brave enough to go out on your own, I won't be far away. If you start to fall, I'll get to you in time to catch you." He leans in closer to whisper. "I don't know if you know this about me, but I'm kind of quick on my skates." He gives me the lightest kiss on the cheek before pulling back. "Besides, I thought kittens were afraid of water, not ice."

Laughing, I give his arm a friendly shove. "Such a jokester. All right, all right. Let's do this."

CHAPTER THIRTY-ONE

JACKSON

I honestly can't remember the last time I had this much fun. I love playing hockey and spending time with my family, but this - goofing around on the ice with Kitten - this is my new happy place. I feel like a tool just thinking that, but I don't care. It's true.

I've lost track of time, but I think we've been here for over an hour. Kitten is better than I thought she'd be, especially after her story about the rollerblades. We started with her standing still and me pulling her around. But she quickly graduated to skating under her own power, while holding my hand.

I'm trying to not show off too much. I'm enjoying the anonymity of being here, skating around like two normal people on a date. I've stopped trying to figure out what date number this is. Our track record is a little weird, but I know it feels like I've known Kitten forever. She's so easy to be with. Easy to talk to. Easy to touch and hold hands with. She just feels so right.

We've been talking while we skate. Mostly sharing stories from growing up. I don't remember a time when I wasn't on the ice. My dad took me skating from the time I could walk. I was playing hockey at that young age when the kids just try to not fall the entire time, and you call it a game.

Kitten talked about going with one of her friends to their brothers' games when she was younger, but admitted to spending most of their time at the concessions - eating candy and flirting with the older boys. Even being a full-grown adult, I find myself jealous of the teenage shits that got my Kitten's attention all those years ago.

We're skating side by side, when Kitten sighs and pulls out her phone. I don't mean to spy, but I can see a whole list of notifications on her screen.

She groans. "My stupid brother has been texting and calling me nonstop. He must've gone online and seen the videos at some point in the past hour." Before she can put her phone away it lights up with another call from *Big Brother*.

I grin. "This might be fun."

"Huh?"

"Hang up on that and use FaceTime to call him back," I tell her.

"Seriously? He's going to freak if he sees you."

"I know. It'll be hilarious. He'll probably get all flustered." Kitten laughs and I nudge her. "Don't tell him I'm here. I'll wait out of view, then come around behind you to surprise him."

"You're right, this will be fun. You're sure you're okay with opening this door? There'll be no going back."

"I'm sure."

Kitten holds the phone up so it's only framing her then calls her brother. The call rings once before it's answered.

She jumps right into it and I have to swallow down a laugh. "Jesus fucking Christ, Alex! You know if there's an actual emergency you're supposed to dial 9-1-1, not blow up your sister's phone."

"Ha. Ha. Very funny," a deep voice answers her. I'm standing off to the side, so I can't see the man on the screen.

"I figured I'd call you back like this, so I'd have some proof of life. Based on the number of missed calls and texts I have, I'm guessing you've been kidnapped and need some ransom money."

"You want to talk about body snatchers! Why not tell me how in the hell I woke up in the Twilight Zone this morning to a video of my sister making out with Jackson fucking Wilder! How long has this been going on?"

"Hmmm?" Kitten pretends to think. "Jackson Wilder, isn't he a baseball player or something?"

I hold in another laugh that turns into a snort. Kitten's eyes flick to mine, full of amusement.

"Seriously, Kay. What's going on? Are you dating him? How long have you been going out? And why didn't you tell me? You know how much I love him!"

"I don't think I knew that. I mean, I know you babble on about hockey this, and Sleet that, all the time. But I didn't know you were a fan of *Jackson*."

"Ugh, goddamnit, woman! Don't you ever listen to me?"

"I try not to."

I can hear a heavy sigh on the other end of the call, and I imagine Alex is trying to rein in his annoyance. Kitten is being pretty sassy. If our positions were reversed, I'd be exasperated too.

"Katelyn, dearest sister, please tell me, do you really know Jackson Wilder?"

"Yes." Kitten grins.

"Holy shit! Wow! Okay. Okay, can I meet him?"

"I don't know..." She looks over to me. "What do you think?"

Taking my cue, I glide over so my body is partially behind Kitten, with my head and chest clearly visible over her shoulders. She has to angle the camera up a bit to get us both on the screen but there's no mistaking that we're together in person.

"Hey, man," I direct my greeting to the guy on the phone screen, who is clearly Kitten's brother. He's mid-thirties, same shiny brown hair, same hazel eyes. Only he looks to be in a state of shock at the moment. His eyes are unblinking, and his mouth is hanging open. Bending to Kitten's ear, I whisper loud enough for the phone to pick it up. "Did we break him?"

Kitten bursts into laughter and the phone shakes in her hands. "Alex, wipe the drool off your chin, and say hello to Jackson."

"Oh, wow. Uh, hey. I mean, hi. Nice to meet you." Alex is stuttering out the words, and even though I feel a little bit bad, it's pretty funny.

"I hear you're a bit of a Sleet fan."

Alex shakes his head, as if to clear it. "Aw, man, this is... You're the best! I watch every single game. The way you move the puck down the ice... it's gold, man. Pure gold."

Kitten is giggling. "Geez Alex, way to play it cool."

Alex is looking at Kitten now. "There's no being cool when it's Jackson *fucking* Wilder. You don't even appreciate how awesome he is, do you?"

"Oh, I think I do..." Innuendo in her voice.

Alex makes a face.

I can't help myself. Grinning, I put my arm around her shoulders and pull her tight against my side.

"So..." Alex drags out the word. "Where are you guys?"

Kitten shakes her head. "No. No way in hell am I telling you. You're not crashing our date. This isn't high school."

"Wait," I interrupt. "He crashed your dates?"

Kitten looks up at me. "He always had one problem or another with the guys that wanted to date me. He would get Dad to tell him where I was going, and then he would *always* show up and ruin everything." Looking back at the phone she says, "Never again, dipshit."

Alex laughs. "Those were the good days."

"I think I like you, Alex." I completely approve of his tactics. "I want to hear more about these dates you ruined."

He beams. "Dude, I'll tell you whatever you want to know."

"Okay, this has been fun and all, but I'm going to hang up now." As Kitten says this a pair of kids come flying past us, so close that I have to pull Kitten back a foot to keep her from getting crashed into.

Alex must have gotten a view of the background when the phone shifted because his next words come out as a shout. "Ohmygod, are you seriously ice-skating with Jackson Wilder?!"

I can feel Kitten rolling her eyes at her brother's excitement. But before she can say anything, Alex continues. "Oh shit, Jackson, my man. I have a huge favor to ask you!"

"What?" Kitten sounds appalled. "You are not asking Jackson for favors. Bye, Alex."

Before she can hang up, I snatch the phone out of her hands and skate backward.

"Jackson! Give that back. Don't fall for his nonsense."

"Kitten, you stay right there," I point at her feet. "I just need a moment. And don't try to chase me down. If you start to fall, I'll have to drop this phone to catch you. Then some kid will trip over it and break their arm. You don't want that on your conscience, do you?"

"Oh, for the love of-" is all I hear her say before I skate off to the other side of the rink to talk to Alex.

CHAPTER THIRTY-TWO

JACKSON

Reaching the far side of the ice, I pull a quick stop then lean against the glass. This way I can keep an eye on Kitten while Alex and I chat. It's probably not necessary. I'm fairly sure she'll respect our privacy and stay put. Actually, I'd put it at about fifty-fifty.

Bringing the phone back up I decide to break the ice, so to speak. "I heard about the time you made Katelyn believe she peed her bed when she was younger. That was diabolical. And kind of genius."

Alex just stares at me for a moment before grinning. "She told you that? I was sure she'd go to her grave with that story. It was pretty fucking funny. She got me back though, so I think we're even."

"Did she? She left that part out."

"Seriously! I figured she'd have started with that. She was an evil mastermind when it came to revenge."

"Let's hear it!" I say, but he's already nodding.

"I think I was sixteen when she found out the pee thing was fake. I don't remember how it got revealed, but I'd kept her going for years on that one. Coincidentally, it was just a few weeks later that my first-ever girlfriend came over to our house. Kay had apparently been planning her payback for a while. She'd made up a fake label for one of those creams that you put on cuts. Antibacterial whatever it was. Anyways, when my girlfriend went to use the bathroom, Kay somehow snuck in ahead of her and left it on the counter." Alex grimaces. "Fuck man, I almost forgot about this. So, my girlfriend comes back from the bathroom and makes up some dumb excuse about needing to go home for a study group. It was the middle of summer, I might add, and she was not in any classes. And it's not like we had cell phones for her to get a reminder on. But I don't argue. I try to walk her to the door but she's practically running ahead of me. Then she dodges my kiss goodbye, and takes off. So I'm heading back to my room to sulk, and I find Kay curled up on the hallway floor. It looked like she was crying, so I ran over to see what was wrong. She was fucking crying alright. She was laughing so hard she had tears running down her face and she couldn't stand."

By now, I'm smiling like a fool. Happy my Kitten got her licks in. "What did the label on the cream say?"

"She still couldn't talk so she just pointed to the bathroom. I had no idea what the hell was going on, but I went in and that's when I found the fake tube on the counter. She did a damn good job of forging a prescription label. It was complete with my full name and address and the name of our actual doctor. Oh man, what was the wording?" He looks skyward. "Something like: for topical use only. Apply to the affected area on the penis, two times daily. For treatment of skin-eating bacterial infection. If condition worsens, or if skin starts to flake off, discontinue use and contact your doctor immediately."

"Wow... that's disgusting!"

"That's not even the best part." Alex is laughing by this point. "What Kay couldn't have known was that my girlfriend had given me a blow job the night before. So along with the discarded cream on the counter, there was vomit in the sink."

"Holy shit!" I try not to gag at the visual.

"Yeah. I'd have puked, too, if I were her. I can only imagine what was going through her mind. She probably ran straight to her own doctor."

"Dude. I don't know if I should laugh or dry heave."

He gives me a look of understanding. "I did a lot of the latter when I saw the vomit. I may have broken up a lot of

Kay's dates after that, but I never played any more pranks on her."

"Shit. I don't ever want to get on her bad side," I say, meaning every word.

"No. No you do not." Alex stops laughing and gives me a studying look. "Clearly, I have no idea what's going on between you and my sister. And even though I'm a huge fan, I don't know you. My sister might be a royal pain in the ass sometimes, but she's my sister. I know there's nothing I can threaten you with, so I'll just say, don't jerk her around. I'm an adult, maybe what you guys have is just casual," he holds up a hand as if to stop me, "and - please - I don't ever want to know even the vaguest of details about my sister's sex life." He shudders. "All I ask is that you be straight with her. I don't want to have to hate you. You have a sister, right? You get it."

I nod. "I do have a sister, and I most certainly get it. I met Katelyn the night of your cousin's party, and he saw us together he said nearly the exact same thing to me. Even including the part about her being a pain in the ass." Alex smiles. "What we have is still new, but I care about her. Probably more than I should after such a short amount of time."

He hums for a moment. "I appreciate your honesty."

"Always." I nod. "So, what was this favor you wanted to ask me?"

"Oh, right!" He perks up. "My school is having a career day, and you would make me the king of campus if you could make it. It's like a week and a half from now. You guys don't have a game that day, so you should be in the Cities. I know this is a big ask, but the kids would absolutely love it."

"Send me the details. As long as we aren't playing, I'm sure I can stop in. Would I need to give a speech?"

"For real? Oh my god, you are the best! I can get you as much or as little time to talk as you want. It's a whole school-assembly thing, in the afternoon. We have a bunch of parents and relatives coming in. Kay will even be there to talk about books and stuff."

"Sounds good. I'll get your number off Katelyn's phone and text you."

Alex pumps a fist into the air. "Awesome!"

"Well, I look forward to meeting you in person at this career-day thing. In the meantime, we'll be in touch. I best get back to Katelyn before she cooks up some revenge plan for me for stealing her phone."

"Thanks, Jackson. Seriously, it was a pleasure to meet you. Talk to you. Whatever. You know what I mean."

"Same to you, Alex. See ya later."

Hanging up, I see that Kitten has started to slowly skate my way. Slipping her phone into my pocket, I take off in her direction. I see her eyes go wide when she realizes that I'm coming in fast. Putting her hands up in a stopping motion, she lets out a little squeak as I skate right up to her.

She was trying to stop me, but she put her hands in the perfect spot for me to grab her forearms as I angle my skates. Putting my weight onto one leg, I execute a quick spin, taking Kitten with me. Gripping her tight, I use the momentum to pull her body against mine.

Coming to a stop, she looks up at me - clearly shocked. My legs are slightly spread, with her feet between mine. This lowers me enough that I only need to tip my head forward to seal my lips to hers. So I do.

I have an instant to enjoy the feel of Kitten's lips curling into a smile, before she returns my kiss with vigor. As her lips part for me, I release my grip on her forearms so I can wrap my arms around her. Kitten's hands find their way under my jacket, roaming, until they grab a hold to my sides. The feeling of her little fingers digging into my ribs has me losing control on the groan I was holding in.

Pulling back slightly, I rest my forehead against Kitten's.

"You're too good at that, darling."

"Too good at what?" Kitten's voice is barely a whisper.

"Too good at kissing me. At touching me. At causing involuntary responses."

She huffs out a breath. "Pretty sure I could accuse you of the same thing."

"I was going to suggest that we get out of here and warm up with a hot drink. But that little kiss got me plenty warm."

"True. But I could still go for a hot drink." Tipping her head back, Kitten looks up at me. "And - let me guess, you have a place in mind."

CHAPTER THIRTY-THREE

KATELYN

Skating with Jackson Wilder was a bucket-list item I didn't even know I had. He was so calm and patient with me while I got used to being on the ice again. I didn't do terribly, but he did prevent me from falling a couple of times. Not that I'm complaining, since that just meant he had to touch me. But even when he wasn't supporting me, he was holding my hand or pushing against my back, making me go faster. I was so jittery with excitement that I felt like a silly kid with a crush. Until he kissed me. Then I didn't feel like a silly kid anymore. I felt like a silly woman. A woman in way over her head with a guy who still seems too good to be true.

We're back in Jackson's car, headed to yet another mystery location. This one apparently serves hot drinks, so my guess is a coffee shop. But I should probably stop assuming things when it comes to Jackson.

I tap my fingers against my thigh and look out the window. "So, you and Alex talked for quite a while."

"Did we? It didn't seem like that long," Jackson replies innocently.

My eyes drag over in his direction. "Uh-huh. What was the favor he wanted to ask you? I hope you turned him down."

"I agreed to it actually. I already texted him, while you were turning in your skates."

"What? Jackson, you didn't have to do that. Whatever it is, I can get you out of it. He doesn't need you giving him tickets to games. He can buy his own."

"That's a good idea. I should send him some tickets. He can go with you to the next home game."

"Umm, no. To all of that. If he didn't ask for tickets, what did he want?"

"I agreed to"—Jackson takes a long pause—"speak at his school for career day."

Oh. Huh. That's not at all what I expected from my brother. It's actually a surprisingly great idea.

Slowing to take a turn, Jackson reaches over and places his hand on my forearm. "Kitten, your silence is worrying me."

"I was just thinking how nice that is. And how mature of my brother to use that as his favor. Not that you owe him a favor. Not at all. But I assume people ask you for stuff all the time. And now that you're doing *that*, he knows damn well he can't ask you for tickets or anything else."

"Interesting theory. Not too many people have the 'only ask for one thing' mindset. But I bet you're right about Alex."

"I'm sorry, Jackson."

He looks over at me, brows furrowed. "What for?"

"For humanity in general. It must suck to have people asking you for things all the time. I know you're very generous, but it's still a burden. And I hope you know that I've loved coming to your games, but I'll gladly buy my own tickets to come watch you play. In fact, I insist on it. You can't keep giving me expensive tickets."

Jackson turns down an alley and pulls into a small parking lot. Turning off the engine, he unbuckles, gets out of the car, and circles around the front. He didn't say a word after I finished talking about the tickets, but I did see his jaw clench. I'm not sure how to read this mood, but staying put seems like the safest option as he approaches.

Jackson pulls open my door, reaches across my body to unbuckle my seatbelt, then grabs my knees and spins me so I'm facing him.

Jackson has to duck down to avoid hitting his head on the doorframe. But he does, and he doesn't stop until his face is just a few inches from my own.

Hands still on my knees, Jackson talks in a quiet but firm voice. "You have to stop being so fucking perfect, Kitten. I'm trying to make it through this day in a civilized manner. I'm doing my best to resist the urge of throwing you over my shoulder and taking you back home. But if I'm going to succeed, you need to stop saying all the right things, making all the right sounds, and looking at me like I hung the damn moon. We have this place, then dinner, *then* I'm taking you home. Not a moment before. Nod if you understand what I'm saying."

My mouth suddenly feels very dry, but I'm able to give him a small nod.

His hands slide up a few inches until they're covering my thighs. "And I'll give you tickets to my games. I'll do so as often as I please, and I'll give you as many as I please. I'll dress you up in my jersey, and any other item of clothing I can think of, branding you as mine. You'll take them, you'll wear them, and you'll be fucking happy about it. Nod if you understand me."

I nod.

His stare doesn't get any less intense. "Good. Now get your fine ass out of the vehicle."

I bite my lips closed, afraid that - if I open them - the bumblebees banging around in my chest will fly free.

Jackson dips his head out of the car but doesn't back up. Slowly, I slide out of the passenger seat until my feet hit the ground, keeping eye contact with Jackson the whole way.

He gestures for me to move so he can shut the door. As I step past him, he smacks my ass.

I let out a yelp, spinning around to face him. He just smirks and takes my hand.

I feel like I'm getting to know the hidden Jackson a little bit better… And I like it.

We walk around the corner of a building and, just like with *Squeeze Me*, we're in what looks to be a mainly residential neighborhood. Looking up at the establishment ahead of us, I see the name is written in big wooden block letters above the doorway. The letters are chipped and painted in yellow, while the rest of the storefront is a dark green. The name reads *Cuppa Chapters*. From the style and overall feel of the building, I'd say we are going into a bookstore.

As always, Jackson holds the door open for me to go through first. Stepping inside, I'm immediately hit with the wonderful aroma of fresh-ground coffee beans—and books. I stop so suddenly that Jackson bumps into me.

He chuckles. "See something you like?"

"*Like?* I'm in love. What is this place? I feel like I stepped into Narnia... or Diagon Alley! How did I not know about this?" My pitch hits a high note as I finish my ramble, but I don't even care. This is absolutely my new favorite place.

"Come on," Jackson says, placing his hand on my back. "I'll show you around."

Jackson leads me through a maze of bookshelves that reach all the way to the ceiling. From what I can tell, there is everything from brand new best sellers to heavily worn, decades-old texts. The sections aren't labeled, so you'd either need to ask for assistance or just take your time strolling through.

Every time we turn a corner, there's another cluster of chairs. Some with tables, some with ottomans, and some large overstuffed chairs you could read in for hours. Reaching the back of the store, we come to a larger, semi-open space that has an eclectic mix of tables and chairs, surrounded by an outer ring of loveseats and couches. In the far corner is a slightly raised platform that holds a single high-back chair. Along the rest of the back wall is a coffee bar. With the espresso machines on proud display, the setup is very steampunk-meets-grandma's-library.

We haven't said anything since we started our wander through this little slice of heaven. Jackson has obviously been here before, but I appreciate that he's letting me take it all in on my own terms. Like all our interactions, this feels familiar.

Standing in front of the menu board, Jackson moves to stand directly behind me. With his hands on my shoulder, I know he's close, so I lean back into his body. Jackson slides his hands around to my collarbones before bringing both arms around my upper chest in a loose hug. Being intimate like this shouldn't be so easy. But since it is, I let myself melt into his embrace even more.

When he rests his chin on the top of my head, I'm thankful that I left my hat in the car.

"This is one of Steph's favorite hideouts." I can feel the rumble of his chest against my back. I force myself to focus on his words, not the vibrations, so I don't slip to the floor in a boneless pile of female hormones. "When she brought me here for the first time last year, she made me promise to keep it a secret. She says it does well enough already, and that if my "meathead friends" started showing up, it would ruin the vibe. But I have a feeling she'd be okay with me bringing you here, though."

"I can't believe I've never heard of this place. Seriously, I'm in awe. And you can tell Steph that you're the only meathead I'll ever come here with."

Jackson gives my body a squeeze. "Know what you want to drink? I can promise that there are no wrong choices here."

Reading back through the menu, I see that - along with coffee and tea beverages - they have an extensive selection of wines.

Deciding to be decadent, I choose the coconut matcha latte.

Tipping my head back and to the side I look up at Jackson, "I know what I want."

His eyes travel to my mouth. "Me too."

Placing our orders, Jackson having a decaf cinnamon latte, I once again try to pay, and he literally growls at me. I relent.

Waiting for our beverages, Jackson keeps an arm slung around my shoulders. "Every Saturday evening they have someone do a reading at the top of every hour. It's usually only about fifteen minutes or so." He glances to the clock behind the bar. "We have about twenty minutes until the next one starts. Would you like to sit here at the tables? They don't do microphones, so if you want to listen, we should stay close."

Glancing around, I spot a comfortable looking loveseat in the corner and gesture toward it. "How about there?"

Mugs in hand, we settle onto the overstuffed cushions. I don't bother pretending that I'm not going to cuddle up against Jackson. I'm pressed against his side, with my legs crossed so I can hold onto the mug by the handle and rest the bottom on my knee. Jackson places one hand on my thigh, while his other holds his drink.

We watch as some of the tables fill up in anticipation of the reader.

"Do you know what the reading is about?" I ask.

"No idea. I think they have a sign-up sheet somewhere so anyone who wants to read can do it. The times I've been here before it's been poetry, but I think that was just random chance. Steph says some are authors, and others are just people reading a chapter out of their favorite book."

"It's a clever idea. I can definitely think of some books I'd like to read from."

"If you sign up, you have to tell me."

"Will you wave around a foam finger, cheering me on?"

Jackson squeezes my thigh. "Absolutely. I'll be your biggest cheerleader."

Looking at him out the corner of my eye, I give him a once-over. "Biggest is an accurate description." He winks, and for the sake of my sanity, I ignore it. "Hmm, I think I'd want the full experience. Pompoms, a little crop top... some hot pants."

He nods. "So, you *did* go snooping around my house the other night."

"Oh my god!" I say laughing.

Before my mind can wander to *that* mental image, a woman steps onto the platform and takes a seat in the single chair. She looks to be around seventy, give or take a decade. *I'm bad with age.* She has a definite hippie vibe with her long grey hair secured by a knitted headband, and her windchime looking earrings so long they reach her shoulders. She has jangly bracelets lining each wrist, and a long-sleeved, floor-length dress tie-dyed in ranging shades of blue. And from all the way back here, I can see a giant turquoise ring on her finger. I instantly want to be her friend.

As she digs around in her oversized bag, I take the first sip of my drink. And I moan. Holy secret coffee shops, how is this so good? What the hell is it made from, pixie dust and pheromones?

As he leans down to whisper directly into my ear, Jackson applies pressure to my thigh. "You're going to need to keep those sounds to yourself, Kitten. We've flown under the radar so far today, but if I maul you right here, right now, someone is bound to make another video of us." He uses a finger to tilt my face toward him. "You have a little something..."

Then instead of using his thumb, or a napkin, or his goddamn sleeve, he licks the corner of my mouth.

Literally. *Licks.*

A small, slow lick that I feel *everywhere.*

I blush as I clench my legs together.

Jackson chuckles.

Damn him.

Thankfully, the lady upfront clears her throat. "Good evening, lovely people. My name is Lily, and I'm going to read an excerpt from the book that my granddaughter just published." The gathered crowd lets out a communal *aww*. "The title is *Laird of My Heart*."

That's so sweet. This cute grandma is out here supporting her family and doing it in a very personal way.

When she starts, I let myself fall into the tone and lilt of her speech. She has a great reading voice. You can hear her age, but it's still strong enough to be understood clearly. She started her reading midway through the book. I'm only half paying attention to the words, mostly listening to the tune of her voice, catching enough of the story that I can tell it's a historical romance. Probably set in 1500s Scotland. I've read a few dozen from this genre, so I'm familiar.

I'm also familiar with the typical buildup to a sex scene. And... Oh. My. Grandma. I feel my heart rate pick up, and the warmth of Jackson's palm on my thigh suddenly feels hot.

I tense.

Jackson must've felt my shift, because he quietly asks, "What's wrong?"

"Umm... you'll see," I murmur, suppressing a giggle.

Looking back toward Lily, I brace for what comes next.

"The sound of her slap against his face echoed around the bed chamber. She was so upset with him for risking his life, and she only just now realized why. She was in love with him. And she felt the truth of it deep in her bones. Why it had taken her so long, she'll never know. The look he gave her in return was new... different... hard to read. She held still for a moment, while she waited to see how he would retaliate for the slap. But instead of striking her as she expected, he crushed his lips against hers. She had never felt a passion like this before, and for the first time ever, she felt a dampness forming between her thighs."

I force myself to keep looking forward, as I hear Jackson choke on a laugh.

"The girl pressed her body against his, wanting to get closer. Her body knew what it needed, even if the girl didn't understand. With their bodies together, the girl felt a strange hardness pushing against her belly."

"Oh, for fuck's sake," I hear Jackson mutter under his breath.

Stealing a look at him, I see he's tipped his head back against the couch and is staring at the ceiling.

"When the girl releases a needy moan, the man grabs her bodice with both hands and rips the fabric straight down the middle. Tossing her onto the bed, the laird growls, before following her." Lily stops.

Looking up, she closes the book and smiles. "Thank you all for coming. If you'd like to hear what happens next, please purchase the book."

There isn't so much *applause*, as there is a smattering of stunned, slow-clapping from a few individuals. One man, though, stands suddenly, claps vigorously, then grabs his date by the hand and rushes away. I have to put a hand over my mouth to keep from laughing.

Looking back over to Jackson, I see he's still staring at the ceiling. Aiming my gaze south, I notice there's a bit of a bulge in his jeans where there wasn't before. I can't blame him. I'd be lying if I said I wasn't a little turned on right now. I get all sorts of worked-up by books, all the time. But it is a little weird for it to happen in public. While hearing it read out loud. By a sweet old lady.

Leaning my head on Jackson's shoulder, I smile at him. "You gonna be okay, big guy?"

"Yep."

"You want me to go buy you a copy of *Laird of My Heart*?"

Jackson barks out a laugh before looking down at me. "Only if you promise to read the rest of it to me out loud."

I bite my lip. "Tempting."

Letting out a sigh, Jackson shakes his head. "Seriously, Kitten, I don't know why all the strangest things happen when we're together. I swear to you, every other time I've been here it's been very PG. And Steph comes here all the time. I'm positive she would've told me if she ever sat through a reading like that before. I mean, I think she'd be thrilled, but she still would've told me about it."

Patting his knee, I force myself to stay focused and avoid the temptation of running my hand up higher. I still vividly remember the feeling of Jackson between my legs when he pressed me into the wall last night. I know what he's hiding down there. And after Lily's little reading, I'm tempted to skip dinner and get to the part where we lose our clothes.

"Earth to Kitten."

I shake myself back to reality. "Huh?"

"I think I lost you there for a moment."

"Oh sorry, just thinking about that laird." I wink.

"Well, that just won't do." Jackson clicks his tongue. "Let me take you to dinner. I'll make you forget all about the laird and his lady."

As I follow Jackson out of Cuppa Chapters, I send Grandma Lily a quick wave and a thumbs-up.

CHAPTER THIRTY-FOUR

JACKSON

I'm not sure what's worse, fighting an erection on a date, or fighting an erection from listening to an old lady read from a book. It's a fucking toss up at this point. Thankfully, the drive to dinner is going to be a short one. I've gotten Kitten strapped in her seat, and I'm willing my body to settle down as I climb into the driver's side.

Kitten clears her throat. "So... is dinner going to be at some exotic strip club?"

"I'll admit, after that show, the restaurant is going to seem extremely tame."

"That sounds just fine to me. Honestly though, after hearing that excerpt, I'm going to amend the list of books I'd like to read from. If I knew erotic scenes were on the table, I'd choose differently."

I glance over to Kitten. "Wait, was that normal? Are books really like that?" At her laugh, I add, "I mean girl books, or romance, or whatever that was. I don't mean to sound like I don't read, because I do, when I can. And I mean, there's nothing wrong with romance… I just haven't read any." I slam my mouth shut. I sound like an idiot.

Kitten reaches over and pats me on the arm. "Well, I hate to throw out a spoiler, but most *romance* books have sex in them. And not just fade-to-black sex, some have very graphic, super-hot sex. And sometimes there are many of those scenes all in one book. And some books are made up entirely of erotic content." She pauses. "But those are best for reading alone. In your bed. At night."

Something about her tone has me going back over her words.

Reading in bed. At night. Alone. *Oh... holy shit.* Now I'm picturing Kitten, reading dirty stories, touching herself.

My body instantly reacts. Closing my eyes, I think unsexy thoughts before I'm stuck dealing with a full-on boner like some dweeb on his first date.

Ice skates. Hockey helmet. Goalie stick. Water bottle. Penalty box.

"Penalty box?"

"Uh, yeah. I was just, uh, thinking…" Crap. I said that last one out loud. "Oh, look. We're here."

I park, turn off the engine, and get out of the car faster than I ever have before.

Just before I slam my door shut, I hear the music of Kitten's laughter following me.

CHAPTER THIRTY-FIVE

KATELYN

I find myself, yet again, walking through a door held open by Jackson, as we enter a hole-in-the-wall establishment. Reading the name written across the glass on the front door, I smile: *Impasta.* Cute. The place is small, but packed. Jackson must've gotten a reservation because we're immediately brought to a table.

I'm distracted by the amazing smells as I slide into our booth in the back corner. The lighting is dim, and I'm definitely getting a classic Italian vibe from the décor. Dark wood, white cloth napkins, little tea candles lit on every table, and our booth seats are a deep red. It's perfect.

I'm still taking in the surroundings when our server appears at the table.

"Mr. Wilder! What a pleasure to see you, my boy!" Hmm, not the server. His hair is jet black, and he has a perfect Mario mustache. Exactly like that Nintendo character.

"Hi, Mario." *Shut the front door. That is not his name!*

"I'd like you to meet Katelyn." Jackson gestures to me. "This is her first time visiting your fine restaurant."

Turning to me, Mario takes my hand and kisses my knuckles. "Ciao Bella. I promise you'll fall in love with my food faster than you can fall in love with Mr. Wilder."

He shoots a wink over at Jackson, who looks as startled by the L-word as I feel.

"Mario, I've told you a hundred times, call me Jackson."

"Si, si. Now, you'll be having your usual?" Jackson nods. Turning to me, Mario asks, "Do you have any dietary restrictions, my dear?"

"None at all," I grin.

"Splendido." And with that, he snatches the menus off our table and leaves.

Jackson looks a little sheepish. "He's kind of a character."

I snort. "Literally. Mario? Seriously?" I rub under my nose with my finger, as if it's a mustache.

Jackson starts to laugh, but then catches himself as our actual server approaches the table. We stay quiet, biting back smiles while the server presents us with a basket of bread and pours both waters

When the server leaves, I lean into the table. "How is it that I've lived in this area my whole life, and yet you're the one showing me all of these amazing places?"

Jackson shrugs. "I can't take the credit. Steph and my mama have always been food crazy. Whenever Steph would come to visit us, wherever we were living, the two of them would scour the city looking for all the hidden gems. I don't even know how they find all these places, but I guarantee they only share half of their finds with me. Steph seems convinced that I'll share every location with the whole NHL, and that they'll be overrun with jocks in no time."

"Maybe I can convince her to share the other half of her finds with me. I mean, I won't be able to share them with you, obviously. Girl code and all that."

"Obviously."

I sigh. "I'm gonna tell my brother to step up his sibling game. He got to FaceTime with his hero because of me. And what does he do for me? Nothing. That's what."

Jackson's lips pull back into a full grin.

"What?"

As I bring my water glass to my lips, Jackson replies. "Alex told me about the dick cream."

I pause a beat, trying to put the pieces together. Then it clicks. I break out laughing so hard I slosh water out of my glass and down the front of my shirt. Jackson reaches over and takes the glass from my hand, before I can spill more.

"He told you that?! Ohmygod, I can't believe I forgot about that part. You should've seen the look on that poor girl's face when she ran out of the bathroom." I crack up again, laughing so hard I can feel tears on my cheeks. "He kept that tube in his pocket for weeks, hoping he'd see her again and would be able to explain that it was fake. Except one day, it fell out of his pocket in the locker room where he worked as a lifeguard. Another boy found it and turned it in to the lost-and-found. But as luck would have it, one of Alex's friends was running the desk. So he got on the loudspeaker and asked Alex Brown to come to the front desk to pick up his penis medication." I can hear Jackson laughing as I wipe at my eyes. "At that exact moment, Alex was flirting with one of the popular girls from the grade above his. When the announcement happened, he said it was like slow motion as he watched her eyes track down to his name tag. He didn't even try to explain it to her, he just turned and ran. Oh man, that was just the gift that kept on giving."

Wiping away the last of my tears I look up to see Jackson staring at me with a soft smile. "You're so fucking beautiful."

The last of my laughter dies away, instantly replaced with the now-familiar buzzing of bees.

"Thank you," I whisper.

"You're also wicked. I don't know what it says about me, but I seem to like that combination."

Perfectly timed, our food arrives, allowing me a moment to catch my breath. Both from the laughter, and from the compliment. Having Jackson's attention so focused on me fuzzes out my brain. And now I'm distracted by the gorgeous food on our plates.

Mario's special selection for me is some sort of herby tomato dish with angel-hair pasta and perfectly cooked shrimp. Looking over, I see Jackson's usual consists of wide noodles, grilled chicken, and what smells like a white wine and lemon sauce. After just one bite, I decide that this Mario is fabulous. And that he was *almost* right. I'm definitely falling in love with this food. But - and I know this is crazy - I think I might already be in love with Jackson Wilder.

CHAPTER THIRTY-SIX

KATELYN

Dinner passed quickly while we devoured our meals and talked about our careers. I told Jackson more about what it takes to edit romance novels and how much I love working from home. I told him about some of the favorite books that I've worked on, and how it can be difficult to juggle deadlines.

I learned more about the demanding schedule Jackson has during the season. He had practice early this morning, which is why he was able to spend the rest of the day with me. He has practice again tomorrow morning, before flying out East for two nights of away games.

It's no surprise that he spends most of his off season traveling with his mama. In the past, they'd go visit Steph, but - now that she's here, too - they go wherever they want. Which of course lead to us discussing the places we've been and places we would like to go.

It was a nice dinner. A *great* dinner. The entire day, since the moment he picked me up, has been a dream. I feel like I can talk about anything with Jackson. And I find myself anxious to hear what he has to say in return.

He's just so... good. A good guy. Good son. Good brother. Good kisser... Which is where I feel like I slip from reality and into fantasy. The sexual chemistry, and tension, between us is like nothing I've ever experienced. Just a single look from him. One press of his hand. One kiss, and my heart is racing. Even just his voice, the brush of air against my neck when he bends close to talk. The sensations keep compounding, and I feel like we've been on the precipice of tipping past foreplay all day. He is driving me home right now, and if he decides to drop me off, ending our date at the doorstep, I think I might die.

We've driven back in relative silence. Both feeling the unseen webs of lust building between us. When we got in the car, Jackson turned on the radio for the first time all day, letting the quiet music fill the space. Then he took my hand, interlaced our fingers, and has been holding it ever since.

I force myself to stop biting my lip when the car slows and Jackson pulls up to my house. He puts the car in park and shuts off the engine. Looking over to me, we make eye contact for the first time since leaving the restaurant.

I slowly release the breath I've been holding. "Would you like to come inside?"

He doesn't hesitate. "Yes."

It's torture waiting for him to walk around to open my door. When he does, he holds his hand out to help me down. He's looking at me like he wants to kiss me. But he doesn't. Instead he leads me to my door and waits for me to unlock it.

Silently we enter my house, removing our jackets and boots. I always leave a few lamps on, so the house is filled with dim lighting. And tension. So much sexual tension.

We're still standing near my front door, facing each other. Eyeing each other.

I wet my lips. "Would you like a drink?"

Jackson shakes his head. "No."

"Would you like to sit?"

Jackson steps closer. "No."

"Would you like a tour?"

Jackson steps closer still. "No."

"Would you like to see my bedroom?"

"Yes."

Smirking, with my heart nearly beating out of my chest, I take off running down the hallway.

I'm not even sure why I do it. The anticipation between us was too much and I couldn't think of a mature way to respond.

I don't make it more than a few strides before Jackson's arms are cinched around my waist, and he's lifting me off the ground.

He growls into my ear, "Now, now, Kitten, you shouldn't have done that."

He nips the side of my neck.

I suppress a giggle. "My, what big teeth you have."

"Mmmm, all the better to *eat* you with, my pretty."

Fucking hell.

I feel a tremble run through my body at his choice of words.

With only a couple doors to pick from, Jackson chooses correctly and carries me into my bedroom. Stopping at the foot of the bed he loosens his grip and oh-so-slowly slides me down his body. His chest to my back.

As my ass slides down against his straining cock, I arch into him. With his hand spread across my stomach, Jackson pulls me tight against him. I can feel him rock his hips into me. His other hand is sliding up my stomach, reaching my breast, where he squeezes just hard enough to send a jolt straight to my core.

"Kitten." He kisses my neck. "My sweet, gorgeous Kitten." Another kiss. "I can't wait to have you bent over, ass in the air, your hair wrapped around my fist, as I fuck you from behind."

My words come out as a choked whisper, "I want that too."

Jackson drags his nose up the side of my neck. "But not tonight."

"Jackson, I swear to god, if you think you're just going to finger me again and leave, I might have to hurt you."

Releasing me, Jackson slaps my ass, then turns me around to face him.

"Don't you worry, Kitten." He grabs a hold of the bottom of my sweater and pulls it up over my head. "I'm going to fuck you tonight." He reaches back and unhooks my bra. Letting it fall, he lets out a groan. "But it won't be from behind." He cups both my breasts in his giant hands, running a thumb over each nipple. He groans again. Louder. "I want to be able to look at you." He drops to his knees in front of me. Gripping my sides, he kisses my stomach. "I want to see the look on your face when I slide into you." He unbuttons my jeans and pulls them down, helping me to step out of them.

With his hands on my ass he pulls me forward and kisses me. Right where I need him. If his hands weren't on me I would collapse. Or combust. There's only a thin, lacy layer between his mouth and my skin but instead of dulling the sensation, it adds to it. The friction is nearly too much.

I grip at his hair, making sounds I'll later be embarrassed for. I can feel his dark chuckle vibrate against me before he pulls away. Leaning back, he slowly - tortuously slowly - drags my panties down. Revealing all of me to him.

Sitting back on his heels, Jackson traces every inch of me with his eyes. Jackson Wilder, on his knees in front of me, fully clothed, while I stand here naked.

Looking back up into my eyes, Jackson stands. "Get on the bed."

For once, I do as I'm told.

Sitting on the bed, I slide back until I'm in the middle before lying down. Jackson doesn't look away as he starts to strip. With one hand, he reaches back. Taking hold of his sweater, he pulls it off in one swift motion. *Fuck me.* He's big and broad and completely male. He has dark chest hair and a hard body. The real, muscular body of a man.

He starts to undo his pants, then pauses. I prop myself up on my elbows. What the hell is he pausing for!? He extracts a condom from somewhere in his pocket, and tosses it on to the bed next to me. Oh, okay, smart man. Mine are in the bathroom. Which is a dumb place for them now that I think about it. But I'm no longer thinking about it, because now Jackson is kicking his pants off. He's left in just a pair of black boxer briefs. And they're doing nothing to conceal his very large, very hard cock. I don't have long to fantasize though, because a second later he tucks his thumbs in either side of his briefs and pulls them down.

Um... Yikes.

This man is huge. Everywhere. I mean he doesn't have a weird freaky dick that I'm afraid won't fit. But it's big. Like *really* big. And although I'm sure it will fit, I'm also pretty sure it will hurt. It's been a while since I've slept with a guy, and now I'm starting to question if this is a good idea.

Jackson must sense my hesitation, because he grins. "Don't worry, Kitten. I'll get you good and ready for me." Then he strokes his cock. One slow, long stroke from tip to base. And holy fucking fuck gods, I've never been more turned on in my life.

Jackson steps to the foot of the bed and looks at me for a long moment. "Spread your legs for me."

I do. I'm feeling uncharacteristically obedient.

Jackson kneels on the bed, towering over me, staring at my exposed sex.

I've never been more on display, but I've also never been less self conscious of myself. The way Jackson is looking at me is filled with reverence. And heat.

Lowering himself, I see where this is going, and I could not be more excited. With his face just above my pussy, Jackson slides an arm under each of my legs. Reaching around, so his hands are on my inner thighs, he pulls them open even further. I'm pretty sure I am an embarrassing level of wet right now. But I don't care. And Jackson kills every thought in my brain when he presses his tongue against my pussy and licks, with one long, sweeping motion all the way up to my clit.

I let out a cry of surprise and involuntarily try to bring my legs together. Jackson's grip holds firm, keeping my thighs spread for him. I knew exactly what he was going to do, but the feeling was electric. I wasn't prepared. I'm still not prepared as he does it again. And again.

I can feel Jackson's groans as they roll through my core. "You taste so fucking good." Lick. "Like sex and sunshine." Lick. "And everything sweet in the world."

Just when I think this can't possibly get better, he grips my legs tighter and presses his face harder against me, focusing all of his attention on my clit. I quickly begin to lose my grip on reality. I think I'm chanting his name, or pleading, or maybe it's all in my head. But when he slides one of those big fat fingers in me, I come undone. I moan, and shake, and see stars, and he doesn't let up until the last tremor has left my body.

I don't know when I shut my eyes, but when I pry them open I'm instantly met with Jackson's gaze. I didn't feel him untangle himself from me, or crawl up my body, but he's right there. Using his large muscled arms to brace himself over me.

"Watching you come like that was the sexiest thing I've ever seen," he pants.

Then he kisses me. Hard.

I can taste myself on him. It should be weird, or gross, or shocking, but it's not. It's hot. Carnal. It's a reminder of what he just did. How he just made me feel. Having a man like Jackson marvel over *me*, gives me a high like I've never experienced.

Too soon, he's breaking away from the kiss. I want to tug him back to me, but then he reaches for the condom.

Ohmygod, this is it.

He rips open the package and slowly rolls it on.

Squeezing the base of his cock, he exhales a loud breath. "You have no fucking idea how badly I've wanted this. After having my fingers in you last night, this is all I've been able to think about. Getting to taste you just now, that was fuel on the fire. I'm gonna try to go slow with you, Kitten. You just make sure to tell me what you like."

I nod. I'm beyond words right now. With his dick in his hand, Jackson looks down and rubs himself up and down my entrance a few times. As he pushes the head of his cock into me, I feel the slight burn of stretching. He's big. I'm dripping wet, but he's still really big. With just the first couple inches inside of me, Jackson leans down and braces his weight on either side of my head. He presses in another inch.

"Open your eyes, Kitten. Look at me."

I didn't even realize that I had squeezed them shut again. Looking up, I stare directly into Jackson's pale blue eyes.

"Relax."

I do. He bends down to kiss me. As I open my mouth to deepen the kiss, he pushes in the rest of the way. *Oh holy shitballs.* I can't help it. I cry out. I'm gripping his back so tightly, I can feel my fingernails digging into his skin. I don't think he cares, or notices. Jackson has his forehead pressed against mine, and his body is still, giving me a moment to adjust.

"You okay?" he breathes.

"Yes. Yes, yes. You're so big."

He groans. "Fuck, baby."

Then he starts to move.

My body hasn't adjusted fully, and even though he feels like heaven, I feel myself tensing. But then he's kissing me. His mouth moving against mine in time with his body moving inside of me. The magic of his lips against mine calms my body. There's no pain left, just Jackson.

He's surrounding me. I feel him everywhere, and I feel my heart shifting along new faultlines. Making room for him.

This doesn't feel like he's fucking me. This feels like he's making love to me. I'm stunned when I suddenly feel tears pricking my eyes. So I hold Jackson tighter and kiss him harder, in an effort to hide my overwhelming reaction to him.

CHAPTER THIRTY-SEVEN

JACKSON

This doesn't feel like fucking. This feels life changing.

I've been with women before, women I really liked, even ones I thought I loved, but it's never been like this. When I first buried myself into Kitten's sweet pussy, I thought I might lose control. I was doing everything I could to keep from blowing right then and there. Her tenseness, even though it made her squeeze my dick even fucking tighter, helped me to focus. I was hurting her, and that was the last thing in the world I wanted to do. So, I did the only thing I could think of, I kissed her. And now she's kissing me back like her life depends on it. She's moving against me, with me, and I feel her everywhere.

Her moans are seeping into my soul. I don't think I'll ever forget the sound, or this moment. Every inch of her feels amazing, but it's more than that.

Kitten scratches her nails down my back and I want more. I want deeper.

Breaking away from the kiss, I put my weight onto one elbow and reach the other hand under her ass. Pulling her lower half up off the bed, I push in harder. Farther.

Her gasp tells me she feels it. Her moaning my name tells me she likes it.

Keeping a tight grip on her, I use my other hand to brush the hair out of her face. Her fingers are still scraping for purchase on my back.

I kiss her again.

She's breathing harder, and I can feel her muscles start to clench around me. She's close. And I want her to come with me.

Releasing my grip on her ass, I push her into the mattress with my hips and slide my hand around to apply pressure to her clit. She's panting my name louder now. And I know it won't take much.

One swipe of my thumb. Two. And she's coming. Hard. Her legs wrap tight around my waist, and I feel her pulsing around my cock. I can't take any more. I pump into her once. Twice. And then I'm following her release with my own. I pull her tight against me, as I bury myself inside her as far as I'll go.

My ears are ringing, and I can barely make out the sound of our heavy breathing. We stay wrapped around each other for several minutes. Days? I don't know. Slowly, we start to untwine ourselves, and - when I pull myself out of her - we both wince. Spotting a garbage can near the bed I carefully pull the condom off and toss it in.

I don't know about Kitten, but there is no way I'd be able to walk right now. I don't even try. Instead, I roll onto my back and pull her with me. With a few tugs, I'm able to get the blanket out from under us so I can pull it over our naked bodies.

Kitten doesn't protest my obvious desire to sleep over. She tucks her head against my shoulder, and hikes her leg over mine.

Pulling her in tight, I kiss her on the forehead.

She sighs. "Jackson, that was..."

"I know." I kiss her again. "I know."

Surrounded by the heat of my Kitten, I drop into sleep.

CHAPTER THIRTY-EIGHT

KATELYN

The bleeping of a phone alarm jolts me awake.
What the hell? That's not my alarm tone.
I feel the mattress move, followed by a loud thump and a, "Shit!"

Smiling, I realize Jackson just fell out of my bed.

My eyes snap open. Jackson. In my bed. Memories of last night pour into my brain, heating my blood. And cheeks. I can't believe I slept with Jackson. I can't believe how good it was. No, not good, wonderful. Magical. Orgasmic. Well, I suppose *Duh* to that last one.

"Sorry, Kitten." Jackson's gravelly morning voice pebbles my skin. "I didn't mean to wake you."

"It's okay," I say through a yawn.

It's still dark in the room, and I can hear the shuffle of Jackson getting dressed. When the mattress dips right next to me, I blink my eyes to find him sitting on the edge of the bed.

Jackson reaches over and tucks my hair behind my ear, then bends down and kisses me gently on the lips. A shiver slides down my spine and I choose to ignore the fact that I have morning breath.

Jackson bumps his nose against mine. "I need to head in for practice. I'm sorry. I wish I didn't have to go."

I give him a sleepy smile. "I understand. Don't apologize."

"I had a great time with you last night." I can feel the blush on my cheeks deepening. Even in the mostly dark room, I'm sure Jackson can see it. "I don't just mean that part, I mean the whole day." Running his finger down the length of my exposed arm he smiles. "Though the ending was pretty spectacular."

I shrug. "Yeah, I guess it was all right."

"Hmmmm." Jackson narrows his eyes at me before pressing his lips to mine. Forcefully, this time.

As I make a move to sit up, Jackson puts a hand on my shoulder, holding me down. "Stay put. Just because I need to be up, doesn't mean you have to be. I'll lock the door behind me on the way out."

I give him a sleepy grin. "I'd argue, but that sounds like a great idea."

With one last quick kiss on the lips, Jackson rises from my bed. "We're flying to Philly tonight for our game tomorrow. Then over to Boston for a night. I'll be back the following night." He pauses and just watches me for a moment. "I'd like to see you again."

"I'd like that too." My voice sounds breathy, but I'm blaming it on the early hour.

"Take care, Kitten."

And with that, Jackson stands and walks out of my bedroom. A minute later, I hear the front door open and close. One night. I've spent one night with the man, and I'd swear he just walked out of the house with a piece of my heart in his pocket. Am I crazy? Is my imagination exaggerating the feelings I swear I felt for him last night?

I slap a hand against my bedspread. Ugh, how am I supposed to fall back asleep now?

Sitting up I reach over to the side table and grab my phone. Bringing it to life, I see that it's not even 6:00 a.m. yet. Who the hell wakes up this early? Oh, right, a professional athlete with the body of a god. That's who. I also see that I have about a dozen more messages from my brother. *Idiot.*

My phone chimes in my hand. It's a text from Jackson.

Jackson: Go back to sleep, sweet Kitten.

With a smile on my face, I flop back onto the bed. Hugging the pillow that now smells faintly of Jackson, I do as he says and fall back asleep.

-

I'm once again woken by a phone, only this time it's mine. After Jackson left, I must've fallen into quite the coma, because I feel like that was yesterday already. Snatching up my phone, I see that it's nearly ten. A much more appropriate time to wake up on a Sunday.

"Hello? Katelyn? Are you there?"

Shit. I must have answered the phone when I picked it up.

"Katelyn honey?"

Even better. It's my mom. Who better to kill my post-night-with-Jackson lady boner.

"Yeah, hi, Mom." Wow I need some water. I sound terrible.

"Honey, you sound terrible. Are you sick?"

"Not sick, mom. You just woke me up."

"You were still sleeping? Are you sure you aren't sick?" She asks again.

"Did your concern for my overall health cause you to call, or did you need something?"

She ignores my tone. "Go make yourself some coffee while we chat. It'll make you feel better."

I'm not sick, but she's not wrong. Coffee makes everything better.

Being overly dramatic I let out a loud sigh as I pull myself out of bed and make my way to the kitchen. At some point in the middle of the night, after sex and before Jackson left this morning, I woke up to use the bathroom. On my way back to bed, I pulled on one of my sleep shirt/dress things. They always make sleeping naked with someone look so sexy in movies, but the realities of all that bare skin pressed against bare skin is sweatier, and stickier, than it is cuddly.

"How was your weekend?"

I'd put the phone on speaker, and set it on the kitchen counter, then forgot all about it. I nearly jump out of my skin when my mom starts talking again.

I slowly release my startled inhale. "It was fine," I reply, deciding to play dumb.

"Well, your father was watching ESPN last night. And imagine my surprise when he starts yelling for me to *come look at the TV*."

Is it too early to start day drinking? It's not that I'm trying to hide Jackson from my parents. Hell, they're going to like him more than any other guy I've ever brought home. But that's the problem, I don't need them going all goo-goo eyes over him before I even know what we are. I mean we've been on dates. He's given me the best orgasms of my life. Are we dating? Sure. Is he my boyfriend? Am I his girlfriend? I don't know. Does he want a long-term committed relationship with me? I have no flipping clue.

If my mom is going to torture me with this, then I'm going to drag it out, too.

"Oh yeah? Did they have another one of those sports bloopers segments on again? I know how much Dad likes those."

She makes an unamused sound. "It was actually a segment on the Minnesota Sleet and their recent winning streak."

"Cool."

"Yeah, it was *cool*." Mom says *cool* as if she's never used the word before in her life. "They talked quite a bit about Jackson Wilder."

"Oh yeah?"

"Yeah. And interestingly enough, they had a clip about him from the Kiss Cam, from one of their recent games."

"Hmm. I don't really like the Kiss Cam."

"Really? You seemed to like it just fine when Jackson Wilder was sucking your face on national TV!" She's nearly shouting by the end.

"Sucking my face?" A snort escapes me. "No one calls it that."

"Well, how would I know? It seems that no one tells me anything anymore! By the time I got into the living room after all your father's hollering, I missed the clip. But don't worry, they played it again. After they played the 'Candyman' video." She whispers the last few words. Like they're profanity.

Now I'm laughing. I'm picturing my mom and dad, sitting in the living room, watching that ridiculous mashup music video, stunned out of their minds.

"I'm glad you find this funny. Your uncles were calling your father all night to ask if he could introduce them to Jackson Wilder. He had to tell them he didn't even know you were dating that man. You *are* dating him, right? It looked like you two knew each other. And Alex said that he talked to you both yesterday."

"Alex told you that already?"

"I'm glad someone did!" She's back to yelling.

I try to tamp down my laughter. "I'm sorry, Mom. I wasn't intentionally hiding him from you."

"So...?" She trails off.

"So, what?"

"So, how on earth did you meet him?"

"We met at Daniel's party."

She squeals into the phone, making me glad it's still on the counter and not pressed to my ear.

Rather than waiting for more questions, I continue, "So, we met there, and then he invited me to his game."

"The Kiss Cam game?"

I cringe a little, she's going to be more pissed when she finds out how much she's missed. "Well he invited me to that game too, but he had one the day after Daniel's party. He gave me a ticket and I went." I decide to edit out the part where I met his mother. Learning that might send her right over the edge. "And then I went to his house for dinner a few nights later."

When my mom gasps, I roll my eyes.

"Our dinner got cut a little short since he had some team stuff come up." I really should tell her about meeting his family, but I'll save that for some evening when I can loosen her up with wine. "Then I went to the Kiss Cam game. And yesterday he took me on a date." There. No lies. Not the entire truth, but enough.

"And your date yesterday was ice-skating." It's like I can hear her batting her eyelashes and swooning from here.

"Yes. And we went to lunch beforehand."

"Ooooo, lunch and skating." If she were a cartoon, her eyeballs would be hearts.

Screw it. I'll make her day. "Then we went to a coffee shop after skating and listened to a book reading."

"Seriously?!" my mom whisper-shouts the word. She loves books as much as I do.

"Yeah, it was a really fantastic place. I'll have to take you there."

"I would love that. What a romantic day." She sighs.

"And then he took me to dinner."

"What?! You spent the entire day together?"

Fuck it. I'll shock her socks off. "And night. He left this morning."

There's a loud clatter on her end of the call. Pretty sure she just dropped the phone.

It's nearly a minute before I hear my mom's voice again. "Warn a woman, would you? You gave me a hot flash."

"I don't think it works that way," I chuckle. But I'm damn proud of myself. Alex and I always compete on ways to surprise our parents. I think I'll be ahead in the tally for quite a while after this.

I can hear my dad's muffled voice in the background. It's getting clearer as it gets closer, and I hear him say, "Is that my Katie? Put it on speaker!"

I give my mom time to comply before saying, "Hi, Dad."

"Katelyn Jean Brown. If you're going to be kissing this boy on TV, I need to meet him." I picture Jackson in my mind and *boy* is not the term I'd use.

"Dad..."

"And I don't want to meet him for a stinking autograph or some such bullshit. I need to make sure he's good enough for my baby girl. I know how those fancy athletes can be. Always playing the field."

I'm not sure what to react to first. It's super sweet that he wants to vet Jackson, but *playing the field*? Where do my parents learn these things?

"Dad, it's still new. If it starts to get serious, I'll make sure you can meet him and give him the stink eye."

"Fine," he grumbles. "Is he treating you right? Is he good to you?"

I can hear my mom giggle in the background.

"Good grief, woman. Don't be over there giggling. It ain't right."

Now I'm giggling.

"Ugh, fine you broads can stay here cackling. I'm sure I don't want in on the joke. I'll be in the garage." I can perfectly picture my dad tossing his hands up in the air and shaking his head as he walks away.

My mom gets back on the phone. "Honey, he seems like a very nice man. Just make sure you have the same standards for him as you would for anyone else. Just because he's rich, and famous, and smoking hot, doesn't mean he gets any extra leeway."

"I understand. And Mom, please let that be the only time I ever hear you call Jackson *smoking hot*."

"Oh, sure. Whatever you say. Love you, honey."

"Love you too."

Hanging up, I take my coffee to the couch. Jackson is going to be out of town for the next two nights and I already miss him. If I didn't have any of my own responsibilities, I'd love to go to his away games to cheer him on. But alas, reality bites. Luckily, I have a TV.

CHAPTER THIRTY-NINE

KATELYN

"Get the door!" Meghan yells from two feet away.

"Wait... is that what you're supposed to do?" I reply with sarcasm heavy in my voice.

Meghan is busy at the stove popping the last of her homemade kettle corn. The counter is littered with chocolatey snacks and bottles of wine, and on the other side of the door is Steph, with a stack of pizzas. Izzy should be here soon, she's running a few minutes late.

Jackson texted me yesterday evening, before and after his flight to Philly. His game will be starting in a few minutes, and I'm glad the girls are here to watch it with me. Meghan made me give her the full rundown of our date together. I figured Steph wouldn't want all of the dirty details, so it was good that Meghan came early to gossip and make munchies.

Tonight's game is a little different vibe than the others, since Jackson used to play on the Philly team. Most of the guys have changed since then, but there are a few that are the same. And he'll be back in the first arena he ever played in as a professional. When I asked him about it last night, he seemed surprised that I remembered, and that I would think it might be a big deal for him to go back. He pointed out that he ends up playing there nearly every year, but that it will always be one of his favorites arenas to play in. It makes me picture post-college Jackson, putting on his professional jersey for the first time, making his mama proud.

Shaking away my gooey feelings, I find the right TV station while Meghan and Steph organize the food in the kitchen.

A knock at the door signals Izzy's arrival and - just like that - it's time for hockey.

-

"Does this get any less stressful?" I'm whining. I know I am.

Steph laughs at me. "You get used to it. I think our mom would eat a whole roll of antacids during each game for the first couple of years. But you've seen her now, she's upgraded from antacids to beer and junk food."

"Hear, hear." Meghan raises her slice of pizza as a toast.

Steph passes around the opened bottle of wine. "A little more liquid courage to help our *Kitten* get through the game."

I groan as the rest of the girls laugh. Calling me Kitten is their new favorite thing.

With the help of calories and alcohol, the game blurs by and the Sleet win 4-2. Steph made up a rule after the first point that we needed to drink at least half a glass of wine every time the Sleet scored. Steph's plan did take away my anxiety, but it also made me a little drunk.

CHAPTER FORTY

JACKSON

Tonight's game was tough. Philly's always been a strong team, and they played hard tonight. We just happened to play a little bit harder.

Since I have some history here, we're doing a group dinner of sorts. It's really just half of a bar that's been blocked off, but the food is decent, and the music is chill.

Making my way through the crowd, I keep getting stopped by old friends. It's nice to see everyone, it really is, but all I want right now is Kitten. I want to be in her apartment, under her covers, tangled in her like a horny octopus. And I'm not just thinking about the sex. I mean, yes. Yes, I want more of that fantastic sex. But really, I just want to be with her. Feel her warmth and smell her scent. But since I'm halfway across the country, I need to settle for a phone call.

Looking at the time, I hope it's not too late. I asked her to wait up for me, but I didn't think it would take this long to break free. Piling my plate with chicken skewers, I find a high-top table in the back and take a seat. Pulling my phone out of my pocket, I catch the movement of someone sitting across from me.

Glancing up, I see it's Luke and sigh. "Hey. Not trying to be a dick, but can you go away? I need to make a call."

"To your mama or to your Kitten?" he smirks

He's lucky I need him to play tomorrow, because I'm tempted to hit him. "Kitten."

He matches my stare for a moment, before tossing up his hands and rising from his stool. "Okay, okay. Call your girl. I'll come back when you're done."

He's only just turned away, when I hit Kitten's contact.

She answers almost immediately.

"Hi, Jackson."

She even sounds cute. And kissable as hell.

"Hi, Kitten." I keep my voice low, not wanting people eavesdropping.

"Good job tonight."

My chest fills with pride. "Did you watch?"

"Duh." She giggles. "The girls were over. We watched together."

"The girls?"

"Yeah, Meghan and Izzy and Steph. They all say *hi* by the way."

"*Hi* back."

"They're gone now, but I'll let them know you said so. It was fun having them over." Kitten sounds a little extra breathy and sleepy. "Steph's really smart. She wanted to help me, and her idea definitely worked."

"Oh, did she? What did you need help with?"

"I needed help making the nerves go away. I'm always so stressed during your games."

I cut in, "Why are you stressed?"

She huffs out a breath, like the answer is too obvious to need explaining.

"Because, Jackson... Because you could get hurt. Or you could do great. Which you always do. Be great I mean. Because you're so good... at everything. But I just worry. There's a lot of pressure on you out there. And... And I worry."

This girl. She doesn't even realize she's doing it, but she always goes straight for my soft underbelly. Her compassion and concern for me is overwhelming, and I'm stuck somewhere between a smile and a frown. I love that she cares so much, but I hate that I'm causing her stress.

Unaware of my mixed emotions, Kitten continues, "So, Steph made us drink."

I'm back to smiling. "Kitten, tell me the truth. Are you drunk right now?"

She's quiet for a few seconds before she drags the word out. "Mayyybe..."

"Are you alone?" I ask.

"Jackson Wilder! I'm not having phone sex with you." She started strong but she got pretty wistful by the end of her statement.

You and your dirty mind. You're gonna get me in trouble." I shift in my seat. "I wasn't going to suggest *that*... but, now that you brought it up..."

"Oh." Kitten sounds mildly disappointed. "What were you going to suggest?"

"Well, if the girls are gone, I was going to suggest you go put your pretty self in bed and let me lull you to sleep."

"Oh!" her tone perks up. "That sounds nice."

"It does, doesn't it. Then at least one of us can be comfortable and relaxed. I'll be stuck here for a little while longer, until the bus leaves." I hear rustling. "Where are you now?"

"Just put you on speaker."

"Are you under the covers?"

"Yep."

"Lights out?"

"Yep."

"Naked?"

"Jackson!" She laughs. But she doesn't answer the question.

I growl, "Answer me, Kitten."

"I'm sorry to dissatisfy, but no. And I'm extra sorry to report that my pajamas are not sexy."

"Describe them to me. I'll decide."

"Well... I'm wearing a large, grey, long-sleeved sleep shirt that goes to my knees. And a pair of fuzzy neon-pink socks."

"Hmm, I don't know. Still sounds sexy to me. Are you wearing any underwear?"

"Oh. Um." She starts to giggle.

"Kitten. What aren't you telling me?"

"So, do you remember that last game I came to, afterward, in the hallway?"

"Remember? I relive that encounter every time I take a shower."

"Oh. Um… Wait, what?"

That has me chuckling. "I'm sorry, did that visual distract you?"

She groans, and it goes straight to my dick. "Jackson, you're the worst."

"I know, darling. Now tell me about your panties." I really shouldn't be pushing this. She's going to talk me right into a raging hard-on. Then I'm going to be stuck sitting here, hiding myself beneath the table.

"Okay, so you were a bit busy and didn't get to see what I was wearing, but I'm wearing the same ones again." A slight pause. "I washed them. Obviously."

I laugh. "Obviously. Now I like the idea that you're wearing a pair of panties that I've had my hands in, but I don't see why that's so funny."

"Well, you know how I had those new mittens and hat and stuff?"

"I remember."

"Well I bought them with the girls at the mall. And Meghan found this pair of undies… Sleet undies… They're blue and they say '*Biggest Fan*' across the butt."

I take a moment to process this. Actually, I take about three moments. She's wearing panties with my team name on them. Panties that say *Biggest Fan*. And she was wearing them when I fingered her behind my locker room.

"Jackson?"

I swallow to clear my throat. "Yeah. I'm here."

"Sorry, was that weird? I thought you'd find them funny, but it's weird isn't it. I didn't want to buy them. I tried to refuse, but Meghan said—"

I cut her off. "Kitten, that's the hottest fucking thing you could possibly be wearing. Your pussy is literally branded with my team name. Tell me where you got those, and I'll buy you one for every day of the week."

"That's... that's not the reaction I was prepared for. *Damn it, Jackson!* You're getting me all worked up with your alpha-male crap. And that deep sexy voice." I hear her take a long breath. "I wish you were here. I miss you."

I feel my chest puff out at that. My Kitten misses me. And I'm turning her on without even trying.

Fuck. We need to wrap this up before it gets out of control.

"Kitten, darling. I need you to go to bed. Pretty soon you're going to distract me past the point of no return."

"Okay," she whispers.

"Good night, beautiful. I'll call you again tomorrow."

"Night, Jackson. I love... Um. I love talking to you."

Kitten hangs up the phone.

Time stops.

She caught herself before saying *I love you*. I'm stunned. Was she going to say that out of reflex? Was it from Steph feeding her wine all night? Or... Or was she really going to say it, because she meant it? Because she loves me?

Realizing that I've stopped breathing, I force my lungs to pull in a full breath.

The thing is, the more I think about it, the more I want her to say it. I want to hear those words from her. And even though it's too soon, it's *crazy* soon, I want to say those words back to her. It would explain everything. It would explain why these feelings I have for her are so overwhelming. So unlike anything I've ever had with another woman before. Could we really be in love already?

A body settles into the seat across the table, shaking me out of my thoughts. I'll ask Luke. He'll make fun of me, but he'll listen.

Looking up, I open my mouth to speak, only to find myself staring at Lacy.

My eyes are seeing her, sitting across from me, but my brain won't register the facts. This place and Lacy do not belong in the same realm. *She can't be here.*

I'm still confused about what the fuck is happening, when she reaches over and places her hand on my forearm. Leaning in, she rests her fake tits on the tabletop, where they're on full display in the low-cut black minidress that she's wearing.

Looking at her now, I wonder how I ever thought I was in love with this woman. She was never right for me. Katelyn, *my Kitten*, that's what's right for me. Getting engaged to Lacy was the dumbest decision I ever made. Getting Kitten's number from her cousin, that was the smartest decision I ever made.

"Hi, Jackson. You're looking handsome tonight," she purrs, as she slides her hand further up my arm.

That snaps me out of it. She probably thought I was checking her out when, really, I was trying to remember what I ever saw in her.

Pulling my arm away, I push my stool back from the table. Her appearance worked better than a bucket of cold water.

"What the fuck are you doing here, Lacy?" I try to keep my voice down, but the sight of her makes me furious.

"I was in town and heard your team would be here." She gives a little shrug. "I thought maybe we could catch up. You and I."

"Catch up on what?" I scoff. "We aren't friends."

"You can't still be mad at me," she pouts. She actually fucking pouts.

"*Mad!?* I was more than mad. You were screwing some photographer douchebag while you were engaged to me. Or did you forget?"

"Don't be like that, honey. Can't we put that behind us?"

Shaking my head, I can't believe how blind I'd been to her shitty personality. Well, I'm not blind anymore. "Don't call me honey. I always hated that."

"Really?" She looks as surprised as her Botoxed face allows. "See, Jackson, you never told me anything! You never shared! You're the one who pushed me into another man's arms!"

She's not wrong. I mean, she's wrong about blaming me for her cheating, there's no excuse for that. But I never really opened up to her. I wasn't trying to be distant, but looking back, I was. Somehow, over the past week I've shared more with Kitten than I ever did during my entire relationship with Lacy.

I shake my head. "You're right. I'm sorry. But that doesn't change anything."

"It could. We could try again. Pick back up where we left off." She slides her hand across the table, as if she thinks I may take it. "We've both matured. We could make it work."

I don't have the energy, or headspace, to deal with this.

"Goodbye, Lacy."

Without looking back, I get up and leave.

CHAPTER FORTY-ONE

KATELYN

I'm trying super hard not to freak out right now. I'm trying, but I don't think it's working. I think I need a paper bag to breathe into. Can I use a grocery bag? That seems too big, right? On TV they always show someone grabbing like a paper lunch bag from way back when kids used paper lunch bags for school. But seriously, who the fuck has those anymore!? How am I supposed to stop this panic attack when now I'm also worried that I should own paper lunch bags!

I need some female help.

"Hey, Katelyn!"

"Oh, thank god." I reply, so relieved Meghan answered on the first ring.

"Uh, okay, what's going on?" Her tone turns hesitant.

"I need you to talk me off a ledge."

"You have a bad meeting at work or something?"

I shake my head even though she can't see it. "No. I, um, I almost told Jackson that I love him."

"Wow, really? Wait, like right now? It's like two in the afternoon."

"What? No. Last night. Not that the time of day matters. Wait, does it?"

"Well, it kind of matters. Things said in the dark, or in the heat of the moment, can be forgiven. But saying something big like that, in broad daylight, in the middle of the week, that's a little harder to take back."

"Strangely, that makes sense," I agree.

"Of course it does. I'm brilliant. Now explain."

I take a slow breath. "We were talking on the phone last night. It was after you guys all left. It was a while after actually. Anyways, it was a nice conversation, a little flirty—"

Meghan interrupts. "You had phone sex and then you told him you love him?" She sounds thrilled.

"Uh, no, wrong on both accounts."

"Oh, boring."

"Anyways." I roll my eyes. "He wanted to put me to sleep. I mean, talk to me as I fell asleep. Crap, why does that sound so weird?"

"He just wanted to be able to picture you lying in your bed."

"Ohmygod, not the point! I need your help!" I feel my panic creeping back. "When we were hanging up, I started to say it. And not just the L sound. Nope. I said '*I love*' before I realized what I was doing. So then I said '*I love talking to you.*'"

"Hmm." Meghan hums. "Like you paused a little after saying *love*?"

"Well, yeah, I paused. But then I started the sentence over."

"Say it for me, exactly like you did for him."

"Okay, I said"—I pause for strength—"I love. Um. I love talking to you." I pause again. "There's no way he didn't catch that."

"We can work with this. It was late, right?"

"Yes."

"Alright. It was late. You were obviously tired. We'd had a decent amount of wine last night. Did he know you were tipsy?"

"Yes. Freaking Steph..." I grumble.

"*Freaking Steph* indeed. So, it was late, you were tired, you were a little drunk, and he was flirting with you. It's completely reasonable to have a slip of the tongue like that. It's no big deal. Did you hang up right afterwards?"

"Of course I did! And, shit, right before that I'd told him that I missed him."

"So?"

"So, I told him I missed him and he didn't say it back. In fact, it was immediately after that when he said he should let me go. Then that's when I said goodnight and the *love* thing. Shit shit shit. I fucked up twice."

"It's not that bad." She doesn't sound convinced. "What was his mood like when he texted you today?"

"He hasn't texted me today! I sent him a *good morning, good luck tonight* text and he never replied!" I'm back to nearly hyperventilating.

"Damn. Okay. You need to breathe, girl. Do you have a paper bag or something?"

"NO, I DO NOT HAVE A PAPER BAG!" I somehow find enough air to shout.

"Yikes, okay, I was just asking. In through the nose." She takes a noisy inhale as though she's my breathing coach. "Out through the mouth. Good, okay, do that again."

I follow her directions and even though I feel like an idiot, I can feel myself calming a little.

"Honest moment?" Meghan says. "It could be one of two things. He could be acting like a typical man, where he's a little freaked out about the whole commitment/love thing."

"Or?"

"Or he's just been busy, because he's a busy guy. They have that press thing going on today and another game tonight. And they probably got in late last night. I know it's easier said than done, but try to put it out of your mind. Either way, he'll be back tomorrow. You can talk then. But if he is being a little standoffish, you don't want to smother him. Men are delicate creatures."

"Okay, you're right." I sigh.

She *is* right. We both follow the Sleet social media pages now, mostly just for fun. One of the sites mentioned there were a few press events today before the game. I don't honestly don't pay too much attention to those; I prefer the entertainment geared sites. I like the snippets of behind the scenes videos and pictures of the players off the ice. And of course, they all have clips from the games. There are also a few unofficial pages that I'm following, since they have the more silly content. Including the "Candyman" video. Which I've watched at least once a day.

"All right, I've got to get to a meeting with my caterer. I wish I wasn't hosting this event tonight, so I could come watch the game with you."

I press my fingers against my temple. "No, it's okay. I'll be fine. Maybe seeing him play will be a good reminder that he's busy with life and stuff. It's not like he's just sitting in a cubicle somewhere ignoring me."

"Exactly. You got this! I'll call you tomorrow."

-

I managed to get a few hours of work done. But I was only able to do this by turning my phone all the way off. That way I wouldn't be tempted to check it every few minutes. Luckily the manuscript I'm working on came to me pretty clean, so hopefully my distracted mind didn't miss too much.

Calling it good, I turn my phone back on and I see that I've missed nothing. Crud.

Well, the game will start in about an hour, so I'll waste some time clicking around on the Sleet sites. Maybe if I catch an interview with Jackson I'll feel better about this whole situation.

The more I think about it, the more I believe Meghan's right. Jackson is a busy guy. He's got more going on than any other person I know. His schedule is demanding, and when he's on the road he doesn't have much down time. I know he likes me. We've always had a great time when we're together. I'll let it grow naturally and stop overthinking it.

Opening the browser on my laptop, I go to my favorites. Deciding I need something fun, I visit the unofficial site first. It doesn't take much scrolling to find a short clip of Jackson's interview today. The title of the video is *Jackson's Girls*. Girls? As in plural? Wondering if it's a clip about his mom and sister, I click on it.

Jackson is sitting at a table with a cluster of microphones in front of him. He doesn't look happy. In fact, he looks pissed.

A reporter calls out a question. "Jackson, will you tell us if you and Lacy are back together?"

What the fuck?

Seriously. What. The. Fuck!

Jackson's firm expression doesn't change. "No comment."

Another reporter shouts, "Jackson, what about the Kiss Cam girl?"

Jackson keeps his angry gaze locked on the man without answering.

The reporter clears his throat. "Was that all just a publicity stunt? Did you plan it?"

"No comment." Jackson turns his attention away and the video stops.

Umm, excuse me? What the fuck was that about?

Thinking there's got to be something I'm missing, I look further down the page. It doesn't take me long to find the catalyst. I click on the post. And I come face-to-face with a handful of still shots. Photographs of Jackson. With Lacy. They're sitting close together, in what looks to be a bar. Her giant perfect boobs are propped on the table, and her hand is on his arm. In one image he's clearly staring right at her overinflated tits.

I don't know how long I sit staring. They look real. *The photos, not her boobs.* There's a timestamp in the corner showing that these were taken last night, right after we got off the phone.

So it's true. She was there. She was in Philly, with Jackson, last night.

How? Are they really back together? Oh right, no comment. Just like *I'm* a "no comment," too. Was she there when we were talking on the phone? No, no way. He wouldn't have asked me about my panties if she was sitting there. Right? And that video of us kissing has been all over the internet, she has to have seen it... Either way, I know she knows about me. I mean we met that day in the mall.

When Steph told me about her she just said that Lacy was Jackson's ex and that they all hated her. I'd been assuming that included Jackson, but that was an assumption. He's never once brought her up. Not ever. I guess I didn't talk about any of my ex-boyfriends during our dates, either, but he heard about Bradley that very first night we met. And he was the only boyfriend I've had in a long time.

I remind myself that I don't have any little paper bags, so I need to try to be reasonable about this. It's just a few pictures. It doesn't tell the whole story. Sure, she's touching him and he's looking at her chest, but maybe... I don't know, maybe she spilled some of her venom down her cleavage. And maybe right after those shots were taken he told her to go fuck a porcupine before storming away.

My fingers hover over the keyboard. I've kept my promise of not Googling Jackson. But was it really a promise? It was really just a decision I'd made.

Fuck it.

I type *Jackson Wilder and Lacy* into the search bar. I don't want to read any articles about them, so I click the option for image results. This is what the phrase *careful what you ask you for* refers to.

My entire screen is filled with photos of Jackson and Lacy together. I don't see any candid shots. They're all red carpet type images from a variety of events.

I want to deny it, but they look beautiful together. The perfectly sleek model and the rough, sexy hockey player.

They look like a power couple. They look like they belong together.

Glancing down, I see my hands are trembling. Without looking at more, I slam my laptop shut and squeeze my hands together in my lap. I feel sick.

This is the reason I didn't look up personal information on Jackson after we first met. It's hard to know what's real. I mean I believe those photos are real, but it doesn't tell me what really happened. And I already knew she was his ex, so seeing old photos of them doesn't prove anything either. I need to give him the benefit of the doubt, or at least the opportunity to explain himself to me.

And if he is with her? the Devil on my shoulder asks.

Technically we didn't have any discussions about our relationship status. There were no promises of commitment made on either side. He could be seeing multiple other women and I couldn't really hold it against him. Except just the thought of it makes me want to puke.

Shutting my eyes, I take a deep steadying breath. I will not cry. I will not freak out. I will watch this game, and I'll talk to him later.

-

It's later, the game is done, and the Sleet managed to keep their winning streak going.

I haven't heard from Jackson, and I haven't tried to reach out again. He has my text from this morning. I'm not going to bother him for attention.

I did get a text from Meghan. And a call. But I ignored both. I know she saw the photos. Her text said as much. But I can't deal with it right now. I need more information before I react.

I'm climbing into bed when my phone chirps with a text.

Jackson: Hi Kitten. Sorry, it's been a long day. We're about to get on the plane home. Come over tomorrow night? I'd like to talk to you.

None of what he said tells me what's going on. But it still feels like a pair of strong hands are pressing down on my chest.

Me: Okay

Jackson: I hope you had a nice day. Goodnight, beautiful.

Not responding, I set my phone face down and wait for sleep.

CHAPTER FORTY-TWO

KATELYN

This has officially been the day from hell. I had a work file that I apparently didn't save correctly, so I spent most of the day redoing something I'd already done. Then, I was heating up a cup of coffee in the microwave and hit the wrong button, putting way too much time on the timer, scorching the coffee and making my entire house smell like burnt asshole. After that, I stubbed my toe on the edge of the bathtub. And later, I jabbed myself in the eye with my mascara wand. Thanks a lot, cosmic mayhem; what a perfect day to pile on the stress.

I've also been avoiding calls from everyone. They've all seen the pictures of Jackson and Lacy. I even got a call from Steph, which I also ignored. I don't want to hear anyone else's thoughts on this. I need to hear what Jackson has to say. And I'll be honest, his text about wanting to talk to me sounds a lot like *we need to talk*. And we all know what that means.

Am I falling for Jackson? Yes. Did I think this thing between us had potential to be real? Yes. Possibly a forever type of thing? Yes, I can admit that now. Am I worried that he doesn't feel the same way? Am I worried that this talk tonight will ruin everything? God, yes. I hope I'm wrong. I hope he can explain, but I'm working to build up my armor. Just in case.

I haven't talked to Jackson today. His text said to come over tonight, and the last time he invited me over it was for dinner at seven. He didn't say anything about dinner, but since we didn't set a time, I'm just going to stick with the same as last time.

Not wanting to deal with traffic, I opt to take a Lyft to Jackson's condo.

I opted to stay casual with jeans, an oversized chunky-knit sweater, and ballet flats. It's a cute outfit, but mostly I chose it because I feel comfortable in it.

When the car pulls up in front of his building, I force myself to take a few deep breaths before exiting the car. Except now, walking towards the front doors, I'm wondering what I'll do if he's not home. I don't really want to sit and wait in the lobby, looking like a desperate idiot. Whatever, I'll figure this out one step at a time.

Once inside, I walk to the security desk. It's the same guy as last time. Reading his name tag, I say, "Hi, Henry."

"Good evening, Miss Katelyn."

"You remember me?" I'm surprised.

"Of course. Mr. Wilder put you on his approved visitor list."

"Oh, um, that's nice."

He smiles. "You can use the elevators on the left."

"Thank you."

Hitting the Up button, I wait. I'm taking it as a good sign that I'm still on his approved list. If he wanted me gone, he probably wouldn't have done that.

When the elevator arrives, I step in. Pressing the button for the top floor, I will my body to relax. I'll see Jackson in a moment, and he'll clear all of this up. He'll hug me in his wonderfully huge man arms. I'll sniff his neck. And all will be good in the world.

The elevator stops and the doors open. Okay, this will all be okay. Relax.

I pause in front of Jackson's door and take one more calming breath before I reach out a fist and knock.

A moment later, I hear the lock turn and the door opens. The smile that I've forced onto my face freezes. Standing before me is Lacy. In a thin silk robe.

It's like in a movie, when time slows down and the hero can watch a fly's wings flap or the slow blink of their enemy. It's like that, only awful.

I can feel it as a piece of that armor I built around myself cracks right down the middle. And instead of a slow blink, I watch Lacy's gaze glide over me as her lips pull into a smirk. She's still perfect, just like the last time I saw her. Perfect hair, perfect makeup, perfect body. Her robe is white, nearly see-through, and obscenely short. From the amount of skin on display, I'd say she's naked underneath. But somehow the worst thing about her appearance is the fact that she's barefoot. She looks completely at home. In Jackson's home.

"Oh, it's you." Her tone is so incredibly condescending that under any other circumstance I'd be tempted to roll my eyes. But not now. Not like this. And I can hardly blame her for her obvious sense of superiority. From her model stature, she literally looks down on me.

I have to swallow twice before I find my voice. "Is Jackson home?"

It's such a stupid question. But I can't think of anything else to say.

"He's... unavailable." As she says this, she waves her left hand to indicate back into the condo. And that's when I see it. The sparkle. The glint of light reflecting off the giant diamond on her left ring finger.

She sees what I'm looking at, her eyes also going to the oversized stone. "I know you and Jackson had your little tryst. But playtime is over."

"No." It comes out like a question and I hardly recognize my own voice. This can't be true.

"Yes. We got engaged long before Jackson ever met you. We took a break for a bit, but we've *reconnected*." Her meaning is obvious.

I don't know what to say. I can't even begin to sift through my emotions. And that's when I see the switch in her eyes. They're still predatory, but the look is mimicking pity.

"Oh, sweetie, you didn't think that you and Jackson were actually going to be a couple. Did you?"

Her words strike me like a slap. I did. I really did.

"I'm sorry, but maybe aim a little lower next time." With those parting words, she shuts the door.

I sense myself backing away from Jackson's apartment. This must be what shock feels like. I know where I am, but I don't feel like I'm here. This doesn't feel like a real moment.

A sound creeps up my throat.

There's a crackling sensation inside my chest and I can almost hear my bits of armor as they slip away, falling to the floor. And as they fall, they allow the pain to start seeping in.

I need to get away from here. I need to get out of this building and away from this feeling. I don't even remember pressing the button to call the elevator, but as the doors slide open, I hear my phone chime with a new text.

I don't even know why I pull it out, but I do.

Jackson: Sorry to cancel last minute but I won't be able to see you tonight. Hope you haven't left your house yet. Can you talk after the game tomorrow?

My chest clenches and it's suddenly hard to pull air into my lungs. And in one painful moment, the rest of my defenses disintegrate.

I stumble into the elevator.

How was I so stupid? Why did I ever think that what we had was special? In what world would Jackson and I really be together? He got what he wanted. He got a viral video to build his popularity. He got a night of sex. Now it's back to his previous lover. A woman who is the exact opposite of me, in every way possible.

Remembering how Lacy looked standing in Jackson's doorway... I've never felt more worthless. More insignificant. And finally, with that realization, the tears start to fall. One after another.

I can't control them. I'm so mad. I'm mad at Jackson. I'm mad at everyone he introduced me to. I'm mad at Lacy. But mostly, I'm mad at myself. I'm *fucking furious* at myself. I should have known better. I should have known that I wasn't made for this kind of life. That I wouldn't have been enough.

A memory slams into my consciousness, and I have to pinch my lips together to keep from screaming. He heard me almost say that I loved him. I stopped, but he knew what I was going to say. God, he must have cringed so hard. There I was missing him, and loving him, and he was already done with me. Embarrassment washes over me, somehow making me feel even worse.

The doors open and I'm in the lobby. There are people here, but I don't look up. I just run. I run like the foolish child that I am, straight out of the building. I think I hear Henry call my name, but I don't stop. I don't even stop when I get outside. I need to be somewhere else.

Anywhere else.

Rounding the corner, I slow to a walk. The only thing that would make this moment more terrible would be tripping and falling onto the pavement. I feel pathetic enough without adding torn jeans and a bloody knee.

I reach up to rub away another cluster of tears. I've done this so many times already that I can feel the mascara staining my cheeks.

Using the edge of my sleeve, I try to scrub away the evidence of my despair. I can tell I'm getting looks from the other pedestrians, but I keep my gaze on the sidewalk. I can't add their opinions to my current list of concerns.

Finally, I stop walking and force myself to take a deep breath. Pinching my eyes closed I tip my head back and suck in another ragged lungful. You'd think after 30 years I'd learn how to guard my heart better. You'd think I'd know how to protect myself from pain and sorrow. You'd think I'd be smart enough to not just hand out pieces of my heart like tickets at a fair. I should know better. And yet... and yet I did just that. I willingly gave my love to Jackson, and now it feels like my heart is falling apart.

How can something so new, someone so new, make me feel so much. So much hurt.

The clenching in my chest is back. Opening my eyes I look down, as if I might see my heart crawling up and out of my sweater. But all I see are my hands trembling, so I tighten my fingers into fists.

The sky picks this moment to open up. The temperature has been holding right around freezing, so the snow comes down as a rainy half-frozen mix. Most commonly referred to as sleet.

Fucking fitting.

I give up. I'm done fighting. I sit down right there on the curb. The tiny icy daggers dropping from above pinch at my exposed skin.

I hear myself let out a huff of laughter. Then I lower my face into my hands and cry.

CHAPTER FORTY-THREE

JACKSON

The last forty-eight hours have been an absolute disaster.

First, Lacy shows up in Philadelphia, acting like there's even the slightest chance in hell that we could try again. There's not. I'd rather quit hockey and join a monastery than spend one single night in her toxic presence.

After I walked away from the table, I wanted nothing more than to call my Kitten back so I could hear her voice, like a palate cleanser. But we'd already said goodnight and I didn't want to wake her.

To make matters worse, seeing Lacy completely killed the buzz I'd gotten from Kitten almost saying she loved me. I know that's what she was going to say. And I know that she knows that I know. And I want her to know that I liked it. That I wanted to hear it. But no, *she* hung up, *Lacy* sat down, and *my* mood went to garbage.

Fast forward to yesterday, and the pile of shit that was seeing Lacy officially hit the fan. Thank the hockey gods for my sister and her warning. Steph called me about five minutes before the media conference that was scheduled right ahead of our game. She doesn't call often, so I answered. And I'm glad I did, or else I would've been blindsided by that asshole reporter.

When Steph called me, it went a little something like this:
Me: Hello.
Steph: What the fuck is wrong with you? *Lacy*? Are you serious! That vile plastic hoe bag? You're picking *her* over Katelyn? Fucking Hell, Jackson, what is wrong with you?
Me: Uh, what?

Steph: The pictures are everywhere, Jackson.

Me: What pictures? What are you talking about?

Steph: Of you and Lacy, last night, getting all cozy. She's got her hands all over you and you're staring at her tits like a baby waiting for a feeding.

Me: You've got to be fucking kidding me!

Steph: There better be a damn good explanation for this. And you need to tell me. Like right now.

Me: I'm not with Lacy. I would never pick Lacy over Katelyn. Fuck, I wouldn't pick Lacy over an enema. She showed up at the bar last night. I got off the phone with Kitten and then all the sudden Lacy's sitting across from me. I didn't even know she was there. And I don't know what those pictures look like, but I sat there shell-shocked for about half a second before I shoved away from the table. If she was touching me in those pictures, then they were taken the moment she sat down.

Steph: Do you promise?

Me: Yes, Steph, I fucking promise. I swear on Dad's grave. And if it looked like I was staring at her chest... well, it's hard to miss. But I wasn't looking. Honestly, I was wondering what I'd ever seen in her.

Steph: Well, no shit. I wonder that every time I see her.

Me: When do you ever see her? Last I knew, she was in New York with that photographer guy.

Steph: We ran into her at the mall, just this past week.

Me: We? You and mama.

Steph: No. Me and the girls. Izzy, Meghan, and Katelyn.

Me: Are you serious?

Steph: Yep.

Me: Why didn't you tell me? Why didn't Kitten tell me?

Steph: Lacy stopped us in the hall so she could flaunt her tits in our faces and ask about you. I said how great you were and introduced Katelyn as your girlfriend. Then we ditched the hag.

Me: And you told Kitten who Lacy was?

Steph: I said she was your ex.
Me: Shit.
Steph: Have you told her anything about Lacy?
Me: No.
Steph: What do you expect is going through your Kitten's mind right now? Looking at these shots of you and Lacy from last night, knowing that she's your ex?

And that's when I had to hang up to start the media panel. All with a sinking feeling in my gut, worried about what Kitten might think.

I hadn't told her about Lacy yet because I didn't want to think about Lacy. I didn't want to poison a conversation with her name. And I sure as shit didn't know that Kitten had met Lacy, let alone knew about her existence. I trusted Kitten when she said she wouldn't snoop about me online, but it was obvious that those stupid photos wouldn't require snooping. They'd no doubt be all over the place by the time our game started. And no doubt Kitten would see them. She'd see the pictures. Pictures from the night when she almost said she loved me.

So, I said the only thing I could. *No comment.*

The game followed the day's theme of shit show. We managed to pull out a win, with a one-point lead, but we lost a defenseman and a center to freak injuries by the end of the night. So, by the time I was getting on the plane to fly home, the best I could think of was messaging Kitten and asking her to come over so we could talk. She agreed but didn't say anything else. No goodnight, no nothing. I tried not to read into it, but that sinking feeling I'd been having started to feel more like drowning.

Continuing the slide downhill, I bring you to today. I had meetings with the coaches all morning, practice all afternoon, and this evening has been consumed with strategy. It started hockey related, dealing with injury replacements and a coaching change for the team we're playing against tomorrow. Luckily, it's a home game so at least I don't have to travel.

But now Coach just told me I have to hang on and talk with the team's publicist. This thing with the pictures, right on the heels of the Kiss Cam videos, has gotten more traction than I thought it would. Being that I have a bit of a "golden boy" image, according to Coach and the publicist, it means that this is turning into quite the scandal. It's total crap, but now I need to wait for yet another meeting so we can fix this.

As I sit here waiting, all I can think about is Kitten. I just want to see her, and hug her, and smell her hair. I wish she could be with me right now, just to hold my hand and tell me she's not going anywhere.

Where is this goddamn publicist? Looking at the time I see that it's just after seven. Then it hits me. I asked Kitten to come over to talk tonight. Fuck fuck fuck. There's no way I'll be done with this and home in time to see her. She said she'd come over, but we didn't discuss a time. I should call her.

I'm pulling up her contact when the door to the conference room opens. Coach and the publicist are here. Shit. I'll have to settle for a text.

Me: Sorry to cancel last minute but I won't be able to see you tonight. Hope you haven't left your house yet. Can you talk after the game tomorrow?

That will have to do for now.

CHAPTER FORTY-FOUR

JACKSON

If I never have to sit through another publicity meeting, it'll be too soon. That bullshit took hours. I don't even understand how. I literally want nothing to do with the one woman and I want everything to do with the other woman. Just let me go out with Kitten, ignore Lacy, and all will be right in the world. I don't even know what the final plan of attack was, but I'm done. I'm going home.

Walking through the lobby of my building, I spot Henry over at the front desk. One of the chattier residents has parked themselves in front of him, so I just wave. The wave he gives me back is a little *off*. Kind of hesitant? Or maybe my brain is fried and I'm going crazy.

Getting off the elevators, I feel some relief at being home. I need to put this day behind me, get some rest, kick ass tomorrow, and then convince Kitten to come home with me after the game.

As I open the door to my condo, I pull out my phone one more time. Still no response from Kitten. Damn it. I know I'm skating on thin ice at this point, and I hate it.

I'm locking the front door when I see it. Sitting on the floor, next to where I'm standing, is some gaudy designer overnight bag. That's not mine. And none of the women in my life would be caught dead with a bag like that. But I do know one woman who'd love a status symbol like that. *Lacy*.

Slowly, I turn around and face the living room. Standing there, silhouetted by the windows, is the devil herself.

"Hi, Jackson. Welcome home," she purrs.

Lacy's wearing some sort of tiny robe, and for a moment, I'm stunned into silence. What in the hell is going on? Is this some sort of waking nightmare? Then in one fluid motion, she unties the robe and lets it drop to the ground.

She's entirely naked.

I'm no longer stunned into silence. I'm fucking furious.

"What the fuck are you doing in my house?!" I nearly yell. "Put your fucking clothes on, you psychopath!"

Lacy looks confused. How is it possible that she'd think this was okay?

She takes a step toward me, and I hold up my hands. She's still twenty feet away, but I don't want her naked body a single inch closer to me.

"Lacy, I swear to god, if you don't put some clothes on, right now, I'm calling the police."

"Are you serious?" she questions me, but she bends down and snatches her robe off the ground.

"Am I serious? This is how fucking serious I am." I pull my phone out and call down to the front desk. "Henry? Yes, this is Jackson. Please send someone up from security. *Now*." I hang up, and continue to look Lacy in the eyes as she reties her robe.

"What's wrong with you, Jackson? I love you. How can you not see that?"

"NO!" The denial shouts from my lungs and ricochets around the room. "No." I say again. "You never loved me. You loved *this*." I gesture around my penthouse. "And to be fair, I don't think I ever loved you either. I was a fool to ever think I did."

"How can you say that?!" She screeches, more affronted than hurt.

"Katelyn." The answer is simple.

Her face distorts. "That -"

"Don't you fucking dare." I point a finger at her. "Katelyn is twice the woman you'll ever be. And she loves me for *me*. And I love her."

The truth of it washes over me and suddenly the fight and anger seeps from my body.

Lacy tries to speak but I cut her off. "How did you get in here?"

"I used my key." She props her hands on her hips.

That's when I see it.

I shake my head in utter disbelief. "Jesus Christ, Lacy. I don't give a shit what you do with that ring, throw it in a lake, donate it to charity. I don't care. But take it off your fucking finger. We're over. We've *been* over. You wearin' it like that... it's just... pathetic."

She's crying now. Not actual tears. I don't think her face knows how to do that anymore. And it's not like she truly wants to be with me. She thinks I'm an asshole. And - to her - I am.

It's been less than a minute since I called, but there's already a knock at the door. Since I'm still standing right here next to it, I pull it open. Perfect. They sent the big guy. I've seen him wandering the halls. He's nearly as big as I am, and I've never seen him crack a smile. I'm positive Lacy's shifty crybaby shit won't work on him.

Keeping my back to Lacy, I address the security guy. "This woman broke into my apartment. I would like her escorted from the building. I'm not sure if I'm going to pursue a restraining order, but I'd like for you to report this so I have an incident to reference."

"Jackson, you piece of shit!" Lacy starts shouting, in a pitch so high I'm sure dogs all over the city are trembling.

We both ignore her outburst. "Absolutely, sir. We take the security of our residents very seriously."

"Thank you. Oh, and she claims to have a key. Please have that confiscated."

I thought I'd done it before, but now I'm sure. I've finally wiped my hands of Lacy. She'll never interfere in my life again.

CHAPTER FORTY-FIVE

KATELYN

I'm wondering how long I can ignore the knocking at my door before the police are called. I'd say about ten more minutes. But it's also just as possible that would Meghan call the cops herself. Conceding defeat, and with a great deal of effort, I rise from the couch.

As another round of knocking starts. I do my best to yell, "I'm coming!" But my voice is weak and scratchy from dehydration. My downfall didn't end sitting on that curb. Nope. When I got home, I decided to Google the shit out of Jackson and Lacy. So I did. And I found a lot.

I found articles about their relationship, commentary on their attendance at fancy events, photos of them side by side. And the salty icing on the wound, I found their engagement announcement. She wasn't lying. There was even a close-up of the ring. A ring I was able to recognize from last night. She also wasn't lying that it all happened before I met Jackson. From the dates on the posts, it looks like their last public appearance was more than two years ago. Until, of course, just the other night.

I don't know anything about their breakup. Based on the disappearance of information, it seems clear that they did end things. But when asked about it, Jackson's response was always the same. *No comment.*

The more I learned, the worse I felt. It was bad enough that Jackson never brought her up when I thought she was just an ex-girlfriend, but it's not like he can claim they weren't serious. She was more than just an ex. She was his ex-*fiancé*. There's a difference, and one is a much bigger deal than the other.

He was planning to marry her. Her! That she-devil of a woman. How can someone, who wanted to be with a woman like that, want to be with me? It's like I don't even know him.

I finally texted Meghan last night, or this morning, around two. The text didn't say much. I don't even really remember what I wrote, but it was along the lines of *He's back with Lacy and we're done.* Then I didn't answer, or even read, any of the four million texts that she sent as a response. I had meant for her to see my message later in the morning, not for her to respond immediately. Unluckily for me, I work from home and she's her own boss, so even though it's a Thursday, she's at my door before noon.

I've barely turned the locks, when Meghan shoves through and wraps me in a hug. She moved so fast that all I saw was a reddish blur of curls.

I had almost convinced myself I'd gotten past the shock and sadness of it all. That I was on to the anger phase. But being wrapped in a hug from my best friend... that unleashes the tears. Again.

"Oh, sweetie. It's okay." She's stroking my hair, like I'm some sort of pet. It does feel kind of nice. "Let it out. It's okay."

I do, and I feel stupid all over again.

Once I get myself under control enough to talk, I pull away. Meghan looks me in the eye and winces. I guess heartbreak doesn't look good on me; go figure.

Meghan guides me back to the couch. "Sit down. Take a breath. And tell me everything."

When I drop myself onto the couch, she goes back to the door, grabs the giant bag she brought with her, and carries it to the kitchen.

When she starts digging around in my cupboards, I cave. "What are you looking for?"

"Found it!" She pulls out a tea kettle.

"You're making tea?"

She adds water to the kettle and places it on the stove. "Sure."

"Sure?"

"Yeah, sure. It's kind of like tea." Then I watch as she unloads a pile of lemons, a thing of cinnamon sticks, a jug of honey and a bottle of whiskey. What the hell sort of tea is she making?

Meghan lets me just sit there and watch her as she combines everything she brought with some steaming hot water.

Filling two mugs, she joins me on the couch. "Go on, try it."

I look between her and my mug. "You put booze in here."

"Yeah?" She raises her eyebrows at me.

"It's still the morning."

"And? Are you really going to sit there and tell me that you were having a productive work morning? Because you look like shit."

"Thanks," I deadpan.

"You love me *because* I'm honest. Now drink up and tell me everything that happened."

I take a sip of the non-tea boozy drink. It's surprisingly delicious. "Huh. What is this witchcraft?"

"It's called a Hot Toddy. It's good for colds. And broken hearts." She gives me a sad smile. "Now spill. Start from when you first saw those pictures online."

So I spill. I tell her everything, every detail, every feeling. She shakes her head, and gasps, and tears up, but she doesn't stop me. She does refill my drink though. By the time I'm done recounting my tale, we are both two toddies in, and I'm feeling the effects.

"Fuck, girl. I'm so sorry," Meghan says, shaking her head for the hundredth time.

"Me too."

"I wish I had something clever to say that would help. Have you talked to Steph? She seemed to hate that Lacy bitch."

"No, I haven't. And I'm not going to."

"What, why?"

"Because they're family, her and Jackson." My voice cracks a little when I say his name, and that just pisses me off. Using that anger, I continue. "I don't need her trying to make up excuses for her brother. And I really don't need to cause problems between siblings. They're a family of three. I can't be responsible for damaging that."

"Fuck that noise. If this were to hurt their relationship, it would be Jackson's fault - not yours."

"Yeah, I know. But you know what I mean. What's the point? What's the point in calling her?"

"If she calls you, will you answer?"

"I don't know."

"Has she called you?"

"I don't know."

With that answer, Meghan tilts her head. "You don't know?"

"I turned my phone off after I texted you last night, and I haven't turned it back on. I didn't want to talk to anyone."

"That explains why all my calls this morning went to voicemail, you bitch."

I smile a little at that. "See, that's why I turned it off."

We are both startled by a knock at the door. I look wearily in that direction but make no move to get up. Rolling her eyes, Meghan goes to the door. I can't see if anyone's there from this angle, but I see her bend down to grab something. When she turns back, she's holding a white envelope, wrapped in a green ribbon.

My heart stops. What the fuck is he playing at? Why would he send me something today, after his night with Lacy?

Coming back to the couch, Meghan sits down and sets the envelope between us. We sit there for a solid minute, then she nudges it closer to me. "Aren't you curious?"

When I don't answer, Meghan grabs the envelope and rips it open. She takes a game ticket out of the card and sets it on the coffee table. It doesn't take her long to read the letter. When she's done, she looks at me, her brows furrowed. I just stare back at her for a bit, before holding my hand out.

> *Dearest Kitten,*
> *I'm sorry I missed you last night. I know that was poor timing. I need to see you, so I can explain everything. Here's a ticket for my game tonight. I'm hoping we can talk after.*
> *Yours, Jackson*

I don't know how long I've been holding this letter, staring at it. The words are getting hard to read, and it's only when I see the tear drops streaking the page that I realize why.

I'm so confused. "Why?" I croak out. "Why the hell would he want me to come to his game? He could have just explained in the letter. *Dear, Kitten. I suck. I want a plastic bitch. Bye.*"

Meghan grabs the letter from my hands and reads it again. She's thinking.

"What?" I ask.

"You didn't see him last night, right?"

"Right. The nearly naked door guard made sure of that."

"Well, what if . . ."

She doesn't finish. It's like she's trying to think of a logical *what if*. I sigh and lay my head back against the couch. "Trust me, I've gone through the whole list. But there's too much that adds up to one big steaming pile of he-didn't-pick-me. Can we not talk about this for a little while? I just need to forget about Jackson, and this entire clusterfuck, for one day. I'll turn my phone back on tomorrow. I can deal with reality then."

"If you're suggesting that we continue day drinking, avoid the topic of dicks, eat food, and go to bed extremely early, then I'm in."

Meghan takes the card, and the ticket, and stuffs them under a pile of magazines. Then she fills our mugs once more.

We stick to the plan perfectly. We drink just enough, we eat too much, and I'm fast asleep before Jackson's game even ends.

CHAPTER FORTY-SIX

JACKSON

The ticket I sent to Kitten was for the seat next to my mama. The same seat Kitten sat in the first time she came to see me play. A seat that I can find in a heartbeat. A seat that remained empty the entire game.

My mama was in her usual spot. I told her I'd be giving that other ticket to Kitten, so she knew who would be joining her. But Kitten didn't come. And every time I looked over, my mama just cheered harder. Like her cheering might distract me from the fact that my girl didn't show up to my game.

When I first saw that open seat, I was worried. Then as the game went on, I became annoyed. Now that the game is done, and she *never* showed, I'm worried again. I don't want to be one of those people who automatically think of the worst-case scenario. I'm trying to stay positive, telling myself that she's alright. That she's not lying in a ditch somewhere. She just didn't come.

She also didn't answer my call this morning, or the text I sent this afternoon. If I were a betting man, I'd say she's still upset over those photos with Lacy. And - honestly - I don't blame her. If I saw pictures of her and some guy, and that guy was touching her, and they had a history of getting naked together, I'd get arrested. I'd get arrested because I would lose my ever-loving shit, find the guy, and beat him to near death just for having the audacity to touch what's mine. And she is. Kitten is mine. But I need her to talk to me, so that I can prove it.

And yes, I'm well aware that I could have avoided this whole mess if I'd told Kitten about Lacy from the get-go.

Had I known they met each other in the mall, I would've told her everything. I don't blame Kitten for not telling me about their meeting. It'd be an awkward thing to bring up. And it'd seem like she was digging for details, no matter how casually it was mentioned. Not that I'd care about any of that, but I can see why she didn't say anything.

I'm sure she was waiting for me to tell her about Lacy, but I didn't. And then she sees pictures of us together. And then I've been so busy that I haven't even seen her since the night we shared together. I need to talk to her, in person. And unless I can find her tomorrow afternoon, it'll have to wait, because we fly out again tomorrow night. Goddamnit.

"Mr. Wilder!"

I'm walking through my lobby, so distracted that I almost passed Henry without saying hello.

"Hi, Henry." I keep walking, but I hear the slap of shoes quickening behind me. Halting, I turn to see Henry jogging my way.

"Mr. Wilder, I'm glad I caught you."

"Is something wrong?"

"No. Well, yes. I'm afraid so."

Henry looks so nervous, I'm worried he might vomit. I place a hand on his shoulder. "What is it?"

"It's just... I didn't put it together... then Miss Lacy was brought down last night."

"Look, it's not your fault. She'd kept a key all these years. I didn't know she had it."

"No, that's not what I mean. I'm talking about Miss Katelyn."

A cold sensation works it's way up my fingertips, towards my heart. "What about Katelyn?"

"I didn't know Miss Lacy was upstairs. I never would have sent her up if I'd known. I just feel so awful. She looked absolutely devastated."

My knees want to buckle, and my lungs are working hard not to seize. "Katelyn was here last night?"

"Yes. I'm so sorry." He's shaking his head and looks on the verge of tears. "She came in right around seven. I greeted her and sent her up. My shift had just started. I didn't know you weren't home. And I certainly didn't know that Miss Lacy was upstairs."

"Lacy was already in my condo?"

"Well, I can't say for sure. But Miss Katelyn came back down a few minutes later. I tried to call after her, but she..." He glances away like he doesn't want to say the next part. "She was sobbing, sir."

No. No. No. No.

"I'm sorry, sir. I tried to stop her. I tried to stop her, but she was running."

No.

My Kitten. My poor, sweet Kitten.

CHAPTER FORTY-SEVEN

KATELYN

I've been avoiding Jackson. I can admit it. And I'll continue to avoid him. After my day with Meghan, drinking and ignoring the issue of men and how quickly and completely they can mess with our lives, I was feeling better. I wasn't feeling great, but I was trying to force myself to not care. The long night of sleep, the blocking of every Sleet related site, the unread texts and unopened voicemails from Jackson, it was all helping. I was almost able to pretend that my time with Jackson had never happened.

I didn't want to spend the day sitting at home, side-eyeing my hidden stash of notes from Jackson, so I spent the day working at a coffee shop. A random one that I'd never been to before, so as to not taint it for future use with bad memories.

It half worked. It worked until I overheard a pair of young teens watching the "Candyman" video. I was so instantly thrown into a mixture of longing, rage, and sadness, that I clutched my pumpkin-spice latte, which was in a paper cup, to my chest. Newsflash, for all you dummies like me, you can't really clutch a paper cup. If you try, you don't so much clutch it as you do crush it. So, there I was, waging a war against my emotions, while my sweatshirt waged a war against milk, espresso, and pumpkin-spice flavoring. Thus, bringing my status one notch below basic bitch to *pathetic* bitch. Luckily for me and my wardrobe, no effort was put into dressing for today. My black leggings and already-stained University of Minnesota sweatshirt will continue to live another day.

Drink disaster aside, I'm glad I left the house today.

I'm scrolling on my phone, shopping for candles I don't need on Etsy, when a text from Jackson comes through. I've done a good job of not reading his messages, but this one popped up while I was already staring at my screen.

Jackson: Kitten, if you're home, please answer the door.

Instantly, I put my phone face down on the table. As if me looking at the text would somehow alert him to my location. Why would he be at my house? What does he really need to say to me?

There's a part of me that still finds it hard to believe that he's a bad guy. He always seemed so genuine when we were together. And if he was being his true self with me, then it might stand to reason that he feels bad about how things went down. Maybe he really loves Lacy, and her coming back into his life was just terrible timing for me. But does apologizing for it really help *me*? No. The answer is a resounding no. In fact, the absolute last thing I want to do is look into his face while he tells me that he's in love with Lacy. He could just text me that he's sorry. I have to admit that maybe he has.

Once again, I have an internal debate on whether or not I should read his messages. Ultimately, I decide on not. Not yet.

Of course, now I'm worried about going home and finding Jackson on my front step. Being a total baby, I call Meghan to have her check the game calendar. We both know I could've done that myself, but I didn't want to go online and possibly come across more Jackson drama.

I feel like I should be comforted knowing that Jackson will leave town tonight, for another pair of away games. Meaning he won't be back home until late Sunday night. Which gives me the whole weekend to worry about him, while I don't have to worry about running into him.

-

I'd like to say that's it - that I forgot about Jackson, and I moved on. I met a hotter guy, and we fell happily in love. But I can't say that. Because it'd be a lie. A big fat fucking lie.

It's Sunday. The Sleet are playing another away game tonight. Meghan told me as much on Friday, but I double-checked this morning. While online, I looked at the score from last night's game. They lost. Their winning streak cut off by a single point. I also saw several articles about Jackson. They weren't related to his *women*. They were about his playing. The first one read: "Jackson's Anger on the Ice." The next one included a video: "Punishment by Penalties." There was also a fan-written piece: "Women Make Him Wilder." I'm definitely not reading that one.

The overarching theme is that Jackson's not happy. But if he got his dream woman back, wouldn't he be thrilled? Would my reaction to his rekindled relationship really be causing that much of an effect on him? I would think that he'd be playing better than ever... Is it possible that I've been wrong? That I read this all wrong?

I told myself that cutting contact was the right thing, but maybe I was wrong there, too.

I need to know. I open my texts from Jackson and start with the morning after I found Lacy in his home.

Jackson: Good morning, Kitten. Sorry again about last night.

Jackson: Kitten, please answer your phone. I saw Henry tonight. He told me everything. I need to talk to you.

Jackson: I'm so sorry. Please call me back.

Jackson: Kitten, if you're home please answer the door.

Jackson: Kitten, I have to fly out tonight. Please trust me when I tell you I'm not with Lacy. I know this looks bad but I promise it's not like that. Call me anytime.

Jackson: We've landed. I'm thinking about you. Goodnight, Kitten.

Jackson: Good morning, baby. I'm not giving up.

Jackson: I know we need to talk in person but I hate not having any contact with you. So I'm going to keep texting and calling. Goodnight, Kitten.

Jackson: Good morning, Kitten. I miss you.

I'm frozen in place. That last text was from this morning. He's not with Lacy? How? And what does he mean he talked to Henry. Like the door guy? What does he have to do with anything? I'm so confused. Is this really all one big misunderstanding? One big naked-woman-answering-your-front-door type of misunderstanding?

I'm still skeptical. But I feel something in my chest that's been missing since I first saw those photos. I feel hope. It's so small, yet it's so consuming, so overwhelming, that I need to sit down.

Wanting to push this feeling to either grow or disappear, I open the texts from Steph. There were fewer of them. Ultimately, they said that she understands why I'm avoiding Jackson, but that she knows the full story, and that Lacy was an evil stalker bitch. She ended with a plea for me to call her.

I tried to pretend that I didn't care about Jackson anymore. But if I were on reality TV, someone would be shouting at me, "And the lie detector determined that *that* was a lie!" I more than care about him. I love him. That's why these last few days have hurt so much. Because sometime between our first meeting and our night together, he crawled into my heart. And I can't get him out. I did my best to claw him out of there after seeing Lacy in his home, but he stayed. He has residence in my chest. And I owe it to myself to find out what really happened.

I check the clock and see that his game is about to start. I can't call him now. Then he'll be flying home and landing late. Tomorrow I have an early meeting at my boss's office, then Career Day at my brother's school. I haven't talked to Alex since he interrupted our ice-skating, but I imagine that Jackson has opted out of attending. I wouldn't blame him, since I've been refusing to talk to him. Plus he's been swamped with the fallout from those pictures.

So, after Career Day, I'll call him. But right now, I'll call Steph.

CHAPTER FORTY-EIGHT

JACKSON

I have to win her back. I have to prove to her that I'm the man she needs. I have to show her how much I love her. Which is why I'm here, hiding backstage, in an elementary school auditorium, to make a grand gesture to the woman I love.

Today is Career Day at Alex's school. The team's publicist had been working with Alex to arrange the details, but once I found out why Kitten was avoiding me, I reached out to Alex directly. I explained the entire story, and he agreed to help me.

Kitten is on the stage right now. She's talking about her job, and she looks like a goddamn dream. It's taking every ounce of self-control I have to stay put, rather than racing to her and adhering my body to hers. She's so close, standing tall, and looking like a librarian pinup model. The red dress she's wearing is snug on top, flares out around her hips, and is covered with yellow polka dots. She has a fitted black blazer over the dress, black tights, (stockings, nylons, whatever the hell they're called...) and shiny red heels. She's the prettiest woman I've ever seen. And I'm not leaving here until she's mine.

There's a round of applause, and my focus is brought back to the mission at hand.

Kitten gives a little curtsy, then steps offstage. Since this is a group of elementary students, there are no chairs. The kids are all sitting cross-legged on the floor in front of the little stage, with the adults - teachers and presenters alike - standing against the walls. Alex is hosting, so after taking the microphone from Kitten, he steps up to center stage.

This is it.

"Thank you, sister!" This gets some laughs from the kids. "I want to thank all of the family and friends who came out to join us for Career Day. It's always fun to get a look inside the daily lives of those who work around us. Hopefully some of you have been inspired to think about your futures, and where you might go. Before we wrap up, I have one more guest. He's a new friend of mine, and I think you'll enjoy meeting him. His career is a little different than the ones we've seen so far today. Please give a round of applause for my friend, and Minnesota Sleet right winger, Jackson Wilder."

I step out onto the stage.

The kids start screaming.

Kitten's mouth drops open.

Alex and I give each other a quick bro hug, before he hands me the mic mouthing *good luck*.

"Hello!" I smile and wave, causing another round of screams. Once the kids settle down, I start. "Thank you for that warm welcome, it's an honor to be here. Like Alex, sorry - *Mr. Brown* - said, being a professional athlete isn't a very common career. But it's also not impossible. If you really want something, the first thing you need to do is set your mind to it. Mindset and drive play a huge role in the outcome of effort. Now there are a lot of really great athletes, and not every one of them will end up playing on the professional level, but that doesn't mean they shouldn't try. It doesn't mean they should give up. If you love doing something, you should always keep it as a part of your life. Even if it's not your career, it can still be your hobby. And sometimes, you'll find that you're really good at something, but you don't enjoy doing it. If that's the case, let it go. Life is too precious to waste time on things that don't bring you happiness." I hold a hand up - "*That does not include homework.*" As expected, the kids laugh. "If there's one piece of advice that I can give anyone, it's *find your passion*. Find what you love, find what makes you happy, and cling to it. Keep it close. Surround yourself with positive people who believe in you, and you'll be able to achieve things you never even dreamed of."

"The unfortunate part of life is that there will always be people trying to bring you down. Some people only want what other people have. You can't let them get in your way. You can't let them ruin what you've worked for. You can't let them keep you from what you love." My eyes lock on Kitten's. "But sometimes, even if you try to prepare yourself, one of those bad people will find a way to break-in and break down what you have. They'll look for the tiniest crack in your armor, and they'll push, and push, until they think that they've won. But we're stronger than that. We can withstand that. You just need to trust in yourself. Trust those you care about."

I step off the stage, striding toward Kitten's spot on the back wall.

The kids slide out of my way, creating a path, holding their phones up, recording every second.

My steps get slower as I near Kitten.

Lowering the mic, I talk directly to her. "You, Kitten. You are my happiness. The one who makes me a better person. The one I want to see in the stands cheering me on. You are the woman I want at my side. You are my passion."

Dropping the mic into the lap of some kid in the back row, I don't stop until I'm inches away from Kitten. Placing my hands on either side of her face, I watch as a tear escapes down her cheek. With a soft brush of my thumb, I wipe it away.

"Kitten." It's almost too much to be this close to her again. "I'm sorry. I promise I'll explain everything to you. I just need you to know one thing. I need you to *believe* one thing. I love you. I don't know how it's possible to love someone so much, so quickly, but it's true. I love *you*."

More tears fall from her eyes, and in a move that causes my heart to burst, she smiles.

For as long as I live, I'll never forget that smile.

I drop my forehead to rest against hers as a wave of relief sweeps through me. I need a second to ensure I don't collapse right here on the floor, that small movement of her lips nearly bringing me to my knees. And the irony of my shaking limbs is that for the first time in days I finally feel steady.

I'm sure I've never been happier than this moment.

But then her hands come up, clinging to my wrists, and she whispers, "I love you too, Jackson Wilder."

Immediately, my hands leave her face and I crush her into a hug. *This* is now my happiest moment.

I think I feel her laughing against my chest, but I'm holding her so hard against me, I can't tell. Then the kid with the mic shouts, "She said she loves him!" and the whole auditorium breaks out into cheers and whistles.

I release my hold on Kitten just enough so she can tip her head back and look at me.

My grin is wide. "Hi."

"Hi." She grins back.

Then I'm kissing her.

I want to press her against the wall and kiss her until her clothes melt away, but I'm reminded of our surroundings when we're suddenly in the center of a child mosh pit.

Laughing, we pull apart. And once I spot Alex in the crowd, I give him the signal.

Alex somehow calms the crowd enough to speak over them. "Jackson has agreed to come back another time this school year so he can give autographs and take pictures with you all. But right now, he has to leave." There's a combination of complaints and hoots from the kids. "Thank you again to everyone who attended today. Let's hear it for our presenters!"

To the sound of children screaming and clapping, I grab Kitten's hand and pull her out the door.

CHAPTER FORTY-NINE

KATELYN

I've had a lot of happy moments in my life, but I think Jackson announcing his love for me, in front of an auditorium full of children, takes top billing. What Jackson doesn't know is that I talked to Steph last night. And she told me everything.

She told me about the lukewarm-at-best relationship that Jackson and Lacy had, even in their prime. She told me that Jackson proposed because Lacy pushed him to do it. She told me that Jackson broke it off when he found out Lacy was cheating on him with some photographer who had promised her a modeling career. She told me how much Jackson despises Lacy now. About Lacy surprising Jackson in Philly, and the conversation Steph had with Jackson that next day right before the press interviews. She told me about Jackson coming home to find Lacy in his condo and how he called security. How sad he was when I didn't come to his game. How Henry told Jackson about me running out of his building crying, and how devastated Jackson was when he realized what happened. How desperate he was to talk to me.

What she *didn't* tell me was that Jackson is in love with me.

Jackson still has me by the hand, and he's leading me toward the dumpsters at the back of the parking lot.

"Um, Jackson, where are we going?"

"Home."

Then, as we round the dumpsters, I see his vehicle.

He leads me to the passenger side, opens the door, then shuts it again without letting me inside. "I know I have a lot to explain. But you need to know that everything I said in there was true. Every word. I don't want anything to do with Lacy. Even if I'd never met you, I'd want nothing to do with that woman. But I *have* met you. And - no matter who else is in this world - you're the woman I want. *I love you, Kitten.*"

I place my hands on his chest, trying to calm his worry. "I know. Jackson, I know all of it. And I'm sorry."

"Kitten, you don't—"

I cut him off. "Yes, I do. I'm sorry for not trusting you. For not giving you the benefit of the doubt and for not hearing you out." He's shaking his head, but I keep talking. "These last few days have been truly awful for both of us. There are things we both should've done differently, but it's over now. And before we talk more, can we please get in the car? It smells like garbage over here."

Jackson laughs. "I didn't want you to see my car and leave. So I hid it. Behind garbage."

"Clever boy. But I wouldn't have run."

Jackson leans down and kisses me, gently this time.

Too soon, he's pulling away, but the look in his eyes has changed. Before they were full of softness and love. Now they're full of heat.

"I need to take you home. Now."

CHAPTER FIFTY

JACKSON

I can't fucking believe it. Kitten is here, sitting in my car, holding my hand. And she loves me. She *still* loves me, and wants to be with me, even after the hell I put her through. I know she made a little statement about us both being at fault, but that was bullshit. This was *my* fuck up. *My* series of mistakes. And I'll spend as long as it takes to make it up to her.

We've driven in near silence. The adrenaline of our reunion is starting to wear off, and it's turning into sexual need. I need to get her home, get her clothes off, and get inside her.

I pull up to the front of my building and signal for valet parking. Quickly getting out, I run around to Kitten's side of the car and open her door. She's laughing at me. My impatience clearly amusing her.

Taking her hand, I lead her into the lobby. Henry must have started early today because he's already behind the desk.

He beams as he calls over, "Miss Katelyn, it's so nice to see you."

Kitten changes direction, so she can go talk to Henry. "It's nice to see you, too, Henry. I'm so sorry about—"

That's how far she gets before I snag her by the waist, spin her around, and toss her over my shoulder. She lets out a slight shriek, but I don't let it stop me.

I wave over my shoulder as I walk away. "Have a good evening, Henry."

Striding across the floor, I hear him chuckle. "I'd say you too, but I think that's a given."

Waiting for the elevator, Kitten taps me on the butt. "Uh, Jackson, you can put me down now."

"No can do."

I can feel the deep breath she takes before she sighs. "Will you at least angle me so my ass isn't the first thing someone sees if they happen to be in this elevator?"

She's wearing those black tights things, but she has a point. Instead of turning though, I just adjust my grip so that my arm is banded across her upper legs, holding her dress tight to her thighs. It's a good thing too, since a moment later the doors open, and an older couple steps off. The woman gives me a disapproving look, while the man looks about a heartbeat away from a heart attack. The good kind.

Nodding in greeting, I step past them.

I don't put Kitten down until we're in my condo. And I don't actually put her down. I slide her down until we are eye level. Then her instincts kick in, and she wraps her legs around me and slams her lips against mine.

I respond in kind.

Her lips part, and I take advantage, pushing my tongue against hers. She tastes like promises. She feels like the future. I'm not letting her go. I'm not sure if I'll ever be able to let her out of my sight again.

With memories of the past few days resurfacing, emotions overwhelm me. Never taking my lips off hers, I stride across the floor toward the kitchen. Finding the island, I lower Kitten until she's sitting on the edge.

I feel frantic. I feel like - if I don't hurry - she's going to disappear. And when she bites my bottom lip, the ache of it shoots straight down to my cock. I'm already straining against my zipper, but feeling that little nip has me ready to burst. Catching her lip between my teeth, I slowly swipe my tongue across it.

She moans and I rip off her blazer.

I heard it actually rip but I don't care. I'll buy her a dozen new ones. She fumbles with the buttons on my shirt, and I give it the same treatment I gave her blazer. I think I hear a tear, but it's now on the floor and that's all that matters.

"Kitten, baby, we can go slow next time. But right now, I need you. I can't wait. I need to be inside of you."

She's nodding and her hands are on my belt. "Yes. Yes, Jackson, right now."

She has my belt off and my pants unbuttoned. I'm falling behind. Reaching my hands under her dress, it takes me a moment to remember. Tights. *Shit.* I slide my hands up higher to where her panties should be. Still tights. I slide my hands higher up her sides. Still *fucking* tights. Pulling back, I lift up her skirt and look down.

"How the fuck do I get these off?"

Kitten starts to laugh. Like really laugh.

I don't have time for this.

Somehow, she managed to put my wallet on the counter before my pants fell to the floor. While she laughs, I grab a condom out of my wallet, drop my briefs, and roll it on. Then I grab the seam of her tights, right at her center, and pull. Her tights rip open, revealing her tiny lace panties.

She's not laughing anymore.

Using one hand, I push aside the material and slide a finger into her pussy. She's slick, and hot, and ready. I want to taste her again, but not now. Not this time. Keeping her panties pulled to the side, I use my other hand to guide my cock to her entrance.

"You ready for me?" My voice is hoarse from restraint.

She looks me right in the eye, lust filling her gaze. "I love you, Jackson."

I feel those words roll through me, and I push myself all the way inside her. My body temperature spikes and I can hear the blood racing through my ears. She's so tight. Her pussy is pulsing, and its pure heavenly torture.

I give myself half a moment to gain control of my body. Then I lose control on hers.

CHAPTER FIFTY-ONE

KATELYN

Jackson is so big, and he's so hard, and he's fucking me like I'm the only thing keeping him alive.

Watching Jackson rip my tights open was the hottest fucking thing I've ever witnessed. Then he pushed his giant cock into me in one swift thrust. And that was just as hot as the clothes ripping thing.

This feels like it's the first time. Like I've never experienced him inside of me before. It's new and intense and different.

I feel like I'm on that razor edge, between dying and ecstasy. His arms are around me. He's holding my body against him, with my ass barely touching the edge of the counter. Jackson's mouth is on my neck. He's biting, and licking, and sucking. My hands are in his hair, pulling him closer. I've wrapped my legs around his hips, and I can't contain my moans as they grow louder and louder.

I'm close. I can feel it coming. And I think Jackson can feel it too.

His grip on me loosens, and I remove my hands from his hair. Leaning back just enough, he puts a hand on my chest and pushes. Dropping me back onto my elbows. Jackson grabs my legs, unhooks them from around his waist, and presses them apart, so I'm spread wide. Keeping his grip on my thighs, he tugs until my ass is all the way off the counter.

Then he picks up the pace.

Holy. Shit.

I drop down until I'm flat on my back, then reach up to grab the opposite edge of the counter for support.

"Fuck, Kitten. Fuck. So tight. So good."

I can't talk. There will be no words accompanying the sounds he's pounding out of me. He releases one of my legs, and I feel his hand move to where we're joined. I tip my head up, wanting to see. The dress bunched around my waist blocks most of my view, but I can watch his forearm as I feel his fingers rub across my clit.

The feeling of him inside me. The emotional buildup and stress of the past few days. The feeling of being fucked while still mostly dressed. It's too much. I'm almost there...

"Come for me, Kitten. I need to see it. *Katelyn*, come for me."

I do. I come so hard I think I scream.

My ears are ringing. And then Jackson is leaning over me, pressing his body on top of mine. His lips are against my neck and I think he's chanting "I love you" over and over, until he stills. Pressed hard inside of me, I can feel as his orgasm takes over.

Jackson keeps his promise. The next time is slower.

CHAPTER FIFTY-TWO

JACKSON

Waking up, in my bed, with Kitten fused to my side, is the definition of perfection. I'm so thankful that we found our way back to each other. We talked last night. She told me every detail of her past week, and I told her mine. Our stories were so intertwined, but so far apart, it was hard to stomach. She told me about talking to Steph, and how she was ready to see me even before my speech at Career Day. I needed to say what I said, so I'm still glad it went down the way it did.

Kitten told me about coming to my home and having Lacy answer the door. She got tears in her eyes when she told me, reliving the feelings it had caused her. And my heart broke all over again. I couldn't stop apologizing, and she kept telling me it was okay. That's when we made love again. It wasn't like the first time, or like the frenzied fuck on the counter. It was long, and slow, and full of promise. It was exactly what love making should be. Now don't get me wrong, I still plan to fuck her, hard and often—just not every time.

I hear a change in Kitten's breathing, and I know she's waking up. She has her head snuggled into my shoulder and her legs intertwined with mine. Her face is makeup free, and her hair is spread wildly across my white pillows. She's wearing one of my t-shirts. And she's never looked sexier.

"Good morning, my love." I whisper it into her hair, before kissing the top of her head.

"Mmmm, good morning."

"I want nothing more than to stay in bed with you all day, but we need to get going."

She snuggles her face into my chest. "Huh, why?"

"We need to go clothes shopping."

"What? No. Jackson it was one pair of tights."

"And the panties. Those are ruined."

"Okay fine, you can buy me new panties, you perv."

I pinch her ass.

"We need to get more than just tights and underwear. You'll need a full wardrobe here. I don't want you having to haul clothes back and forth."

She pops up on an elbow to look at me. And she's looking at me like I'm a goddamn lunatic. I'm not. And I *will* be getting my way on this.

She plunks me on the forehead. "Did that last orgasm shake your brain loose? What the hell are you even talking about?"

I smile. She's just so cute. "When I'm in town, we're staying together. We can stay here, or we can stay at your house. I don't care. But when we stay here, I want you to be able to come over and stay. So, we'll go and pick you up some clothes. A little of everything. And we'll get your girly shit, so you can shower, and primp, and whatever it is you girls do. I already live out of a suitcase half the time, but if you'll allow it, I'll leave a stash of stuff at your house too. I want to be able to land back home after an away game, drive to wherever you are, and climb into bed with you as quickly as possible."

"Jackson." She pauses and I can see when she realizes that I'm serious. "That's crazy though... right?"

I brush a lock of her hair behind her ear. "Crazy has kind of been our thing."

My Kitten smirks.

Then she pounces.

EPILOGUE

KATELYN

It's the first home game after Christmas, and the whole family is here.
Like, all of them.

My parents hosted Christmas, and they invited the Wilder family, and Izzy, and Coach. It was chaotic, but one of the best holidays I can remember. My parents met Jackson over Thanksgiving, but this was the first time everyone from both families got together. Of course, my uncles all crashed the party by the time we were eating dessert. They couldn't even pretend to be chill around Jackson and Coach. *It was a little embarrassing.* But the guys are used to fans, so they kept it from being weird.

My mom and Jackson's mama *appeared* to become instant friends. But we later learned that they'd found each other on Facebook and had been chatting for weeks. They even went in on a joint gift for Jackson and me - tickets to a Christina Aguilera concert. And not just tickets; Mary talked to Coach, who talked to the team publicist, who talked to Christina's publicist, who got us VIP all-access tickets. Including a meet and greet with the singer herself. Apparently, there was some talk about getting Jackson on stage during "Candyman," but he shut that down the moment it was suggested. I did notice that the date of the concert was over six months away, so clearly our parents have no doubt that we'll still be together. It was all very sweet.

Jackson's gift to the family was a bunch of tickets to a Sleet game. Front-row tickets. Well, I'm in the front row. There are so many of us, Jackson got a chunk of tickets taking up the first three rows. He gave everyone their own ticket in an envelope, saying we had to keep the seat he gave us. He can be a peculiar man, so I didn't argue even though I thought it was unfair for me to take one of the best spots.

Sitting down, this is just like every other game… I'm nervous.

I told Jackson about how stressed I get, but he just kissed me and told me not to worry. Secretly, I think he likes it. Maybe my stress is just a reminder of how much I love him. Not that he should have any doubts. Since Career Day, we've spent every night together. Minus the ones when he's on the road. We stay at his place a lot, but he also has a key for my house. That way it doesn't matter what time he flies home, he can always come right over.

I've never been happier. I don't know if our routine will change in the off-season, but I hope not. I know we've moved fast, but it works for us. When it's right, it's right.

"Katelyn, you are by far my coolest relative!" One of my uncles thumps me on my back, breaking me out of my daydream.

"Hey!" Alex shouts from a few seats over. "I arranged their little *love reunion* at the school. If it wasn't for me, none of this would be possible."

"Boo!" Daniel throws a peanut at Alex. He might be a fancy city council member now, but he's still my dorky cousin.

They all know the full story. That we were already on the collision course back to each other, but my brother likes to pretend he's the reason we're together.

Among my family, Jackson's family, Meghan, and Izzy, I got the spot in the front row, on the end of the grouping. I don't mind, it's kind of fun to be able to sit back and watch the family be weird.

There's a handful of seats still open on my right side, but I don't have to wait long to see who'll be sitting there. A group of noisy college-aged guys appear and start making their way down the row. Locking eyes with the one closest to me, I feel myself sit up straighter.

"*Shut. up.*" - is the best thing I think of saying.

He smiles. "Well, would you look at that!"

It's fucking Frat Boy. I must be making a face that shows my unease, because he raises his hands, palms out.

"Hey, I learned my lesson. I won't try to kiss you. Ever. I promise." He stretches one of his hands out to me. "Truce?"

I act like I'm thinking about it, but of course I accept. "Truce."

I've enjoyed every game that I've attended, but having all of my family here makes this experience even better. Everyone's reactions are so hilarious; I keep catching myself watching them, rather than the game.

Being this close to the ice is more of a thrill than I expected. Watching the players fly past, or smash into the glass, has jolted me more than once. And anytime I catch Jackson looking at me, I can't help the dopey smile that takes over my face.

The third period just started, and the Sleet are up by 3 points. We should be able to keep the lead, but the opposition has been aggressive the whole game. A player from the other team accepts a pass and heads in this direction. Two Sleet players come in from opposite sides, seeming to trap him, funneling towards me. Then, before I even see it happening, Jackson is on top of the guy, slamming him into the glass, *right* in front of me.

Luckily, the crowd is cheering so loud it covers up my startled scream. One of the other Sleet players snags the puck and takes off.

Jackson moves back from the player he just checked, and before turning away he gives me a quick wink. I try to be discreet when I press my thighs together.

As he skates away, I see there's now a large crack right down the center of the glass panel. I've had Jackson give me lessons on the rules of hockey, so I know that this broken pane will have to be repaired before they can continue the game.

In no time, the teams are at their benches and the maintenance crew has just removed the damaged panel.

As we all wait for the new glass to be brought out, the big screen comes to life. With the Kiss Cam.

I hate that my new reaction is to tense up. Then I see that my mom and dad are centered on the screen. My dad turns beet red as he leans over to give my mom a quick kiss on the lips. Adorable.

Then my aunt and uncle appear on screen. My uncle makes a big show of grabbing my aunt by the cheeks and kissing her hard. The crowd laughs.

Then the screen is centered on me. And Frat Boy. No. Fucking. Way.

My family all starts to laugh and I quickly shake my head. Glancing over to Frat Boy, he just gives me a shrug and slowly starts to lean in.

Before he can get close enough that I'm forced to punch him, we're both started by a loud "HEY!"

Eyes following the sound, I see Jackson skating straight toward us. Fast. He reaches us in a matter of seconds, does that impressive sliding hockey stop right up to the boards, leans over the rail, grabs me under my arms, and hauls me up and over the wall.

I'm a confusing combination of turned on and mortified.

"Jackson!" I whisper shout. "Are you insane?"

He keeps a grip on me, while he gently sets my feet on the ice.

"A little. I think." Then he smiles. A big *I love you* type of smile. "Kitten, I'm crazy in love with you. The thought of a single other person putting their lips on yours is intolerable. I need those lips to be mine. Forever." He looks over my shoulder and shouts, "Alex!"

Huh?

Jackson's hand snaps up as he catches something. It's a little box. And my breath is already hitching when Jackson lowers himself onto one knee.

Oh. My. Holy. Shit.

"Kitten. Baby. Katelyn Jean Brown. I love you. Will you please agree to be my wife?"

On their own accord, my hands have flown up my mouth, and I'm shaking my head.

"Are you shaking your head *No*?" He doesn't look concerned. He knows me well enough by now.

Lowering my hands, I reveal my smile. "I'm shaking my head because you really are crazy. But I love your crazy. So, yes. Of *course*, yes. I'll marry you."

Jackson grabs my hand, and it's only now that I look at the ring. It's a slim band covered in small sparkling emeralds. It's gorgeous. It's my favorite color and one of his team's colors.

It's perfect. It's us.

With the ring on my finger, Jackson stands. Wrapping his arms around me, he lifts me up and presses his lips to mine, in a kiss that I'll remember forever.

IZZY

The sound in the arena is deafening. The crowd is literally going wild.

Katelyn and Jackson are twined in a heart-stopping kiss, while their mothers are hugging each other and crying. Alex is patting his dad on the back, and Katelyn's uncles are celebrating as if they just won the jackpot. All of the players, from both teams, are banging their sticks against the boards. And I can see my dad beaming from the bench.

The organist starts to play the unmistakable beat of "Candyman," and the fans stomp their feet in turn. The world is celebrating around them, but Jackson and Katelyn only have eyes for each other. They have the sort of love that can survive anything. The sort of love that the world only gives out every once in a while.

The sort of love that I want.

About the Author - S.J. Tilly

S.J. Tilly lives in Minnesota with her husband and their herd of boxers. She spends an unhealthy amount of time with her face buried in books, reading and writing. If she's not nose deep in text, or harassing her dogs, she's probably playing with her plants, pretending she knows how to garden. You can find her stumbling around on Instagram @sjtillyauthor

Acknowledgements

I feel like I'm always repeating myself on here. But fuck it, the same people keep helping me! XoxoX

Sleet Kitten is actually the first book I've ever written. It started with a single scene. A fantasy. A moment that my imaginary friends acted out. But then I started to obsess. As I'm prone to do. And that scene turned into two. And that quickly turned into a whole damn book. So I had this outline, and then one night I sat down with my laptop and just started typing. And two months later, Sleet Kitten was real. So I'm gonna go ahead and be *that bitch* and take a moment to High-fucking-Five myself for this one.

As always, a huge thanks to my mom. She's the best. Every night when I finished a section of writing, I'd email it off to her. (A tradition that we have continued with each book.) She's been supportive and excited and overall amazing through every single page. And even though she's not listed as an editor, she might as well be. The number of times she's read this book is probably second only to me. So, thanks Mom. I love you.

Mander Pants. You know what you do and how much I love you.

Husband, oh husband. You probably thought I was crazy when I started writing this book. But you never told me. Thank you for being such a wonderful partner. Life would boring as fuck without you.

James Adkinson, you beautiful brilliant man. I love you to death. Your covers are nearly as stunning as you are. When I first wrote this book, I used crappy clip art images to try and design the outline of a cover. You took that pile of garbage and turned it into art. And I'm not embarrassed to say that I *cried* when you finished this cover. This book is the start of my dreams and you helped bring it to life.

M. Penna, my wonderfully talented friend. Editor feels like such a small title for what you do. Your feedback and notes and thoughts are the final line of defense between me and release day. And even though I'm a total cocky shit, my anxiety flies through the roof before each and every launch. Your goofy "Ha!" and "Dun dun dun" and "Swoon" and "Great Line!" comments help me to feel more confident.

For everyone who has read my Sin Series... I love you so much. I hope you enjoyed Jackson and his Kitten.

And finally, a hockey book wouldn't be complete without a nod to Minnesota. So thanks, state. I may have played a different winter sport, but that doesn't mean I didn't spend hours upon hours in hockey arenas. Like going with my friend to her brother's hockey games, only to spend the whole time near concessions talking to boys. Right Nikki? *Go Hastings Raiders*! In college I'd sit through the games, mostly to harass my roommate who wore the mascot costume. But we'd only leave our seats during the intermissions... to drink beer in the parking lot. *Go Bemidji Beavers*! But now as a real adult, I scream and shout and curse at the refs along with the other 20,000 fans. *Go Minnesota Wild*!

Books by this author

Sin Series
Contemporary Romance

Mr. Sin

I should have run the other way. Paid my tab and gone back to my room. But he was there. And he was… *everything*. I figured what's the harm in letting passion rule my decisions for one night? So what if he looks like the Devil in a suit. I'd be leaving in the morning. Flying home, back to my pleasant but predictable life. I'd never see him again.

Except I do. In the last place I expected. And now everything I've worked so hard for is in jeopardy.

We can't stop what we've started, but this is bigger than the two of us.

And when his past comes back to haunt him, love might not be enough to save me.

Sin Too

Beth

It started with tragedy.

And secrets.

Hidden truths that refused to stay buried have come out to chase me. Now I'm on the run, living under a blanket of constant fear, pretending to be someone I'm not. And if I'm not really *me,* how am I supposed to know what's real?

Angelo

Watch the girl.

It was supposed to be a simple assignment. But like everything else in this family, there's nothing simple about it. Not my task. Not her fake name. And not my feelings for her.

But Beth is mine now.

So when the monsters from her past come out to play, they'll have to get through me first.

Sleet Series
Romantic Comedy

Sleet Kitten
There are a few things that life doesn't prepare you for. Like what to do when a super-hot guy catches you sneaking around in his basement. Or what to do when a mysterious package shows up with tickets to a hockey game, because apparently, he's a professional athlete. Or how to handle it when you get to the game and realize he's freaking famous since half of the 20,000 people in the stands are wearing his jersey.

I thought I was a well-adjusted adult, reasonably prepared for life. But one date with Jackson Wilder, a viral video, and a "I didn't know she was your mom" incident, and I'm suddenly questioning everything I thought I knew.

But he's fun. And great. And I think I might be falling for him. But I don't know if he's falling for me too, or if he's as much of a player off the ice as on.

Sleet Sugar
My friends have convinced me. No more hockey players.

With a dad who is the Head Coach for the Minnesota Sleet, it seemed like an easy decision.

My friends have also convinced me that the best way to boost my fragile self-esteem is through a one-night stand.

A dating app. A hotel bar. A sexy-as-hell man, who's sweet, and funny, and did I mention sexy-as-hell? ... I fortified my courage and invited myself up to his room.

Assumptions. There's a rule about them.

I assumed he was passing through town. I assumed he was a businessman, or maybe an investor, or accountant, or literally anything other than a professional hockey player. I assumed I'd never see him again.

I assumed wrong.

Sleet Banshee

Mother freaking hockey players. My friends found their happily-ever-afters with a couple of sweet, doting, over-the-top in-love athletes. They got nicknames like Kitten and Sugar. But me? I got stuck with a dickhead who riles me up on purpose and calls me Banshee. Yeah, he might have a voice made specifically for wet dreams. And he might have a body and face carved by the gods. And he might have a level of Alpha-hole that gets me all hot and bothered.

But when he presses my buttons, he presses ALL of my buttons. And I'm not the type of girl who takes things sitting down. And I only got caught on my knees that one time. In the museum.

But when my decisions get one of my friends hurt… I can't stop blaming myself. And him.

Except he can't take a hint. And I can't keep my panties on.

Printed in Great Britain
by Amazon